Skin in the Game

Melissa Price

BELLA
B O O K S
2017

Bella Books, Inc.
P.O. Box 10543
Tallahassee, FL 32302

Printed in the United States of America on acid-free paper.

First Bella Books Edition 2017

Editor: Vicki Sly
Cover Designer: Judith Fellows

ISBN: 978-1-59493-559-6

Other Bella Books by Melissa Price

Steel Eyes

Acknowledgment

I would like to thank the dedicated people in the clandestine services. I'm particularly grateful to those who allowed me a glimpse into their world. Along with people in microchip manufacturing, their information allowed me to envision and formulate this story's plot. I remain grateful to the memory of Pierre Bourgeade: French man of letters, playwright, novelist, poet, director, and descendant of Jean Racine. What a gift to have called him a friend: *L'âme de la campagne pense à toi.*

To the noble women at Bella Books—the caretakers of our stories.

To Suzann Brent: True north is always right where I've left it. To Linda Lane and Oana Niculae: If you could sing we'd have been a girl band. To you, my readers: You are my *raison d'être.*

About the Author

Melissa is a novelist, who credits her former profession as a chiropractic sports physician with creating characters who make skillful leaps and bounds. She is passionate about animal rescue. Her novels include *Steel Eyes* and *Skin in the Game*. Melissa's current works-in-progress include: *The Right Closet*—a sociopolitical farce, a children's book, and a May-December lesbian romance. She co-wrote the screenplay *Toma—The Man, The Mission, The Message*. A lifetime guitarist and avid swimmer, Melissa hopes to be reincarnated as a mermaid. Her motto is: Write. Read. Swim. Repeat. While Melissa's happy place is anywhere Caribbean, you can always find her at www.melissa-price.com.

Dedication

Dedicated to the memories of Nancy and Chick Price, who taught me to strive for excellence and originality in all its forms. And Andréa Price Goldsmith—to whose effervescent artistry I remain beholden.

PROLOGUE

2003

Kenna Waverly shivered when the Russian poked her bare back with the cold barrel of his Walther 9 mm. She stumbled on her high heels when he shoved her forward—her head still woozy from his chloroform cologne.

"Get up on the stage now—both of you," he said.

"You don't want to do this, Ivan," the other woman began, "they're going to come looking for us."

Ivan waved the Walther between them. "You'll be gone by then. I take no prisoners."

Kenna glared at him. "And here I thought we had nothing in common."

She and Elana stepped up onto the stage in the abandoned strip club.

Ivan tossed two pairs of handcuffs at their feet. "Cuff yourself to the pole."

"No," Elana protested. "Why should I?"

"Because I can make death quick and painless, or I can make it feel like dying a hundred times. Your choice."

Kenna put one cuff on her left wrist and slapped the other end around the pole. She looked at Elana and flexed her right eyebrow. "Do it, Elana."

Elana stared into Kenna's eyes and then locked herself to the stripper pole, the handcuff scraping against the metal.

The women stared into each other's eyes, grabbed the pole with both hands and Elana followed Kenna's lead as they performed a slow and sultry spin around it.

"Yes," Ivan said. "Now you dance only for me. I am the last person who will ever see you dance." He stood at the edge of the stage and lowered the pistol while he watched them spin sensually in tandem. They stopped.

"Can't dance without music, Ivan," Kenna said.

Ivan lumbered off the stage, trudged to the boom box on the dusty bar and turned it on.

"Pole Melt?" Kenna whispered.

Elana nodded.

"Dance!" Ivan shouted.

"Well, turn up the volume!" Elana said.

Kenna grunted. "You've got to be kidding me."

"What?" said Elana. "'She's Outta Control' by Steel Eyes is perfect for a Pole Melt."

They gripped the pole. "Top or bottom?" Elana whispered.

Kenna hid her smile. "Seriously? Top."

"Dance," Ivan yelled again over the loud music.

Kenna whispered, "Don't move until he's close."

"I said dance!" Ivan stomped back to the stage, his face now crimson with anger when the women still hadn't moved.

"Wait for it," Kenna said under her breath.

Ivan jumped up onto the stage and nudged Kenna again with his gun. She stared at him playfully, seductively, as she and Elana began to rotate around the pole in their skimpy two-piece fringe stripper costumes.

Ivan stood there smiling.

They performed two full rotations and stopped.

"Ivan, I can't hook my elbow to the pole with this handcuff on," Kenna said. "If you want us to do your favorite routine…"

He unlocked the handcuff and Kenna climbed to the top position on the pole, hooked her elbow around it and extended her legs straight out in front of her.

Elana began her Spinning Straddle, holding the pole with both hands. Below Kenna, she spun around it with her legs spread apart. Picking up momentum with each rotation, she pushed Kenna's foot sending her into a spin where she turned upside down. In one perfectly timed simultaneous strike, Elana kicked the Walther from Ivan's hand with her stilettos, and Kenna's calves locked him in a choke hold. Ivan struggled, but not for long before he collapsed on the stage.

Kenna straddled his body and stared down at the Russian. "You're right, El, that is the perfect song for this." Then she thought, though I never would have guessed when I wrote it.

Kenna searched his pockets and tossed Elana the handcuff key while she fished out the keys to Ivan's SUV—the vehicle he had used to kidnap them.

"Is it me or is it damn cold in here?" Kenna said as she slid across the stage toward the Walther.

Elana cuffed Ivan's wrists behind his back. "Not according to the Steel Eyes song. We're so outta control that we're hot."

"Maybe that's not what the lyric really means," Kenna said a little defensively, her register almost a full octave above her natural voice.

They both whipped around toward the clatter coming from outside.

"What was that?" said Elana.

Kenna kicked off her heels, chambered the Walther and slapped Ivan awake. "On your feet!" she commanded him.

"It's coming from the front," said Elana.

"Go out the back and get that SUV. I'll use Ivan to hold them off and then meet you at the door."

"No—" Elana began.

"Dammit, El. Go! Now."

CHAPTER ONE

Three weeks earlier

Sunset at Quarter Moon Resort in Montego Bay was always the end to a perfect day, because any day spent at Quarter Moon was inevitably perfect. Kenna sat quietly beside her old friend Myron—My-*RON*, as he pronounced it. She dug her toes down into the cool, end-of-day sand, then brushed dried Caribbean salt off her sun-drenched skin.

Painfully quiet at times, Myron only spoke when he had something to say, and even then it had to be important to him.

"*Dark-night*, ya know?" he said with a Jamaican accent as thick as his body was thin.

Kenna nodded. "The waxing crescent will be back tomorrow. I miss the moon during dark-night. No glimmer off the waves."

Myron spoke with clipped words that were never kind to the American ear. "A few more minutes and I will be hard for you to see." And even when he joked, his face remained smile-free.

She grinned at the reference to their first meeting, when Myron's title was *Young* Beach Man; when the hair on his head was black instead of snow white. Kenna had long admired his economy of expression, and his keen, mostly silent observations. Tall like a spindly tree, his skin blacker than anyone she had ever seen, a very serious young Myron gave eleven-year-old Kenna her first sailing lesson. Menacingly silent apart from the instructions he spoke, his dark and serious mood had unnerved her. He would observe her, saying little, and even then she could barely understand him.

Offshore enough that everything on land had appeared dollhouse-size, they'd gotten caught—been engulfed—in a squall that swirled up around them without warning. The two-man sunfish they were sailing would have repeatedly capsized in the whitecaps and erratic wind were it not for the sea-savvy Myron.

Frightened by the ominous cloud that had swallowed the sun, young Kenna hoped Myron knew what he was doing. But it seemed to her they were still heading out to sea and she said so. Myron glared at her, seemingly unfazed by the waves, or the wind, or the rain—or her. He fixed his obsidian stare, his expression cold. "Do you want to go to Cuba, little white girl?"

"Myron, take me back to shore!" she answered.

Myron laughed so hard that Kenna could see the spaces where teeth were missing in the back of his mouth. That moment sealed the deal on a lifelong friendship. The Cuba remark had been their private joke ever since. But Myron was much older now. They both were.

They'd never been closer than the past few years, since her rock star alter ego, Steel Eyes, had gone underground. The assassination attempt on her at the height of her fame wasn't part of her life plan, but then, in her experience, life had a crude way of doing whatever the hell it wanted to anyway. She had swum, windsurfed and stared out to sea for longer than she thought possible. At times longing to get it all back, she continually tried to bargain with the universe—tried to make peace in every breath that the music was gone—just up and gone.

Not unlike her parents' fate, an assassin had come after her too—with one exceptional distinction. She was still alive. Kenna questioned if at this point it wasn't sheer fantasy, to think she'd ever find the people who had killed her family—and changed her forever. Then she wondered if revenge and vengeance were the same things, because if they weren't, she wanted to double down on both.

Myron flicked his hand in the direction of their windsurf boards. "You've become a good sailor, you know the *good wind* now."

"Thanks to you."

He reached into the pocket of his sand-coated beach shorts, took out a tiny bag and held it in his closed hand. "Miss Lola gave me dis fa you. The lady come and give it to her like you said." He slipped her the velvet pull-string sack. "Miss Lola said to thank you for the money to fix her house after the storm. And for dat she's going to find you the sweetest sugar pine ever grown on the island."

Still gazing out to sea, Kenna nodded. "Now there's an offer I can never refuse, Myron. No one knows how to pick a sugar pine like Miss Lola." She glanced at him and gave him a wink. "Don't tell her I did it for the sugar pine."

Myron laughed. "You're a good friend."

"You are too, Myron. Thank you for doing this." She slid the sack into her pocket. "I wouldn't have asked you unless it was important."

"Ya know, *everyting* gonna be okay as long as you nuh fall out of da tree."

"Meaning?"

"When you live in da tree, life is good…life is *beautiful* up in da tree…as long as you don't fall from da tree." He reached out with his long arm and patted her shoulder. "You have a dangerous job. Don't fall from da tree."

"I know."

Myron gazed up at the palm canopy under which they sat. Slowly, he lowered his eyes until they met hers. "I remember your parents—you, as a girl. They raised you to live in da tree. You stay in da tree, my friend."

She stood, hooked her sandals between her fingers and looked down at him. "You know what to do if it all goes bad."

"Yea, mon. I nuh fall from da tree!"

"Exactly." Kenna shook his hand and left toward the eastern gate where she had parked her Jeep. She was in no rush to pass the prehistorically large foliage and bright flowers, nor the ackee tree that had survived every tropical storm and hurricane for as long as she could remember. Its hand-painted sign still warned guests to *never* eat an ackee until it had opened naturally.

Poison never looked so artful to her as an ackee. The pear-shaped fruit in all their colorful stages, turning from green to bright red, then to yellow-orange before naturally splitting open to reveal the creamy flesh. It seemed to her that ackee was the erotica of the plant world—both dangerous *and* beautiful. Her favorite combination.

Farther down she stopped and looked hard in every direction. Certain she was alone on the path, she reached up and snatched a ripe naseberry from its branch. From the shadows, Nathan, the young security guard appeared.

"You picked a good one tonight, Miss Kenna."

"Nathan, how do you do that! I was sure I was alone this time."

"Ya can't get *anyting* by me, miss." He smiled. "Have a good evening."

She bit into the sweet fruit and waved as she passed him. The ritual of roaming this property flowed deep through her, slow and sweet like the viscous naseberry nectar on her lips. More than Quarter Moon's inherent and manicured beauty, her bittersweet memories tied her to this place. Indelible flashbacks of her childhood were splashed on Quarter Moon's canvas in fuchsia, yellow, turquoise and every imaginable state of green. The imprint of the way life once was before she was orphaned lived on in this place. Here, her parents were still alive instead of cheaply stolen by an assassin.

The path ahead of her grew darker. The sun had finally set.

CHAPTER TWO

Six months earlier

Ivan Mikhailov made it under the radar into the United States by the pure luck of timing. Russian criminals were neither the thugs *du jour*, nor the commie spies of the Cold War that they once were. Although well beyond September 11, 2001, yet still in its emotional wake, the Eurasian Mafia became small potatoes to national security; more accurately, teeny tiny potatoes.

Titles like *Russian Mafia* were almost irrelevant compared to words like 'al Qaeda' and 'terrorist.' The Soviet Union's collapse more than a decade earlier and the mess that was now Moscow, had rendered Ivan and his organization useless in the eyes of the Americans.

Ivan cleared customs at JFK airport and grabbed a cab to the Russian enclave called Little Odessa, after the port city on the Black Sea. There, he would report to his only superior, and his oldest friend, the infamous Vladimir Sergeyev—the badass of Brighton Beach.

At last—America, Ivan thought as he lit a Sobranie cigarette and stared out the window catching his first glimpse of the

United States. He liked smoking Sobranies because he thought they made him appear sophisticated. It distinguished him from the street thugs back home. They smoked the old-school Russian papirosi-style cigarettes like Belomorkanal, with the cardboard tube filters. A modern man like him smoked modern cigarettes, with *western* filters.

"No smoking in the taxi, buddy," the cabbie said.

Ivan sneered. "I pay you extra."

"There's no smoking in the taxi," the cabbie repeated.

Ivan glared at him in the rearview mirror, then crushed the cigarette outside his window and put the unsmoked portion in his jacket pocket. He stared out at Jamaica Bay as they sped along the Belt Parkway, wondering what this new land of opportunity would bring to an old man such as himself.

He smiled. *Leopard is back!*

His code name in the old days, the KGB had summoned the leopard to do their dirtiest work. It was finally Ivan's moment to become Leopard once again. No longer was he doomed to inhabit the leftover communist tenement apartment. Never again would he suffer such disrespect by the swarm of young gangsters who had flourished in the wake of the Soviet demise.

He had been promoted—the number two man in America! America, where he would finally show them all what he was made of. As the taxi drove through the streets, Ivan read the business signs in his native Cyrillic alphabet. Cafés with names like "Moscow" and "Taste of Russia," were populated with round-faced Russian women and bulky men. He laughed when he read the sign that said, "All dogs must be leashed on the boardwalk." To him, the name *dog* was reserved for the people he'd interrogated.

The taxi turned off Brighton Beach Avenue just short of the Atlantic Ocean. "This is it," the driver said when he pulled into the tony three-building complex.

Ivan looked up to take in the height of the structures. *As big as the communist apartment blocks, but much nicer!* The sign read, *Welcome to Atlantica* and it advertised "Luxury Amenities." Whatever *those* were, if it was a good thing, he was certain that

Vladimir Sergeyev had plenty of them. When he was satisfied that he had seen as much as he could see from the car, he placed the cab fare into the cup in the plastic divider that separated him from the driver.

"Keep the change," he said, parroting his Muscovite superiors. They had reminded him, "Don't do anything to make yourself stand out, Ivan." He did as he'd been instructed. Ivan had been good—he hadn't bashed the driver's head in for making him extinguish his cigarette, even though he wanted to. He carried his heavy suitcase inside the middle building and rolled it into the elevator, following the directions he'd been given.

"Ivan Mikhailov! Come in, come in," said the brick of a man who answered the door to the penthouse. *"Kak dela?"*

"Vladimir Sergeyev! I am well, thank you."

"Welcome to Atlantica, Ivan, where two million dollars buys you a million-dollar view."

They hugged like brothers; still two ambitious boys from the wrong side of the tracks, who had made good thanks to prostitution, money laundering and some new enterprise that had caused Vladimir to send for Ivan.

"Vova, it's so good to see you," Ivan said just before each man tossed back a shot of Stolichnaya vodka—not like the cheap stuff they had grown up on. This was the high-class crap. They sat on the plush sofa in Vladimir's lavish parlor with the gold-leaf furniture and high-back upholstered chairs. The very objects that Vladimir had scorned as a boy, now decorated his million-dollar view.

They reminisced while they drank, reliving their glory days. All the money that Ivan had made in that corrupt cesspool was gone. It was time for new endeavors, in a new land, with more money. And not rubles either, but dollars. Green American dollars.

"You know, Ivan, you are the only one who still calls me Vova. Not even my wife calls me that anymore. And to everyone else I'm *Sir*." He laughed. "It makes me feel young again to see you."

"I can't help it. We'll always be the boys from Vladivostok. Where is your wife?"

"She's in Los Angeles. That's where we live most of the time. I only flew to New York for the weekend to meet you."

Ivan's eyes opened wide. "You only live here sometimes?" Ivan stood and took in the breadth of his surroundings.

"Wait until you see our places in LA. Bring your drink out to the terrace."

Ivan followed his friend outside, and when he looked out at the ocean view, he took stock of the property he was on. Below him sat three swimming pools, two Jacuzzis and signs for a spa entrance. "What luxury, Vova," he sighed. "The ocean is so close I could fire only a handgun and still hit it."

"You can have this too, old friend."

"It's a far cry from the Moscow tenement. So, how is your daughter? Last I saw her she was getting ready to graduate from university."

Vladimir smiled proudly. "After university, she got a big job and then got married." He paused and stared into Ivan's eyes.

"She was always a smart girl. And beautiful too—like her mother, of course."

Vladimir laughed. "Yes, thank God she takes after her mother in that regard." He led Ivan back into the living room. "Have a seat."

"So tell me, Vova, what is it you need me to do?"

"I need someone I can trust, Ivan. I need you to run the strip clubs while I undertake something new, something important."

Ivan smiled. "Strip clubs?"

"Yes, I want you in charge of the money and the women in Los Angeles. I wouldn't trust anyone else with the money. The girls I can replace."

"What is this new endeavor, Vova?"

"I can't tell you yet. I cannot tell anyone. But I promise you that if it works out, you will have great power and more money than you've ever hoped for. The kind of money we used to dream about as boys. You have always been my loyal friend, Ivan, and I want you to be my partner. If you're tempted to accept, we leave for LA in the morning."

"But, Vova, what about the men you already have? How will they take this news?"

Vladimir chuckled. "Don't worry, Ivan. Compared to you, they're like playing chess with a *woman*."

"Then we shall agree to this as two *men* would do!"

Ivan leaned forward and poured two more shots of vodka from the bottle on the coffee table into their glasses, then handed one to his friend. His sinister smile was still almost boyish, mischievous. He raised his glass. "To great power and more money, Vova. *Na Zdorovie!*"

"*Na Zdorovie*, Ivan."

CHAPTER THREE

Kenna rinsed the sticky nectar from her fingers in a Quarter Moon fountain while savoring her last bite of the naseberry. Now, the only place left for her to go was home.

"Good evening, Miss Kenna," said a maid who meandered toward the exit in no apparent hurry to catch her bus.

"You have a good evening, Miss Myrtle."

An American didn't exist who could naturally walk as slowly as a Jamaican—it had taken Kenna years to master the pace. A breath, a thought, a vision—a lack of vision—they all figured prominently into how slowly one should walk, how acutely one should notice every lizard, stray crab or belching bullfrog. She'd learned long ago that in Jamaica, the concept of time was negotiable.

She often wondered if moving that slowly made people live longer, or simply made it seem that way. Regardless, when Steel Eyes had gone underground in Jamaica at the height of her fame, that pace had felt like slamming into a wall doing 150 miles per hour.

But now, after her long and challenging ride out to sea, with Myron's sailboard upwind of hers, Kenna meandered marginally faster than Miss Myrtle. No manner of thought plagued her from her past when she was surfing the faces of waves; steering the board with her feet, tilting the sail to stay in the *good wind* as Myron called it. That's what wind and water were for—to wash away everything but her present moment. No matter how pressing a thought was, to not exist completely in the moment was dangerous offshore, when all that existed between a girl, the forces of nature, and the predators below, was a Popsicle stick and a tall sail.

Kenna got into the Jeep and checked the velvet bag that Myron had given her to ensure the lead-lined waterproof container inside was intact. She stuffed it down into her pocket, then cranked up the engine and headed up the road to her villa.

While eating dinner, she couldn't help but wonder what was on the thumb drive Myron had passed to her. Her handler, the man she had called Uncle her whole life, possessed the encryption codes, and she would find out once aboard his yacht. Listening to a set of waves roll onto shore in front of her veranda, she wished on an early star that Mel, Rich and JJ—the Steel Eyes Band, would come for another visit. Even though Kenna Waverly was no longer the world's anonymous rock guitar legend Steel Eyes, she still missed the band. More than that, she missed her best friends.

Her longtime bodyguard Jean Claude entered the dining room holding the phone, the long black cord trailing behind him. He pointed the receiver at her. "*Bonsoir*, Boss, it's Hunter."

The former Steel Eyes band manager, Hunter van Bourgeade was the handsome man she called her brother—and her espionage partner.

Kenna abandoned her food and took the phone into the other room. "You're early, Hunt. Everything okay?"

"Hi, Wave," he said. "I wanted to ask how you made out today and to remind you to *stay healthy*."

She knew what he meant. Stay healthy was their euphemism for *don't get dead*.

"I saw my beach friend today, and the ocean was clear and calm. I brought home fresh fish."

Hunt would understand that meant she'd retrieved the thumb drive. He remained silent until she finished the code.

"Then I picked a naseberry from a tree at Quarter Moon."

"Huh?" Hunt paused. "A naseberry? What the hell does that mean?"

Kenna laughed. "It means exactly that. I picked a naseberry off a tree and ate it."

"You've been down there too long. You're starting to make as much sense to me as a Jamaican."

"Really, Hunt? You know, sometimes a naseberry is just a naseberry."

Hunt chuckled. "So are you ready?"

"Yes."

"Good. Jean Claude will get you there and I'll see you soon."

"I've been leaving messages for *Maman* but she hasn't called me back."

"You'll see my mom tonight," said Hunt.

"I didn't know Phyllis would be aboard."

"I should probably prepare you. She's going to hit you up to come back to LA and move into the family estate."

"Thanks for the warning, but I could afford a mansion if I wanted one."

"I don't think that's the point, but having you around her is great for me. When she focuses on you, she stops asking me when I'm going to give her grandchildren."

Kenna laughed. "It's part of her DNA. I don't know of a Jewish mother who doesn't want an answer to that question."

"I even told her I was dating someone."

"Is it true?"

Hunt hesitated. "Yes. I met a nice woman last month. I probably should have already asked her if she plans to have my children."

"Now that's just creepy."

"Exactly! You want to explain that to Mom?"

"I'll see what I can do. And Hunt, stay healthy."

After Kenna finished her dinner, she did a final walk-through and stood in the grand foyer.

"It's time to go, Boss," Jean Claude said from the doorway.

She shifted her gaze to his in the mirror before her. "Do I still have what it takes to do something this big, Jean Claude? I mean, I couldn't even steal a naseberry at Quarter Moon without getting busted by a security guard."

"I think if you don't have what it takes then the whole world is in trouble," he replied with his French accent. "If it helps to know, I believe in you." He nodded. "Whenever you're ready."

"Good-bye for now, Jamaica," she said under her breath. She walked to the mahogany French doors of the beachfront villa and paused, knowing that nothing, especially not her safe return, was ever guaranteed. She flicked off the light switch and followed Jean Claude to the dinghy that would usher her out to his sailboat. He would then motor to the offshore rendezvous. The time had arrived, the time was now, and they were waiting for her out on Uncle's yacht—the *Allons-y*.

Jean Claude started the engine and the veil of *dark-night* cloaked their passage.

CHAPTER FOUR

Elana West entered the retro city diner with the worn Naugahyde booths, and walked to the farthest one. She sat opposite the brunette in the suit. "Deputy Director," she said.

"Thanks for getting here so fast," said FBI Special Cases Deputy, "Sonny" Sonnenheim. She signaled the waitress before she began.

Elana ordered a cup of coffee and unzipped her hoodie. "It sounded important."

"I'll get right to it." Sonnenheim opened the manila envelope on the table and slid a photo in front of Elana. "Do you know this man?"

Elana didn't have to think about it. "Nope. Who is he?"

Sonnenheim paused until the waitress served the coffee and left. "His name was Jiang Lee."

"Was?"

"I'll get to that. Have you ever heard of a company called Physio Dynamics?"

"Sure, the silicon chipmaker."

"More accurately, a government contractor who, as it happens, made the chips that wound up in our computer system upgrade."

"What is the FBI investigating?"

"Jiang Lee worked for Physio Dynamics as a Project Manager. His body turned up in a dump with all the signs of a professional hit, including either a lack of, or contamination of the evidence." Sonnenheim swept their surroundings with a glance before she continued. "This is the point where I need to know if you're in or not before I go any further."

"Hell yes, I'm in." Elana took a sip of coffee.

Sonnenheim breathed a sigh of relief. "Thank you. My pool of off-book agents I trust is almost nil at this point." She leaned forward and continued in a hushed voice. "Shortly before Lee was discovered, our new computer system exhibited some glitches that we think could trace back to the chips made by Physio Dynamics. The bad news is that the FBI computer system didn't alert us to a major breach."

"More iced tea, hon?" said the waitress with a pitcher hovering over Sonny's glass.

"No thanks." Again they waited for the waitress to leave.

"We were hacked. So were NSA and CIA, but to a lesser extent since we caught it."

Elana's eyes darted to a man passing by. "Shit," she whispered. "What was the breach?"

"Identities, personnel files, from Social Security numbers to psych profiles, to what those folks eat for breakfast. Code names, stations of covert operatives, and on and on. It's why we really need you. There's no file on you."

Elana's shocked expression ended with a passive nod.

"Exactly, Elana. While we try to shut this thing down, there's something I need you to do."

"Name it."

"Do what you do best. Investigate."

"Investigate what?"

"Sabotage. Jiang Lee was involved with our government contracts, and if that had anything to do with why he's dead, we could already be more compromised than we guessed. He had security clearance for his projects, but Physio Dynamics is a Chinese company. If our American operatives were to be outed, every agency would be devastated. You'll be coordinating with another off-book consultant on this. Someone you already know."

"Who?"

"Sierra Stone. You know her pretty well? I mean…still?"

Elana smiled. "You know how well Sierra and I knew each other. She recruited me for you."

"She didn't just recruit you—you worked at the same club."

"I haven't seen her since we busted the sex trafficking ring a few years ago, if that's what you're asking."

"No, I'm asking if there are going to be any issues working with her. This is a matter of national security."

"No, Sonny, no *issues*."

"Sierra won't be happy about me interrupting her weekend in New Orleans to send her to Montana. I'm ordering her to pick up a thumb drive from a Canadian asset. That thumb drive contains the list of operatives who may have already been compromised. The Canadians made a deal to secure it for us. You'll meet with Sierra after she delivers the package to DC— probably in a few days. I'll let you know when and where."

"Why is the FBI wasting a valuable cyber asset like Sierra Stone by making her an errand girl?"

"We have our own cyber team working on the hack. Sierra's only a consultant. An erratic consultant."

"But how many of your people have lived on the dark web? Sierra eats code for breakfast—and late night snacks."

"It isn't worth the risk."

"You're at greater risk without her."

Sonnenheim slid the manila envelope in front of Elana. "From this moment on, everything that can be, is done on the ground, in real life. No emails, no phone calls unless it's made using the phone in here to another secure phone. Sonny glanced down at the envelope. "To activate the phone, dial three stars, two pound signs, spell out 'sonnenheim' and press the star button three more times. I'm programmed in as Pizza Place.

Homeland Secretary Zwarnick is programmed in as Chinese Food. Watch your every move, Elana."

Elana nodded.

Deputy Director Sonnenheim threw some cash on the table, and as she slid out of the booth she added, "Keep that phone with you at *all* times."

"Even during sex?"

"You won't have the time, even if you weren't kidding." Sonnenheim stood to leave. "Good luck. I'll be in touch."

CHAPTER FIVE

"Welcome aboard, luv. I thought you'd never get here!" Phyllis van Bourgeade barely waited until both of Kenna's feet were on the yacht before grabbing her. Her thick white hair was tied back neatly, and her nautical fashion was more Rodeo Drive than anything else.

Kenna wrapped her arms around her surrogate mother and lifted her off the deck in a big hug. They kissed on both cheeks, as had been their custom all of Kenna's life. "Bonsoir, Maman!" Even though they mostly spoke in English, their greeting was always proper and French.

"The crew will show you to your stateroom," said Phyllis. "After you stow your things, come meet us in the main aft salon. I assume you'll be dressed appropriately by then."

"It was a bit of a bumpy sea getting out here. I'm looking forward to putting on some dry clothes. Tell Uncle I'll be right there. Oh, and here." Kenna pulled the waterproof pouch containing the thumb drive out of her case and handed it to Phyllis.

"Fantastic, our software engineer has been anxiously waiting to get to work on this. Have you eaten, *mon chou?*"

Kenna rolled her eyes. "Yes, Maman."

"Great, because I made your favorite dessert."

"You didn't!"

Phyllis smirked. "*Now* let's see how long it takes you to get dressed, missy."

"Thankfully some things never change," Kenna said while turning to follow the crew member below deck.

She entered her stateroom and placed her case below the porthole. The high-gloss built-in teak furniture flowed seamlessly along the curved hull. Thin polished chrome piping accented a large mahogany bed platform. Soft indirect lighting welcomed and warmed her. "I could get used to this," she said to the legendary old man in the sea. Then she thought, I can afford to live like this—so why aren't I? Shaking off the thought, she changed her clothes while listening to the Brazilian jazz playlist that had been deliberately piped into her room. Then, after only two wrong turns she found the main salon located topside and aft.

"Bonsoir, Uncle!" Kenna said as she entered and went to him.

Uncle stood and embraced her warmly. "My word, for an instant I thought you were your mother!"

Kenna laughed. "It's the gray eyes."

"I'm so glad you're here, *mon chou*," he said.

"Me too. All we're missing for this party, Uncle, is your children, and Chantal and Hunter. This tub is certainly big enough for all of us."

"Chantal," Phyllis said while sipping a cognac. "Now I did something right with *that* child. She's the only one out of all of us who lives a normal life."

"What's not normal about being a spy? Are you insinuating that there's something wrong with me?" Kenna teased. "And I'm telling Hunter you said that he's not normal."

"I never said that, *chou*. But that boy turned out just like his father. It's maddening sometimes. And as for you, I only half-raised you."

"You were married to his father until the day he died, Phyllis, so I can't imagine what you're talking about," Kenna said.

Uncle laughed while he poured Kenna a brandy. "You should know Phyllis by now. Hunter has a lot of you in him too, Phyllis. Have you ever considered that the part of your son that drives you batty is the part that's most like you?"

"Nonsense," Phyllis struck back. "Those parts were all from Maurice, not me. It's *ener-genetic*, like when Kenna does those things her mother did."

"Ener-genetic, Maman?"

"Yes. Part energy, part genetic."

"What things do I do like my mother?" Kenna said before taking a sip of the brandy.

"Wait," Uncle said, "I bet I know what Phyllis is going to say." He sauntered across the salon and answered thoughtfully. "The eyebrow lift of sarcasm," he began. "And that sigh you do when you get annoyed but don't want anyone else to know."

"I do not do that," Kenna protested.

"Oh, he's got you on both counts, kiddo," Phyllis said. "Give it up. We've both known you since you were born, had known your parents forever, and I raised you after they were gone. You *do* have that little sigh of ennui."

"Fine, whatever." Kenna exhaled.

"See? Right there! That's it. That's the sigh of ennui," Phyllis concluded.

Kenna looked between Uncle and Phyllis. "Did you say you have French plum cake for me?"

"I suppose we can break out the cake and coffee," Phyllis said, rising from her armchair.

"Right behind you, *mon chou*," Uncle said to Kenna.

"I promise not to breathe the sigh of ennui if you let me have seconds," Kenna said as she raised the eyebrow of sarcasm.

Phyllis's voice led the way. "You only get seconds if you promise not to tell Hunter that I think he's not normal."

"So you *were* insinuating that he's abnormal."

"Fine," Phyllis began, "and an extra slice to take back to your room."

Kenna shrugged. "Seems fair."

CHAPTER SIX

At three a.m., the New Orleans water plant on Claiborne Avenue experienced a drop in water pressure due to power surges at two pumping stations. It was the latest event in a seemingly random sprint of mishaps in an array of US cities. This pump failure necessitated an official 'boil alert.'

New Orleans officials had delayed the announcement about the problem, which stretched from the muddy Mississippi clear across to the far end of the French Quarter and then some. Most of the thousands of tourists who had earlier sweated past the architecture, the endless party known as Bourbon Street, and the stifling July heat, were asleep. Some would have already risked serious infection by brushing their teeth or brewing their morning coffee with the tainted water, had they not turned on their televisions first thing or answered their phones.

By four thirty a.m., employees from the stack of claustrophobic hotels near the fried oyster-scented Riverwalk busied themselves distributing pallets of bottled water to their multitude of guests. Robo-calls played recorded messages to each room alerting people to not use the tap water, and to advise them to wash and brush their teeth using bottled water only.

Jolted awake by the obnoxious peal of the telephone, Sierra Stone almost rolled out of bed in her sex hangover. She fumbled the receiver, realized she was listening to the mouthpiece and flipped the handset around. Sierra listened for several seconds, and then hung up.

"Who the hell is ringing your phone at this hour?" muttered the girl lying next to her.

"Hotel. Go back to sleep, and *don't use the water.* It might be contaminated."

The girl's eyes opened wide. "What?"

Bleary-eyed, Sierra sat up. "They said there's bottled water at our door. I'm going to get it and put it in the bathroom." She was too sleepy to make much of the call yet, other than the contempt she already held for the drippy, sticky July weather, and the onus of calculating how many bottles of water it took to equal a shower. "Of all weekends," she complained as she padded to the door.

It wasn't until she got back into bed that she had a thought. How did this happen in a major city, a major humid city—in July! Sierra rolled over and spooned her date, the girl she had brought home from the little tavern she had wandered into for dinner the night before.

The girl turned over to face her. "Where did we leave off, Greer?"

Sierra liked being called 'Greer,' even though it wasn't her real name. Real names were reserved for the real world, for Sierra Stone's world. Greer's world was a different matter entirely.

The girl ran her fingers lightly across Sierra's back and then down over the slope of her ass.

"Mmm, that feels wonderful," Sierra said, her brain aflutter with names, "really wonderful…Dani."

Dani wrapped her arms around Sierra and pulled her on top of her. The moment their lips met, the phone rang again.

"What is this, Grand Central Station, Late Night Edition?" Dani protested.

Sierra reached over and picked up the phone. There was no robotic voice chatting her up this time. There was no voice at all. *Damn, the FBI's timing sucks!* "This is Greer."

"So you're not alone," said the Deputy Director.

Fuck, it's Sonnenheim. "No, and would you believe we're on water lockdown due to some brain-eating amoeba in the water supply down here."

"You know why I'm calling," the woman on the phone said in a serious tone.

"Shit. Now? You want me *now?* A weekend off means until Sunday night."

"Not anymore it doesn't. Not since every *known* employee has been compromised—and that leaves us with you," Sonnenheim countered. "Change your plans. Greer's going to Montana at noon on Alaska Airlines. You'll stay at the Glacier Vista Motel outside Glacier National Park. Your cousin from up north has a *gift* for me. See you in DC for the wedding."

Click.

Sierra slammed down the phone, rolled off Dani and onto her back. "I have a work emergency so I have to get on a flight at noon."

Dani turned onto her side and propped herself up on a pillow. "Phone calls on a Saturday at five in the morning? What the hell. Are you like a doctor or somethin'?"

"Florist."

Dani scoffed. "You have a *floral* emergency?"

"I do. Big, very expensive wedding tomorrow."

Dani pulled Sierra closer. "So we still have a little time left."

"A little. Say it for me again, would you?"

"*Etouffé.*"

"No, the other one."

"N'awlins."

"Now you're just screwing with me."

Dani smiled. "*Quawtah*, dahlin'. French Quawtah."

"That is damn sexy, baby. It's so unfair that I have to leave when we're just getting to know each other."

"It's horribly unfair," Dani said with the sugar-sweet accent and matching pout. "But talking about it is only going to take up valuable time we could be using for something else."

Sierra smiled. "Oh, this isn't over by a long shot." She kissed Dani. Then she kissed her again and again.

* * *

Later that day, Sierra checked into the Glacier Vista Motel under the name Greer Stabinow, and paid the clerk to make one phone call that lasted exactly sixty-three seconds. When she returned to her room at the remote end of the gravel parking lot, she tossed her useless mobile phone onto the bed.

I need a Plan B in case anything goes sideways. I'll have a look around outside after dark.

Doused with daylight, the stubborn Montana summer twilight lingered despite the late hour. Sierra used the time to scarf a slice of hotel huckleberry pie and to monitor the winding road from her obscured corner of the curtain. The Glacier Vista sat on a road that had only two final destinations—ahead or behind.

Here and gone, she thought. That's how this is going to go. I'll get the thumb drive from the Canadian, hand it over to Sonnenheim and then I'm going back to New Orleans. She smiled at the thought of seeing Dani again.

Her contact would be there soon and it was finally dark enough to slip out back into a viable Plan B. The Trans-Continental rail cars echoed off the rocks, chugging along tracks that skewered the craggy slope behind the motor inn. Sierra counted her paces, knelt on a patch of weeds and turned on her small flashlight. The train's mechanical racket covered the *ping* of her knife meeting with mineral-laden earth.

"This is no good, it will take forever," she murmured.

Still, she needed to find a hiding spot that an asset might discover in the event something went south during her exchange;

one that an assassin wouldn't have the luxury of time to search for. The rustic room was a better option than the rental car.

Sierra's head swung to the left when she heard the rustling. There wasn't much space between the road in front of her motel room and the train tracks just behind the narrow long building.

Oh God please don't be a bear. She stood slowly and reached for her empty holster. *Dammit!*

Her gun was in the room under her pillow. Keeping her eye trained on the direction from which the noise came, she slinked quietly backward until she reached the adjacent campground, then sprinted to the front of the Glacier Vista. Sierra fumbled with the lock on her door, her heart racing as she bolted it behind her. In the darkened room she grabbed her weapon and pressed her ear against the door. Her .38 revolver hung at her side, but she wished she had a backup piece—of pie.

CHAPTER SEVEN

Twenty hours after Sierra Stone had left her the voice mail from the Glacier Vista, Elana West tossed her knapsack into the back of the four-seat helicopter that awaited her in Kalispell, Montana. She hopped into the front seat, strapped herself in and adjusted her mic. "I'm Elana, thanks for waiting."

"I'm Jesse," the woman at the controls replied. "Any later and you'd have had to drive up to Goat Lick," she said as she lifted up and over the cabins just to the east, heading toward Glacier National Park.

"How long will it take to get there?"

"I should have you on the ground in about ten. The state police said to fly you in when you landed. Was the victim a friend of yours?"

"Yes."

"Sorry for your loss. We don't see murder up here too often."

Elana could feel Jesse's eyes on her cleavage as she reached behind her to grab her knapsack. "Chilly up here." It sounded like a good enough excuse to dig out her hoodie and cover up.

"How long will you be in town?"

"I'm hoping to have some answers by tomorrow."

"You flew in from LA?" Jesse banked to the south.

Elana nodded. For the entire two-hour flight to Kalispell, Elana had pored over the holes in every cloud, meditated on the tip of each mountain peak that poked through, wondering what the hell had happened up here last night.

Now, she stared blankly at the strata of glacier curtain before her. Snow thawed into the streams of summer before her eyes, waterfalls dissolving into creeks and lakes. False summits appeared at every new height—their chasms unknowable to the eye from the ground until one conquered the summit before it.

"Jesse, every time we climb toward the top of a peak, I think it's the summit, until you climb higher and I get to see the one beyond it."

"False summits are quite an illusion."

What isn't? Elana thought. She searched the distance, wondering which valley would be the one where she would have to identify Sierra's body. Her stomach rumbled from the nauseating reality. The lakes and river below her, smug and unyielding, flickered their indifferent shade of glacier-mint in the early evening sunlight.

Jesse pointed downward and to their right, descending like a hawk surfing on wind current, carving the air into layers across the divide. Elana shuddered at the sight of the swirling red dots on the cop cars before noticing the pass that led to them. Visually tracing the winding secondary road, she attempted to calculate the proximity to where Sierra had called her from the night before.

"Jesse, is that the road that leads to the Glacier Vista Motel?"

"Yep, it'll take you right to it."

"So, where we're going now is about how far from the motel?"

"About a fifteen- to twenty-minute drive."

In her voice mail, Sierra had said she thought she might have picked up a tail. She had even joked about what breed of idiot would follow a person into a glacier park in the height of tourist season. Then she left the name of the Glacier Vista; the place where she was to meet her contact to get the thumb drive that contained the names and files of compromised personnel.

Elana would interview the staff at the motel when she checked in. As Jesse zeroed in on her landing, Elana caught sight of a raggedly shedding mountain goat and her kid. She held her breath for the instant that the baby goat leapt below onto a narrow crag of rock high above the ravine floor.

Jesse circled the landing once before setting the helicopter down on a stretch of road just uphill from the crime scene. Elana watched the mountain goats hop farther down the rocks into the ravine, the baby daring a tip of precipice to hold him.

Those goats are probably my only witnesses.

Elana crouched low under the helicopter's main rotor and moved beyond it until she had cleared its thrum. She slung her backpack over her shoulder and strode toward the man who approached.

Deliberate in his step, he waited until the helicopter lifted off and then extended his hand. "Ms. West. I'm Lieutenant Moss," he said.

"Call me Elana." She took note of a sketch artist off to the left who was measuring and then drawing everything to scale. The forensic photographer's motor driven clicks pointed downward into the hillside. There would be time to pore over the photographs and sketches afterward, but unless these shedding mountain goats could talk, Elana had the feeling that witness statements would be her weakest link in the case.

"Sorry if I delayed you. I caught the first flight I could get out of LA," she said as she looked beyond him. She eyed the lump of human form beneath the covering some thirty feet away and wandered out of the conversation before she entered into it. Moving toward Sierra's body, she felt her face tingle and beads of sweat around her hairline. Her body went cold inside.

Moss walked reverently beside her. "There are defensive wounds indicating she put up a fight before she was shot. I'm calling it an intentional homicide. That's Montana-speak for first-degree murder."

"Has your medical examiner cleared the scene?" she asked. Moss nodded.

She stopped and turned to him. "Do you have any clues about the altercation?"

"Not yet."

"Who called it in?"

"A local woman spotted her while on a hike this morning."

"I'd like to speak with her before I leave."

"I have orders to provide whatever you need within reason," he said kindly.

Elana flung a glance toward the lump under the tarp. "Tell me, Lieutenant, is *that* reasonable?"

Silent, Moss led her to the corpse. He bent down and placed his latex-gloved fingers on the tip of the tarp and glanced up at Elana. "Are you ready?" he asked.

She nodded.

Moss slowly peeled back the tarp at the head.

Ripped skin, bloodied, beaten, then shot. Elana alternated between fixation on the lifeless body, and an aversion to viewing it at all. "That's her." The words contained only enough air to be heard.

Moss nodded. "It looks like this is where she died"—he pointed in another direction—"but she crawled from over there. There are bloodstains on the ground beyond the body. We'll let you know what we find."

"Have you finished searching the motel?"

"Yeah, we went through it, but DNA in a motel room? That's a Petrie dish and we just don't have the resources. If the FBI wants to run our samples, I have no objection. But there wasn't any sign of foul play. In fact, the bed barely had a dent in it, but something keeps bothering me. If this is Sierra Stone, then why did she register at the motel under the name Greer Stabinow?"

"To stay alive."

"Huh." He shook his head. "A lot of good it did her. Any history of an abusive boyfriend or partner?" Moss asked.

"Not that I know about."

Moss looked out over God's country. "No one but the bears and goats would have witnessed it. I'll give you a few moments," he said as he got to his feet. "For what it's worth, I'm sorry for your loss," he added before walking away.

"Thanks." Elana laid her backpack on a boulder and unzipped the front compartment. She pulled on her latex gloves and inspected the body. She got low to the ground and turned her head in the same direction as the inanimate eyes, imagining what was the victim's very last view in life, if any at all in the pitch darkness. Once Elana was certain that Moss was occupied elsewhere, she swabbed the victim's mouth and sealed the sample, then fingerprinted her. Sure that she had enough to make an ID, assuming this woman's DNA or prints were in the system, she zipped up the backpack compartment. Elana stood and stared down at the atrocious sight, afraid she would never be able to erase the image.

I might as well see it all now. She pulled off the gloves.

By the time she reviewed all the crime scene photos, Elana was sure she would be able conjure this spectacle in her sleep—as if she wouldn't while awake. Holding tight to her FBI orders, she had identified the body as Sierra Stone's...even though it wasn't hers. If there was a leak inside the Bureau, Sonnenheim wanted them to believe that Sierra was dead until they could find her and the thumb drive containing the names of the compromised operatives. Dead or alive, the game had changed, again.

Who is this woman? Where is Sierra, and what the hell happened to that thumb drive?

* * *

"Number seven," said the clerk as he handed Elana the key. "It's the last room at the end of the building. A-Are you certain you want to stay in there, given that the last young lady who stayed there is dead?"

"Were you here when she registered?"

"Yes, I checked her in. She seemed nice enough. Paid to use the phone in the other room to make a call. Our mobile phone reception is practically nonexistent up here."

"Do you have a record of the call?"

"No, we don't keep a log or anything if that's what you mean."

"Was that the only call she made?"

"As far as I know. I mean, probably. It was pretty short."

Elana nodded as she surveyed the small lobby and restaurant. The call coincided with the timestamp on her voice mail. "And you didn't hear anything unusual during the night?"

"There are always cars on this road. Oh, a pickup truck did pull in but no one rang the bell. It was after hours, so probably about ten o'clock. But it was gone shortly after. People always pull in to look at their maps."

"Was it dark outside?"

"Pretty much."

"So did the driver turn on the inside lights?"

The clerk thought about it. "I don't think so. But I did see long hair so I just assumed it was a woman who got lost. That's all I can think of."

"Did you catch the make of the truck?"

"No. But it was domestic. Ford or Dodge or one of those."

"Did you tell this to the police?"

The clerk rubbed his chin. "No. I didn't remember it until you asked."

Elana slid a fifty-dollar bill across the desk. "If you don't mind, I'd like to keep that between us until I leave town."

He pocketed the fifty.

"Anything else?" Elana asked.

"This is the only road that goes through on this side of the park and it's tourist season, so we hear traffic all the time... except of course when the train comes through."

"What time is that?"

"Which one? There are several. Here," he said, reaching behind him into a cubbyhole. "These are the approximate times they come through at night this time of year."

"Thanks."

Elana entered her room and sat on the bed, thinking it through as she methodically scanned each section. *Sierra was here to rendezvous with a Canadian asset to get a thumb drive and bring it to Sonnenheim in DC. The asset was supposed to be male, but the corpse that I identified as Sierra's was a woman. If she was the woman the clerk saw, and she's dead, where's the truck? There's no way to know if Sierra had even met with her contact. And Sierra's rental car has vanished.* "What if that thumb drive is still here?" She ran her fingers through her hair on her way into the bathroom. She stood on the toilet seat and reached up to unscrew the light cover. Nothing. Next, she examined baseboards, looked behind the paintings and furniture. "Where else could it be?" She yawned. "I'll think about it in the shower."

She turned on the water, stripped and stepped into the shower, her Glock laying on the tub's edge. Elana rinsed off and reached out to pull a towel from the rack before stepping out—and that's when she saw it. *What does that say?* In the steamy bathroom, on the foggy mirror, the numbers written in fingertip came alive.

CHAPTER EIGHT

That first night aboard the *Allons-y*, Kenna slept like a mermaid on a shoal. Her eyes opened to thoughts of the work that lay ahead. At half past sunrise she reconvened in the galley with Uncle and Phyllis van Bourgeade.

"Have you had a chance to see what's on the thumb drive yet, Uncle?"

"Yes, they worked on it for most of the night downstairs. American spyware, including a keylogger program."

"When I penetrate the Chinese Embassy's computers, the Americans will be able to monitor every single keystroke from their keyboards?"

Uncle nodded. "Once Annaliese gets hold of this they will. Every letter, symbol, backspace and deletion. Here you are." He handed her back the thumb drive, except that its case now looked like a tube of lipstick.

She poured a coffee and joined them at the dining table for her debriefing. Clearly unhappy when Kenna answered his first question, Uncle pursed his lips and frowned. "A beach man!" he said. "Encrypted or not, why would you take that risk with such valuable information? For God's sake, Kenna, you allowed the fate of the world to rest in a Jamaican beach man's pocket?"

Kenna glanced up at him from her coffee cup and raised the eyebrow of sarcasm. "Not only a beach man, Uncle. There was also a fruit lady from the hills involved."

Uncle's face flushed. "What? What were you thinking?"

"I was thinking that potentially every known and covert operative in the free world could be already compromised. We're all on the grid. It's why the Americans are staring down a global crisis right now. However, an older lady who walks half a mile each way with a fruit basket on her head to catch a bus in order to sell that fruit on the beach, is about as off-the-grid as you can get—next to the beach man, of course."

Uncle mulled it over. "I'm beginning to come around to your way of thinking."

"Would you like to brief me now?"

Uncle removed his reading glasses and smoothed back his shock of white hair. "Our cousins—your fellow Americans, are in trouble and need our help. As you know they've been hacked, and there's serious concern that their agents and assets have been outed. There are very few off-book operatives that the agency trusts." He smiled. "Your name was first on the list—the unwritten list."

"Who requested me?"

"Your friend in the cabinet, the Secretary of Homeland Security."

Kenna smiled. "Vince Zwarnick is a really good guy. Did the Americans actually catch the Chinese government in the act?"

"You know the Chinese would never be that sloppy. Their business enterprises do their hacking for them."

Her eyes met his. "What's on this drive I'm giving to the asset in Buenos Aires?"

"A counterintelligence back door. In addition to alerting them to breaches, American spyware will allow them to figure out what the Chinese have stolen. When the Chinese try to reenter the system, the Americans will use their backdoor to capture their keystrokes. Right now, the FBI is scrambling to find the extent of the Chinese malware and figure out how it wound up in their computers."

"That could be one or two lines of code out of millions," Kenna said.

"Once the FBI gets their hands on the source codes you'll be stealing in Buenos Aires, they'll use code matching to find discrepancies without even having to open a program to do it. But let's hope the Americans get good at it *quickly*. Future wars will be fought with keyboards, and I fear the future is upon us."

"How long until we get to Curaçao?" she asked.

"A few days. Long enough for us to make our plan fireproof, and for you to heal from the implant."

"I'll be back with the implant in a few minutes," Phyllis said when she left the salon.

"Kenna," Uncle began, "before Phyllis returns, I need to speak with you."

She looked at him quizzically. "Why?"

"Something came my way, a piece of information that you've wanted for a long time. Before I share it with you, I need to know that you truly want to know this."

She stared at the gravity tugging at his expression, the melancholy in his eyes. She had only ever seen that solemnity once before. "It's about my parents, isn't it?"

"Yes, *mon chou*, it is. Weigh it carefully."

She exhaled a hard sigh. "Tell me."

"It's not much, but considering how long it's been—"

"You know who assassinated them?"

"I only have a code name. It came up in one of our recent documents while cross-referencing another case where a British agent was killed in the exact same manner three years after your parents, in Norway of all places. All I know is that the assassin was referred to as *Le Gros Chat*."

"Do you have anything else? A nationality? A description? Anything?"

"I'm afraid not."

"That's it? The Big Cat? That's all you have?"

"Yes."

"The assassin should be shot just for calling himself that."

"I know it's not much to go on, but the case has been cold for over twenty years."

Kenna shook her head. "Sometimes I think I'll never find him."

"I know. Perhaps it's better that way."

Phyllis reentered the salon with a medical bag and a tray of sterile instruments. "It's time, *mon chou*," she said while walking to the table that was draped with a clean tablecloth. She placed the tray on the table, turned on the surgical light and adjusted it after Kenna sat in the chair.

Phyllis positioned Kenna's arm on the table and pulled on her latex gloves. She swabbed the area above the elbow with some iodine. "I'll try to be gentle but the needle has a big gauge. What I'm about to insert is the capsule."

"So how does this little chip work?"

"It's amazing and the GPS feature will allow us to locate your latitude, longitude, direction, speed."

"I'll bet you wish you'd had this when I was a teenager."

Phyllis smirked. "You really think I didn't know what you were up to, Kenna? Mothers *are* the original GPS. But to think that we can now zoom in on a softball from four hundred miles in space is really something." Phyllis loaded the chip into the syringe. "Everyone's in the satellite and GPS race these days."

"Neither the fruit lady nor the beach man have telephones yet."

Uncle glanced up from *Le Monde* newspaper and chuckled.

Kenna continued. "I thought we were at least a decade away from getting this technology to work properly in a human. No one's been able to get that right."

"This chip is GPS and also radio frequency."

"You're talking Radio-frequency identification?"

"Yes, RFID. Wherever you'll need a security code to enter, this chip is already programmed for the readers outside the door. As for reaching satellites, that may be hit-or-miss depending on radio-frequency noise interference."

Uncle poured another coffee from the carafe. "The easy part will be electronic entry, like getting you into the secret club in Buenos Aires to meet your contact."

"Dare I ask the hard part?"

"You'll need to be within eight feet of a computer at the Chinese Embassy for a minute or more for their source code to automatically download onto your chip. Once you're in DC, they'll extract the code and perform the code matching."

Kenna stared down at the microchip still in the syringe. "All of that in that tiny chip? How secure is this thing?"

"The chips were made in the US by government contractors and have met all of our specifications. By the way, we *want* everyone to think we're a decade away from successfully pulling this off." Phyllis squeezed the plunger and inserted the microchip.

"Ouch! *Merde!*" Kenna breathed through the pain. "Holy shit."

"Sorry, *chou*, but in my generation we were trained to take things out of people, not to insert them."

"I suppose that's true." Kenna breathed deeper through the pain.

Phyllis pressed a gauze pad against the injection site. "*Voilà.* That should do it." She peeled off her gloves. "Once in Curaçao, Annaliese will test it and make certain everything is calibrating properly. If anything isn't quite right, she can make adjustments and correct any signal issues. She'll also provide you with your Dutch passport, and she's arranged your passage into Buenos Aires."

"What's my cover and how am I gaining entry into the Chinese Embassy? I don't exactly look the part."

"There's an event scheduled to celebrate the new trade agreement between China and Argentina. As Dutch businesswoman Marleen Spiker, you'll be the date of a wealthy Argentine business supporter. The Argentine asset has an invitation for you and will brief you."

"Blueprints to the offices? Photos?"

"You'll like this, Kenna," Uncle said. He removed the lid from a long jewelry box and slid it to her across the table.

"Elegant, but really, you shouldn't have." Kenna stared down at the watch.

Uncle smiled and removed the watch from the box. He pressed the button on the side. "Point your hand somewhere and keep your eye on the watch face."

She pointed the hand of her chipped arm starboard and then twisted it in different directions. The images came up on the watch's screen.

"Now," Uncle began, "place your hand casually on the table, and then tap your index finger once."

She did it. "Are those our GPS coordinates?"

"Yep," said Phyllis. "I like this one. Tap this sequence: index finger, middle finger, index finger. When the image appears, use your finger taps to navigate. It takes a little practice but you'll pick it up quickly. It's also waterproof."

"You're kidding. Embassy maps, offices, computer server. How do I—"

"Save your big questions for Annaliese," said Uncle.

"Who is this Annaliese? Have I ever met her?" Kenna stood and flexed her arm. "I can feel the implant in there."

"Leave it be," Phyllis said with maternal command. "No, you don't know her…but you'll *like* her."

"Are you trying to fix me up, Maman?"

"You've been alone on that island far too long."

"I do own a house at the Jersey Shore, you know."

"You're rarely there."

"Not true. I've been there a lot lately."

"Besides," Phyllis continued, "Annaliese is beautiful, single and she's on our side." Phyllis smiled. "Shall we go dye your hair now?"

"What color is on my new Dutch passport?" Kenna asked as she followed Phyllis out.

"Black. It will make you a little less obvious in South America."

"Hmmm. A brunette. I might just be the only brunette in Buenos Aires with blond roots."

Deep into the night, Kenna awoke to a gnawing throb in her arm. She lay there pondering the identity of the assassin named *Le Gros Chat*. After turning over in bed for the last time, she pulled on a pair of shorts and a tank top and went topside. She stood on the bow and rocked with the waves beneath her—felt them carry her toward some distant land, under ancient stars where all that had ever been was here now. The waxing crescent sliver reclined on its back, and if all went as planned, she would be out of Buenos Aires before the gibbous moon grew full. Once in DC, she wondered if she could find any intelligence on *Le Gros Chat*. She took a deep whiff of night-sea and pushed the mission from her mind until all that remained was her, the boat and the ocean.

"Good evening," the woman behind her said softly.

Kenna turned. "Bonsoir, Captain Amara." She looked Amara up and down. "You're not in uniform, though I'm not complaining. You look cute like this." They greeted one another with a kiss on each cheek.

"Sometimes even captains need to just breathe."

With short-cropped brown hair, and dressed in yoga pants and a sports bra, Amara neither resembled a captain nor a spy.

"Is there anything more beautiful than sailing through an ocean in the middle of the night, Amara?"

"Look who you're asking. I'm a little biased."

"Me too," Kenna said, shifting her gaze out to sea. "How've you been?"

"I've been afloat for too long I think." Amara stepped closer and leaned on the rail, shoulder to shoulder with Kenna.

Kenna turned to look at her. "What makes you say that?"

"As you know, there are two things I love more than all others. Women and the sea. I've had lots of sea lately."

"And yoga, apparently."

"Apparently," Amara sighed.

"You making a pass at me, Amara?"

"No, it's your turn."

Kenna smiled. "I didn't know you were keeping track."

"I like you as a brunette. It could be a new beginning for us."

"All I can feel is my arm throbbing from that implant."

Amara gently rubbed Kenna's arm. "Get some rest. But I'm giving you fair warning, there are only so many yoga poses I can strike without invoking the Kama Sutra. Just saying."

Kenna laughed. "It's good to see you too and thanks. Sweet dreams." On the way back to her stateroom, Kenna grabbed some ice for her arm.

* * *

"Bonjour, Maman," Kenna said when she entered the breakfast salon.

"How are you feeling this morning, *mon chou?*"

"I didn't sleep all that well. My implant woke me several times during the night."

"And now?" Phyllis continued to arrange the croissants, baguettes, jams and spreads on the table. "Help yourself to coffee. I just pressed it."

Kenna walked to the coffeepot. "Doing a little better actually. It makes me wonder how such a small piece of electronics can have such a huge effect on a body."

"That's why it needs to be implanted a few days before we test it. They've found a variance that can occur with chemicals, some of which occur naturally in the body. It needs to heal a little bit."

Kenna swallowed some coffee. "Am I radioactive?"

"No, but you are radio-active, and I know that Annaliese will be right on your frequency." Phyllis winked.

Kenna laughed. "Hunt was right. You really *do* have a need to marry us off."

"I wish he would find a nice girl and give me more grandchildren. That goes for you too."

"I heard he met a nice woman. As for me, give it up. I'm a lost cause."

Phyllis just smiled.

Kenna took a sip of coffee and sized up her surrogate mother. "Oh, Maman, you didn't! You're already having her vetted, aren't you?"

"Who?" asked Phyllis.

"Hunt's girlfriend!"

"I have no idea what you're talking about."

CHAPTER NINE

Midmorning on the fourth day, Captain Amara entered the galley, poured a cup of coffee and joined Kenna in the salon. "We'll be at the transfer point within the hour. I wanted to wish you easy travels and good luck."

"Thanks, Amara. Can I ask you something?"

"Sure."

"Have you ever heard of any code name like *Le Gros Chat*?"

"Hmm. The only name I've ever heard with "cat" in it is the Cat Team, but they're US Secret Service."

"Secret Service?"

"You know, the tactical guys on the roofs with sniper rifles. What's this about?"

"I'm not really sure. All I have is a code name. Take care, Amara, it was good to see you again."

Amara smiled and kissed Kenna on the cheek. "Stay safe. And…who knows, maybe our paths will cross again soon."

Kenna smiled back. "Good luck with the yoga, and the Kama Sutra." She stood, walked out to the deck and stretched.

Psyching herself up for her long swim ahead, she downed another bottle of water and watched the decrepit and defunct lighthouse on Klein Curaçao come into view.

Uncle joined her. "Are you ready, Kenna?"

She held up her goggles. "Today, I get to cross swimming-an-uninhabited-island off my bucket list. A long swim will be good for me after being on this boat for a few days."

"You'll dive off about a mile-and-a-half away from shore and swim along the coast. Annaliese's boat, the *Queen of Hearts* will be moored on the southwest end. You can't miss it."

"Swimming downwind with the current will make it much easier."

"Once Phyllis and I clear immigration, we'll send your belongings over to her house from Willemstad."

Kenna hugged him. "Wish me luck."

"I have faith in you," he said. "There's a reason you were the one who was tapped for this job."

"Yes, because my identity hasn't been compromised, and Secretary Zwarnick at Homeland trusts me."

"No. It's because you're one of the best tacticians anywhere. Remember that. Your parents would be very proud of you."

"Perhaps prouder if I could find their killer."

"Kenna, don't do that to yourself. You were a child."

"I'm not any more though, am I?"

"It was a long time ago. There's a good probability that the assassin is gone too by now."

"I'll let you know when I find him or her."

"You know, I've always admired your tenacity. You're both the calm *and* the storm—brilliant at it really. How you became so steadfast and fearless is beyond me."

"I wasn't really given a choice now, was I? Besides, being Steel Eyes taught me a little something about that."

"You must miss it—being her."

Kenna smirked. "I miss *wanting* to be her. Does that count? I miss the music most of all."

"Maybe you're not done with her."

"It's been a long time, Uncle. I can't play like Steel Eyes anymore. My guitars might as well be in a museum."

"She was so different from you, and yet your perfect complement. Perhaps it's best to keep an open mind, hmm?"

Kenna shook off the thought and looked out to sea. "What about the tour boats?"

"We chose the location for that reason. There are plenty of day-trippers and people in the water. No one will notice you. Well, as long as you get there before the Coast Guard does its daily run from Curaçao."

"Are you certain about their timing?"

"Yes. Annaliese has a lot of power on the island. The Coast Guard has no reason to question her or board her boat, so all should go smoothly."

"And she has my ID?"

"Yes."

"I take it you're prepared for the Coast Guard to board you?" Kenna said.

"Completely. The software engineers are wearing crew uniforms, and Phyllis and I make the perfect old couple, don't you think?"

Kenna looked at him as though she had considered it for the very first time. "Actually, you do."

* * *

Kenna exhaled when she crossed into the transparent aquamarine unknown. A mosaic of sea turtles paddled beneath her, their necks elongated in apparent curiosity. She bobbed for air, adjusted her goggles and took inventory of the day-trippers from the party boats who were snorkeling to her west. Moored beyond them floated a yacht.

*If that boat looks that big from here...*Kenna interrupted her thought with a deep breath and swam toward it. Her seasoned masterstroke tuned her breath to her body, and tied her body to the rhythmic current. She set her pace, inhaling bilaterally until she could feel the oxygen deep inside her chest. About half a mile into her course came the moment she awaited. Her boundaries blurred and she became at one with the sea; such that she could no longer feel where skin ended and water began.

A school of bright-colored fish scattered as she swam through them, her glance darting around her, ever mindful that small fish attract larger fish. Later, a stingray peered at her from its dorsal-lying eyes before it swam away with its graceful wings. Alone for a while, a small pod of dolphins surrounded her, and she wondered what they were saying about her as they chattered back and forth. She glided above the coral core of volcanic underbelly, the wind yielding more, and the current propelling her as she shifted her trajectory. By the time she reached the *Queen of Hearts*, her breathing was labored.

The crew member who stood by the aft ladder awaiting her, ushered her below deck where she showered and changed. The engines accelerated after the boat turned as they set course back to Curaçao.

Kenna entered the luxurious salon and smiled at the leggy woman with the dangerous curves. Refined and well tended without being delicate, Annaliese Dahl carried herself with poise and grace as she moved across the room. In her forties, with medium-length thick brown hair and attentive hazel eyes, to Kenna she resembled Catherine Deneuve.

"Welcome, I'm Annaliese," she said with a Dutch accent.

"Good to finally meet you. I'm Kenna."

While they shook hands, Annaliese overtly scanned Kenna from head to toe and back again. "It looks good on you—that bikini."

What there is of it, Kenna thought.

"I assume everything went smoothly thus far?"

"Yes, thanks. Phyllis and Uncle send regards."

"You must be quite thirsty after that long swim. What would you like?"

"Water. I've already downed the bottles that your crew gave me."

"Have a seat," Annaliese said as she took a bottle of Evian from the bar and walked it over to Kenna. "In the envelope on the table is your new passport, pocket lint from Curaçao, and some wallet-litter with receipts from last week. At home, I have some tourist items for your suitcase."

Kenna lifted the eyebrow of sarcasm. "Now where would I stash pocket lint in this bikini?"

Annaliese sat next to her and sipped a Bloody Mary. "Sorry, I really wanted to see you in it."

Kenna laughed. "Have any other plans for me I should know about? Like actual clothing maybe? I'd prefer not wearing a bikini when we dock."

"Not to worry, I moor the yacht at home. We'll be there in about an hour and there's plenty to choose from until your suitcase arrives. I'll be testing the chip after dinner and adding the keystroke software to the thumb drive."

"How does that work?" Kenna took a long sip of Evian.

"It's set to tie into their encryption. Whenever someone types anything onto the Chinese servers, we'll be able to see what they're sending."

"So, once you've penetrated their firewall, you'll track the chatter?"

"Yes. I can do it all through a VPN, an offsite virtual private network that can't be tracked—even *if* they knew I was doing it, which they won't."

Kenna picked up the items on the table and looked them over. She grinned and then tossed the passport and all her carefully chosen litter onto the coffee table.

"Is there something amusing about your passport?"

"I'm not used to seeing myself as a brunette. I'm a blonde actually."

"Really? I can't picture it."

Kenna looked into her eyes. *Phyllis might be right. She definitely has something about her. What am I saying? Hunt would never let me live it down if I hooked up with a woman that his mother fixed me up with. Oh, god, fixed up! You've had women throw themselves at you as a rock star and you're letting your surrogate mom fix you up? Pathetic.*

"Are you all right, Kenna?"

Kenna snapped back to reality. "Yes, why?"

"You had a curious expression."

Kenna shook her head. "Oh it's nothing, just making my mental notes."

"I watched you in the water with my binoculars. It was quite enjoyable actually—watching you. Even more so while sipping a Bloody Mary with my feet up."

Kenna tilted her head to the side, observing this woman, trying her on for size. *This is my girlfriend Annaliese*, then, *Yes, Annaliese and I love going there. What is wrong with me!* Finally she spoke. "I hope you were the only one who noticed me out there."

"If you're worried about the Coast Guard, don't. I'm a key figure on the island. Besides, they're after the smugglers who mostly come from Venezuela since it's so close." Annaliese rose from the couch and placed her empty Bloody Mary glass on the bar. "You're welcome to join me on the deck, or if you prefer you can rest up from your swim."

"Thank you for the hospitality, Annaliese."

Annaliese smiled, tossed her hair to one side and moved toward the door.

Kenna slowly drank the Evian with her eyes trained on Annaliese as she sauntered from the salon—watched her until every last bit of her and the Evian were gone from sight.

She then waited a respectable five minutes before she joined the woman on the deck.

CHAPTER TEN

Kenna took the seat across from her host. "Have you lived on the island a long time?"

"About eight years, but I split my time between here and Europe since I have enterprises there. And you live in Jamaica?"

"Is that what Phyllis told you?"

"No, it was Uncle. He mentioned several times—how shall I put this—that you're single, and that he thought we would *like* each other."

"Hmm. They really are a devious pair. I got the same push from Phyllis."

Annaliese laughed. "Looks like we've been double-teamed." She looked away when her skipper approached. "Alfred, are we slowing down?"

"Coast Guard is behind us," he said. "I have to get on the horn but I thought you'd want to know."

Shortly after, the Coast Guard vessel neared, and a man's voice interrupted the music coming through the speakers. "Motor vessel *Queen of Hearts*, this is the Coast Guard. Please switch and answer Channel 20 alpha."

"Coast Guard, this is the *Queen of Hearts*, go ahead, over," the captain replied.

"*Queen of Hearts*, we will be boarding your vessel for a routine check."

"We read you, Coast Guard. Proceed, over."

"Should I be concerned?" Kenna said.

"Yes. Are you clear on your cover?"

"Right down to my lint and litter. How do you want me to play this?"

"You're gorgeous, so just smile…and say as little as possible."

The Coast Guard pulled up alongside the yacht with its officers preparing to board the *Queen of Hearts*.

"This shouldn't be happening." Annaliese's voice was taut.

"You think I'm gorgeous?"

"Now is actually not a good time."

Kenna laughed. "I suggest you laugh too," she said quietly. "Make it look like we're having fun."

"We are having fun." Annaliese laughed along with her, and then turned toward the Coast Guard's boat. "Good afternoon, Captain," she said when he boarded. "Please come in." She led him and two of his men into the salon. "To what do I owe the unusual pleasure?"

"Good afternoon, Ms. Dahl. I'm sorry for the inconvenience but we've been ordered to step up our safety inspections." He shook his head. "Damn drug runners."

"I haven't seen anything unusual, and I've been out most of the day," said Annaliese.

"I take it you boated out to Klein Curaçao today?" said the captain. His eyes scanned the salon.

"Yes."

"I was wondering if everything is okay. You usually stay out longer and you're sailing faster than usual."

Annaliese smiled effortlessly. "Thank you, that's so kind of you. Yes, everything is fine. I need to get home for a call before it gets too late in Europe. Not everyone observes our island schedules."

The captain smiled. "Yes, we do treasure island time."

"My cousin and I were just out for a little cruise," Annaliese said.

Kenna smiled at him coyly. She stood, let the three men drink in the sight of her tanned swimmer's body, and then sauntered toward the bar in her skimpy bikini. "Would you gentlemen care for something?" She gazed into the captain's eyes and waited. "Perhaps…water or soft drinks?"

"Uh, thank you, no. No, we're fine." He fidgeted and diverted his gaze to Annaliese. "So then, I assume everything is in good working order? Signal flares, life vests…"

"Of course. You know what a stickler Captain Alfred is."

"You're lucky to have such an experienced captain. Sorry to delay you," he said.

"Really, it's no bother at all. I appreciate your concern," said Annaliese. "By the way, Joost, I'll have the rest station set up for your crew at the Curaçao Jazz Festival again this year. I'm sure they'll need it with all the drunk tourists."

The captain smiled. "Isn't that the truth! We do appreciate it, ma'am."

"It's the least I can do." Annaliese shook the officer's hand. "Stay safe out here, Captain."

Kenna watched the Coast Guard pull away and then followed Annaliese onto the deck. "Close call."

"You're very good at handling men. He was like a school kid when you stood and strutted your stuff."

"They're all little boys at heart."

"Evidently, so am I."

* * *

An hour and a half later, the *Queen of Hearts* approached Curaçao from the south. They sailed past Jan Thiel and a flotilla of yachts barely smaller than the one Kenna occupied. In the waning day, she watched the sea's color deepen into its richest and darkest shades of cobalt; the waves rolling high and cresting in the wind. Standing in awe, Kenna viewed the contrast of silver *Bouladou* fish, shamelessly outpacing her craft as a school flew through the air above the surf.

Annaliese came up beside her and leaned on the railing. "That's my place." She pointed to the top of a hill where but one dwelling stood.

"Quite impressive," Kenna said, glancing over at her. "It even looks big from this distance."

"It's home. We'll be mooring the boat in about five minutes. I bet you'll be happy to finally set foot on land."

Kenna sighed. "Not really."

"Are you hungry?"

"Ravenous."

Annaliese smiled warmly. "I thought you might be. Dinner will be ready as soon as we get there."

Kenna joined Annaliese on the dining terrace to drink in the bountiful Caribbean sunset—pushing away the thought that it could be her last. They lingered long after their plates had been cleared and the coastal lights came to life below them.

Kenna still felt the rocking of the boat. Every so often, she jerked slightly, as though compensating for a wave, instead of feeling solid land beneath her.

"Steady there, sailor. Are you okay?" asked Annaliese when Kenna did it again.

"This is the first time my feet have been on land in days," she said. "You know that balancing sensation when your brain still thinks you're at sea?"

"I love that feeling. How does it feel to be back on solid ground?"

"Being on land isn't always the same thing as being on solid ground. Although, my mind is clearer than it's been in a while. I'm still thinking about that exquisite meal, Annaliese. My compliments to your chef."

"Yes, she's a gem. Wait until you see what she's whipped up for dessert, which we will have as soon as we've completed the implanted chip tests." She stood. "This way," she said as she led Kenna upstairs. They followed a hallway of stone and glass as they traversed the sprawling hillside home. It led to a separate wing that looked out over the expanse of water, and down at the Santa Barbara lights.

"The testing shouldn't take long if everything goes smoothly," said Annaliese just before she stopped. "Move toward the security door, Kenna."

The door unlocked when Kenna stepped in front of it. "Was that the RFID programming?"

Annaliese nodded. "I thought you should get a realistic view of how it works before you use it in Buenos Aires. RFID readers should be able to pick up the radio frequency within a meter."

Kenna followed her into the large, cool room. "Chilly in here even with clothes on," she said as she took in the panorama of electronics.

Annaliese stepped over to a table full of wands and electronic toys. "I run this room off a private generator to stay off the grid, and to minimize power disturbances."

"Some women just have a sex dungeon for entertainment," Kenna teased.

"That's in the other wing," Annaliese replied dryly. "I've programmed the coordinates for where you'll be going in Buenos Aires as well as the entry code to the secret club off the Plaza Dorrego. Your contact will school you on the Chinese Embassy part of the plan. My job is to make sure you have the necessary tools when you get there. You do need to know that in order to clone the code from the Chinese computers, you'll need to be within two and a half meters of an embassy terminal at the exact time the window is open."

"How will I know when—"

"The Argentine asset will brief you."

Kenna nodded, still surveying the equipment.

"All right, have a seat over here near my expensive toys. You can follow what I'm doing either on your watch or on the big screen behind me."

Annaliese tapped computer keys, picked up the first wand and waved it near Kenna as she watched what came up on her screen. She repeated the process with other devices, making occasional entries into the computer. Finally, she spoke. "This is the progress icon you'll see while the chip is loading the source code from the Chinese computers."

Kenna glanced at her watch. "And if there's no icon?"

"Then get to another terminal fast. Your window to clone the code will close in one minute and twenty-five seconds if you're not in the system by then." Annaliese powered down the equipment. "That should do it. It needed a few tweaks, although I'm not sure why. Then again, that's why we're testing it."

"Phyllis had said that sometimes body chemistry can affect the chip function."

"It's not been problematic, but it is possible since the chips are miniature electronics implanted in a living organism. Your soft tissues are already growing around it and integrating their function to deal with it."

"Comforting. Who's tracking me?"

Annaliese smiled proudly. "We and the Americans are, darling. Haven't you heard? There's a global storm brewing, and you're the agent that the free world is counting on to stop it."

"Oh, good, and here I thought there'd be pressure." Kenna exhaled the hard sigh of ennui as she stood.

Annaliese stepped toward her and stroked her hair. "I think it's time for dessert and then some relaxation from that long swim."

Kenna froze when Annaliese kissed her lightly on the lips. "I have you scheduled for a massage."

Kenna lifted the eyebrow of sarcasm. "I *like* this resort."

* * *

The following morning, Annaliese joined Kenna on the breakfast terrace and poured a cup of coffee from the carafe. "Morning," she said when she took her seat.

Kenna waited before answering, observing the woman. "Did I do something wrong last night, Annaliese?" she said calmly.

"From your reaction last night, I thought maybe I should be asking you that question. Perhaps I've become too used to getting what I want."

"I'm focused on the mission. Maybe another time."

"I understand. Perhaps I'll see you when you get back to Jamaica."

"*If* I get back to Jamaica."

"You're going to do fine. Don't worry. After you're finished with Buenos Aires, you'll be in Washington to extract the code from the chip and then you're done."

"You make it sound easy."

Annaliese reached out, touched Kenna's hand and met her eye. "Just stay safe. You owe me a *date*."

"When does *Marleen Spiker* leave for the airport?"

"Whenever you're ready. The suitcase Uncle had delivered is already repacked and in the car."

Kenna stood and matched Annaliese's perfected and terminal come-on stare with one of her own. Tilting the woman's chin upward, Kenna bent forward as if to kiss her and stopped an inch before. "Do you *really* have a sex dungeon?"

CHAPTER ELEVEN

As Dutch subject Marleen Spiker, Kenna breezed through immigration in Buenos Aires. A city named for its good wind, Kenna hoped Myron had been right when he told her she knew the good wind. She clung to the good wind now in all manner of life's turbulence; surfed it the way a leaf blows free at the close of autumn.

She tossed her carry-on into the backseat of the taxi. "Hotel *Buen Ayre, por favor*," she said. While taking in the sights, she massaged the muscle under her leftover scar from an assassin's bullet. Who she had been, what she still was, each occupied its self-contained world inside her. To have survived all that she had, only to face the consequential loss of Steel Eyes and her music, all but paled in comparison to having lost at love. Although the spy in her knew that every person or situation she encountered was potentially her last, the artist in her lived for the next eloquent moment—what she called, *intangible nuance*.

Once Kenna checked in, she tipped the bellman and stood before the large window of the classical Euro-styled room. The plazas and Parisian facades cinched the sweeping view of the boulevard.

Over empanadas and coffee from room service, she pored through neighborhood maps. Then, disguised in a mousy-brown bob wig and unfashionable glasses, she combed the route she would need to know the next day. She even managed a close-up inspection of the Chinese Embassy across town on Avenue Crisulugu Lairalde.

While timing her route to the Plaza Dorrego, a landslide of recollections bombarded her. Filtered though they were through the sieve of time, they distracted her in no particular order. Thousands of Steel Eyes fans had once welcomed her here. Through the presbyopic lens of years past, the underground rocker could still readily taste the memory. She could still conjure the faint echo of a distant roar—of fans singing the famous chant for the character she'd long ago abandoned: '*Steel Eyes, Steel Eyes, Steel Eyes!*' By the time Kenna made it back to the Buen Ayre, she was sure of her course, ready for what lay ahead.

The following evening, while dressing and getting into character to meet with her contact, she let her mind drift a little in the direction of Annaliese, reaching to feel something real for the woman; anything at all.

How could I not feel a spark with a woman like that? she thought. She's smart, beautiful, fights the good fight.

Kenna exhaled the self-reproach and changed her shirt two more times to prove it. Then she took refuge in reminiscing about Cathérine, the Parisian bartender who had made off with her heart. Cathérine, who had inspired that last performance in Buenos Aires.

Back then, when Kenna had wandered this city without her famous mask, she'd had thoughts of returning to Paris after that tour to see if she and Cathérine could be together. She had even considered removing her mask to reveal her true identity to the woman. Had she not suffered the almost fatal gunshot that ended her career, she'd have done it. She was certain of it.

Except for Kenna's exhilarating nights with a lap dancer named Alice, the magic of Steel Eyes's brief affair with Cathérine was the only relief she'd ever had from lamenting the loss of Alex Winthrop. She remembered thinking how Cathérine had been her one chance to move on with someone else. But now, that spark of attraction to anyone, like the passion for her music, was gone from her.

The heir apparent to the void of love, sex, and fame, was the chilling shadow of peril—peril, and covert meetings with foreign assets on nights like this one.

"I do not look like a Marleen Spiker," Kenna said while tilting her hat one last time before the mirror. She adjusted her ankle holster, and then exited the hotel to work her way along the cobblestone streets. According to her test run, she would be at the Plaza Dorrego in ten minutes.

Buenos Aires's vibrant twilight charm reverberated throughout colonial La Boca and San Telmo, the oldest neighborhoods in the city. Aged and worn, the once immigrant tenements known as *conventillos*, now housed trendy boutiques and cafés. With a nod to their tenement history, the buildings remained splashed with an array of bright colors—a testament to the era when leftover shipyard paint colored the barrio, and dressed up the brothels.

From somewhere down a narrow cobblestone alleyway, beyond a crumbling church, the sad song of a solo *bandoneon* trickled out. Its lonely bellows breathed through aged reeds, drawing Kenna in the direction of its musical dolor. That music. So emotional was its ubiquitous uprising in her body that it made even the *idea* of thinking detestable; loathsome, like playing this music when instead she could let it play her. All she could do when she heard those tragic intervals was to feel their every rise and fall as they had their way with her. She slowed her pace to watch a young couple dancing to the concertina in the street, allowing its melodic story to wash over her before continuing on.

At the end of the narrow street was another street, and then another until the cobblestone alleys eventually opened onto the corner of Humberto Primo and Calle Defensa. She surveyed the ring of tango cafés surrounding the Plaza Dorrego. So far, all had gone as planned.

The crowd of *Porteños*—Buenos Aires residents—filtered in, gathering in the second oldest square in the city. Most of them—*tangueros* and *tangueras*—men and women tango dancers ready to fill the night with smoldering passion, arrogance and flare. They performed with the nostalgic sadness and longing that the dance demanded, to lyrics often sung in *Lunfardo*—the slang of lower classes from another time.

Bathed in dusk, Kenna checked her watch, glad she had time before she would have to meet her asset off the opposite side of the plaza. Knowing that the dancers used eye contact and little else to select their perfect partner, she scanned the faces to observe it in action. In a fraction of a second, the dancers conveyed their interest, or lack of it—glances sweeping from one person to the next without a blink or a hesitation, until they found the *one*.

She smiled. *Without chemistry there is no emotion. And without emotion there is no tango.*

So much was tied to the subtle acknowledgment between potential partners that the eye movements and facial expressions alone seemed to her a dance all their own. Men and women alike turned as Kenna started through the crowd. Their gazes feasted upon her—a tall woman dressed in a man's tailored black suit and a cobalt shirt unbuttoned to her cleavage. Fluidly weaving her way through the square, the two-four beat accented her every step. With her black hair piled up under the fedora, the tilted brim formed a continuous upward sweep from her high and prominent cheekbones. Kenna didn't acknowledge the stares she felt landing on her from every direction.

Although same sex unions were now legal in Argentina, she knew she was pushing it to bend her gender in public, let alone draw attention to herself under any circumstance. The men waited for Kenna to acknowledge their interest, but she continued on not making a twitch of expression in anyone's direction. Instead, she drank in the graffiti art on the buildings, and with every step, felt the infusion of a cadence buried underground for a century. She shivered from the visceral stirring of this beat forever bound to merciless melodies of impure desire. That penetrating tempo had once scavenged sailors for the brothels, in the name of the barrio's wandering patron saint of seafarers, San Telmo.

Kenna halted when the next song began. This one spoke to her, like a wanton embrace, or the wisp of a kiss—the brush of a hand on her waist.

If I existed purely as music, then this is the music I would be— tonight.

The modern tango electronica ignited the evening air when the Gotan Project's haunting "Santa Maria Del Buen Ayre" rose through the loudspeakers. Unable to think when that music pulsed inside her, Kenna granted her longing temporary amnesty from its self-imposed exile.

Ba-DUP! ba da da da
Ba-DUP! ba da da da

Intoxicated by the song's highs and lows, the history of sex in this barrio, she would dance to it at this street tango—at this *milonga*.

Across the circle, beyond the men vying for her attention, the radiant temptress aimed her stare at Kenna. Kenna's eyes flared involuntarily when she saw the brunette with the low-cut red halter dress. A slit along the right leg exposed a shapely calf that ended in three-inch black heels. The woman wore her black hair pulled back tightly. Her distinctive dark eyes and chiseled cheekbones conjured colonial Spain from another century, giving her an air of sophistication.

With a subtle nod, Kenna's *cabeceo*—her invitation to dance—was complete. The returned nod was so slight that Kenna wondered if she had imagined it. The *tanguera* held her gaze as they both stepped toward the circle, the two-four beat taunting them, daring them.

Those eyes.
Ba-DUP! ba da
Those curves.
Ba-DUP! ba da

While the woman's brooding sensuality drew Kenna in, it also locked everyone else out, at least for this *tanda*—the next four songs. As the two women sauntered toward each other, not even the muffled gasps from homophobic aficionados or tangueros could drown out the torrid, punctate rhythm. Nor could it stop their slinky advance to meet in the center of the circle.

Ba-DUP! ba da da da

Their stare was made of fire, at the core of which burned the silent confrontation that defined the tango; that posed the questions: *Will she? Won't she?*

I'll make *her want to!* In that moment, Kenna Waverly owned the Argentine tango—and the porteña in the red dress with the smoldering stare.

Poised and firm, Kenna raised her left hand and awaited her partner's right. She sensually wrapped her right arm around the woman in a close *Abrazo* embrace, their hips touching— her hand resting on the center of the woman's back, below her shoulder blades. Kenna felt the woman's fingers slide up every inch of her arm until they rested on Kenna's shoulder.

Ba-DUP! ba da da da

Kenna pulled her closer.

Ba-DUP! Ba da da da

Their breasts now pressed against each other, their lips were not an inch apart when the dance began. She wondered if their initial pose appeared as artful as it felt; as thrilling as it felt.

Mirroring one another, their first set of walking steps danced the tango.

Slow, slow, quick-quick, slow.

Their second set of steps laid bare the lament of the dance. Kenna's blazing stare commanded her: *Follow me!*

The woman's body answered, "Yes! No! Yes. No."

Slow, slow, quick-quick, slow.

As Kenna moved her across the floor, her eyes spoke: *Follow me to the end! Let me lead you…to the end.*

The *tanguera's* steps answered, "Maybe, I don't know."

The concertina goaded them with its brisk and hypnotic trill. *Ba-DUP! ba da da da.*

Gancho! Their knees hooked around one another's and then flicked a release.

Enganche! The woman wrapped her leg around Kenna's, the slit in her dress parting.

Slow, slow, quick-quick, slow.

Kenna pressed into the *tanguera* from her core and slid her backward in synchronized passion, shifting their weight together, their bodies locked against one another. Their sensual ache was restrained, contained, waiting to break free. Bound by barrio heat, they moved as one, Kenna dipping her backward into a spray of crimson light. She stared down at the graceful neck beneath her and then at the cleavage, longing to place her lips there.

Slow, slow, quick-quick, slow.

As their connection burrowed deeper, the dance played out their artful configurations of trust. Kenna's foot play sensuously displaced her partner's leg; the response of which was the woman's instep rubbing along Kenna's thigh and down her calf. No words. Only the language of tango—the expression of each movement. Their silent conversation played out a series of asked and answered emotions. In the end, their embrace spoke, 'You are mine.'

Slow, slow, quick-quick, slow.

With her back to Kenna, the woman raised her leg behind her, wrapping it behind Kenna's hip. Kenna slipped her fingers around the woman's inner thigh with the same tenderness with which she would caress a guitar, then lifted her and spun in a circle. The woman stroked Kenna's neck as her feet recaptured the ground.

Their eyes in lockstep, they danced until the final note in their *tanda* faded. Silently, they turned and went their separate ways—Kenna disappearing into the crowd to deliver the thumb drive to some asset; the *tanguera* blending back into the night.

Intangible nuance had at last collided with that which could be touched.

CHAPTER TWELVE

Kenna hustled to navigate through the growing crowd in the Plaza Dorrego, weaving around the pack of dancers. Diagonally across from where she had danced, she spotted the spoke of alley—the type that was easily passed over in favor of broader streets with their cafés and shops. The spy followed the GPS on her watch to the second building from the far end of the block on the right, and entered. Across the quaint Spanish Colonial courtyard, she located the red door on the eastern wall. Even though she couldn't see the RFID reader, she watched the red light above the door change to green as she neared. Once inside, she descended the three steps into the dimly lit vestibule of a club so secret, it didn't have a name.

"You have full access," said the man in the tuxedo who greeted her. "Where would you like to go?"

She noticed three hallways: one dead ahead, another to the right, and one farther down on the left. "The blue door," she said. The secret club's secret club, she thought.

He pointed to the corridor on the left and Kenna walked to its end. When the RFID reader sensed her, the blue door opened onto a darkly lit plush club. She scanned lavish tufted sofas off to the right, and dimly lit alcoves in the distance.

Dark red on the walls, perhaps a brothel from a hundred years earlier, it was the secret's secret for a reason. In the center of the room, the dance floor glowed from crimson lighting that matched the walls. Beyond it to the left, a deep mahogany bar, ornate and Spanish. Kenna took it all in and sauntered past the crowd to the far side of the bar, taking the second to last seat facing the door.

Dressed in designer clothing and expensive jewelry, the patrons had bottles of top-tier champagne as their tables' centerpieces, and most members danced a version of tango she had never seen. Sizzling and sultry, every dancer subscribed to the representation of vertical sex set to music, after which they would return to their alcoves where some drew their privacy curtains.

Staggered smiles landed on her from every *tanguera* intrigued by Kenna's brand of gender-bending. The heat behind their eyes intersected with hers in the middle of the room, like two bodies coming together in the Abrazo embrace.

The men turned their backs, but Kenna acknowledged the flirtations anyway. *Now I want to know what's behind the doors down the other hallways. Maybe I should be living in Buenos Aires.* So polarized was she by the beat and the movement to it that she didn't immediately sense the presence on the barstool next to her. She turned slowly to meet her asset.

Her look was met with the penetrating stare of the dark-haired woman with sensual curves—in the low-cut red halter dress.

"You're a very good dancer," the woman said.

The only thing better than staring into this woman's eyes is the sensation of her body against mine in the tango. "You almost made me late for you. Did you know who I was when you accepted the dance?"

The *tanguera* smiled slyly. "Does it matter?"

"Yes, it matters."

"Why is that?"

"Because having you wrapped around me didn't seem contrived."

"It wasn't." The Argentine slipped a scrap of paper into Kenna's coat pocket. "Yes, I knew who you were. We're not safe here."

"The man at two o'clock?"

"Yes. Wait ten minutes and then meet me at this address. Be mindful on your way."

Kenna entered the ladies' room stall and programmed the address into her watch, then flushed the piece of paper. She left the Blue Club and walked for ten minutes to make sure no one was following her, then hailed a cab on a side street. Night fell harder as the taxi rolled through the Centro district and continued on to the affluent Recoleta neighborhood, past the forever home of Eva Peron in the Recoleta Cemetery.

Kenna paid the cab driver, walked a block and then rode the *Subte* subway for one stop. She exited and turned right onto the tree-lined street a few blocks away toward the safe house. On the far left corner stood the curved provincial building that could have as easily adorned a Parisian boulevard.

When her asset answered the door to the posh penthouse, she was no longer the *tanguera* in the red low-cut dress with her hair pulled back tight.

"Come in. It's Pascale, isn't it?" she said.

"Yes," Kenna said when she entered. "And what shall I call you?"

"Trysta. How about something to drink?"

"Trysta. Trust—the agreement between lovers. Vodka martini dry. Olives if you have them."

Kenna observed the woman as she walked to the bar, now dressed in designer jeans with an off-the-shoulder silk knit top and heels. "I like you with your hair down. Frankly, I didn't think you could get any more beautiful than the *tanguera* in the red dress, but I was wrong."

Trysta placed Kenna's cocktail on the coffee table and sat on the sofa. "Join me, Pascale."

Kenna removed the fedora, shook loose her long, black hair and removed her suit jacket. "Thanks." She sat on the sofa near Trysta and took a long sip of the martini. "Business first?"

"*Sí.*"

Kenna nodded, took the thumb drive from the false heel in her boot, and handed it over.

"Hmm, very inventive how they've made it look like a small tube of lipstick."

"I was told you have the instructions for the Chinese Embassy."

"I do. While our asset is uploading this spyware onto the Chinese computers, you'll be downloading code wirelessly from their system onto your microchip." Trysta stared into Kenna's eyes. "This part of the operation must be precisely timed, and your window of opportunity is brief."

"How will I know when the window is?"

Trysta grinned. "I'll be attending the event, so you'll have to keep an eye on me."

"Keep an eye on you?" Kenna laughed. "I'm having difficulty looking at anything else."

"When our Chinese friend loads the spyware, he'll signal me and I'll alert you. You'll then have one minute and twenty-five seconds to get to within two-and-a-half meters of a computer terminal anywhere in the building. Your radio-frequency chip should gain you access to the office reception area, and as long as you're within range of a computer for sixty seconds, we're good."

Kenna raised the eyebrow of sarcasm. "You said the chip *should* allow me to gain access. What if it doesn't?"

"It will. When we arrive at the embassy, all I need to do is get within a few centimeters of any higher official and use my cloner to trap the RFID code from their badge. Then I transfer it onto your chip, which I can do wirelessly."

Kenna nodded and took another sip of the martini. "Who's my wealthy Argentine date for the evening?"

Trysta deadpanned her.

"Really?" Kenna said, amused. "I would think the Chinese frowned on that sort of thing."

"They do. But right now they're courting me in the trade agreements since I represent a consortium, and they don't have a choice. It's strategic on my part really. If they're busy picturing me in bed with you, they won't be thinking of me as the hacker within their walls."

"I can see how picturing that would be very distracting," Kenna said.

"Have you studied the layout of the embassy?"

"Yes. The main ballroom has a back office for the event organizers. According to my research, there's a computer in there for checking in staff and food deliveries. They'll have to leave the computer on during their event and it's most likely integrated with their overall system."

"How do you know this, Pascale?"

"Last night, in disguise, I rented a truck and made a large flower delivery through the service entrance."

Trysta gazed into her eyes. "You're everything they said you'd be—and more. Much, much more."

Kenna took another sip of the martini. "Who is 'they'?"

"Well, Jocelyn, for one."

"I've known her a long time. How do you know Joss?"

"We did an op together in France last year. When she'd heard that I'd be working with you, she called."

"What did she say?" Kenna's gaze danced over the soft skin on Trysta's neck, then along the slope of her shoulders. Already knowing the thrill of holding this woman in her tango embrace, she blinked against the heat behind her eyes.

"Joss said if I had the opportunity, I shouldn't let you get away. So I thought the best way to do that was to spot you before our official meeting, then tempt you with something irresistible." She smiled from the corner of her mouth.

"So you already knew my weakness for sultry women who dance the tango?"

"I took an educated guess. And since I knew where your route would leave you, I positioned myself to be found."

"Well done, Trysta. You've perfected the art of playing on a target's weakness. Now, about the gala tomorrow night. What time do you want me at the embassy?"

"I'll pick you up at your hotel at seven. It's black tie. Any questions?"

"No."

Trysta leaned toward Kenna, held her gaze, and sighed. "Then we're done here, Pascale."

Kenna moved to leave and Trysta reached out to stop her. "I meant our business has concluded."

Kenna looked back at her. "Is that Brazilian jazz I hear trickling through your sound system?"

"*Sí.* You prefer something else, *amor?*"

Kenna smiled, stroked back the woman's long hair, and let her fingertips slide down Trysta's sensuous neck and along her bare shoulder—remembering what the *tanguera* looked like bent backward beneath her, soaked in crimson light. Then, on the second upstroke of the smooth bossa nova beat, she leaned in and placed her lips against Trysta's.

All the denied desire that had been present in their dance exploded the instant that their tongues played against each other. No longer did Kenna feel the back and forth of the emotions asked and answered in their *tanda.* The 'yes, no, maybe' had evaporated, and what remained was the lightning strike—the firestorm of their lips meeting for the first time.

In the plaza, their dance had summoned the saint of twilight lust. That suffocating public restraint now behind them, their passion breathed deep and hard behind closed doors. Here, their craving would take its full and predestined form. Every caress, each kiss, now belonged to a legacy of long-ago brothel back rooms, between Kenna and the woman whose real name she would likely never know; the woman to whom her own identity would remain Pascale. For two women who teetered on the edge of each moment, eternity seemed bland.

Trysta pulled her in closer, unbuttoning Kenna's shirt, touching her round breasts first with her soft hands and then with her lips and tongue. With one intoxicating look, the woman distilled Kenna's desire into surrender. Irreversible. Unstoppable. Inevitable surrender.

It's been so long since I've felt this, Kenna thought. This! Yes...this. She wrapped a mane of Trysta's hair around her hand

and gently pulled back the woman's head. With a shiver inside, she pressed her warm mouth against the neck whose skin she had wanted to devour since the moment she had held Trysta in her arms. That first instant their bodies had pressed up against one another, palpable heat vacillated between their hips, their breasts. A fiery come-on look melted the air between them. Kenna didn't care how dangerous this could turn out to be— sleeping with an asset. She didn't give a damn about any of it with Trysta up against her.

Ba-DUP! Ba da da da

Slow, slow, quick-quick, slow.

Grayscale counted for little in her black-and-white world of life and death. Right here was *all* of the black, *all* of the white, dovetailed, curled around each other in the perfect balance of the yin and the yang. Like Steel Eyes, Kenna Waverly thrived only when inspired; she lived for the rare moments of dangerous *and* beautiful, for neither was nearly complete, the one without the other. Trysta grabbed her, melted her with the smoldering stare of the *tanguera*.

Fuck the rules.

They moved as one, at first in the tango, and later, in bed.

Slow, slow, quick-quick, slow.

In the predawn, Buenos Aires tossed its leftover streetlight through the loft's clerestory window. Trysta whispered from her pillow across the darkness.

"You're a true romantic, Pascale."

"You inspire me, Trysta."

"The way that you took me—it was relentless. Surely some woman in your life would not be happy about it."

Kenna smiled. "There is no other lover. You have me all to yourself."

"But your touch is electrifying." She reached over and caressed Kenna's hand with her own. "It's not possible that someone isn't waiting for you somewhere."

Kenna sighed. "Until tonight when our eyes met, desire had eluded me for a very long time. Until you, I wondered if I'd ever feel it again."

Trysta slid on top of her and lavished her with kisses, dissolved into the sequel of what had already been, her long dark hair spilling onto Kenna's skin. "Once more before you go. Please."

Kenna slid her hands onto the *tanguera's* smooth ass and pressed their naked bodies together.

Trysta moaned. Cheek to cheek, she whispered into Kenna's ear. "I want you, Pascale. Do everything to me—again."

Kenna rolled her onto her back and looked down into Trysta's deep dark eyes. She felt the woman's hips press into hers; felt the thighs beneath her separate an inch. Then another inch.

Slow.

Slow.

Quick-quick.

Slow.

CHAPTER THIRTEEN

Precisely at seven the following night, the chauffeur held the car door when Kenna made her head-turning exit from the Buen Ayre and climbed into the limo.

"Good evening, Trysta."

"Good evening, Pascale."

With their eyes resting in each other's, their night together had yet to fade from Kenna's body.

As they drove away from the hotel, Trysta gently separated the slit in Kenna's cocktail dress and slid her hand along Kenna's inner thigh. "My god, Pascale, how ever am I going to concentrate tonight?"

"Think about what I'm going to do with you after it's over."

"Oh? Are you asking me for a late date?"

"I'm not asking."

Trysta grinned. "So you just take for granted I'll say yes."

Kenna stroked her neck. "Yes, assuming we're not in a Chinese prison by the end of the night."

Trysta leaned into her touch. "Mmm, don't be a buzzkill, *amor*."

Trysta introduced Kenna to the Argentine Business Consortium during the cocktail hour as Marleen Spiker, a Dutch businesswoman looking for Argentine investments. Her cover was as close to her real self as a duck in a relay race. About two hours into the ordeal, and halfway through dinner, Trysta gave her the signal.

"Excuse me," Kenna said. She rose from their table and moved toward her target, confident and relaxed in her gait, with her eyes casually focused on the periphery. She slipped through the service area in the back hallway, and checked to make sure she was alone before zeroing in on the catering computer. Glancing at her watch, she waited for the download to begin.

Nothing.

Nothing.

Still nothing. Something was wrong. Waiting longer than she had time for, still no download icon appeared. *Why the fuck isn't this working?*

"May I help you?" asked a waiter.

"The nearest ladies' room? It seems I've taken a wrong turn."

"Go back through the ballroom and then past the double doors."

"Thank you."

Passing through the banquet, she saw Trysta's watchful eye trained on her while engaged with the Foreign Trade Minister, and Kenna could tell she knew something wasn't right.

Thirty-four seconds gone.

Continuing to the other side, Kenna had fifty-one seconds to find and engage with a different terminal. When she exited the double doors, she saw a stairwell to her immediate left. She tried the door to no avail. *Dammit! The door's secure!* As she crossed in front of it, with forty-seven seconds remaining in her open window, she heard the lock click open and she slipped into the stairwell. She raced up one flight, following the blueprint on her watch face. Thirty-nine seconds to go. The door to the floor of offices one flight up clicked open when the RFID reader sensed her, and she raced to the first terminal in the nearest cubicle. *Twenty-eight.* The download icon appeared on her watch.

While the Chinese code downloaded, she counted down the sixty seconds she needed. *Eighteen seconds more.* She heard faint voices coming from the corridor that led to the elevators.

Come on, come on! Thirteen. Twelve. The voices grew nearer until they were finally on the other side of the office door.

Two. One.

Posthaste Kenna slipped back through the stairwell door behind her as the front office door opened. She fled down the steps, and seconds later she smiled while tasting the sorbet intermezzo. She finally exhaled when Trysta's hand grazed the side of her thigh under the table.

They waited until the after-dinner dancing began before making a clean exit and getting into a taxi.

"What about our limo, Pascale?" Trysta asked as the cab pulled away.

Kenna opened her mobile phone, dialed and handed the phone to Trysta. "I don't speak Spanish. You can tell him we won't need him the rest of the evening."

Trysta did so with a smile on her face. "Where are we going?" she asked when she hung up.

"I took the liberty of renting us a room at a low-profile place. A very low-profile place."

"Oh, Pascale—I like it already."

The worn *pension* Kenna had found for them was way beneath either of their dignity, if they'd had any. No one would ever look for women like them in a place like this. Dingy with sordid clientele, the place was both unworthy of, and yet perfect for their kind. Gritty, with bare lightbulbs illuminating its shabby hallways built upon creaky floorboards—it was the type of seedy hotel where people stayed for an hour, not for a night.

"What is this place?" Trysta asked when the hotel room door closed behind them.

Kenna pressed Trysta to the wall with her body tight up against the woman, sensually restraining Trysta's arms—her heartbeat outpacing her. Their smoldering stares collided—their breath fell on each other's lips.

"It's the place where one-night stands become immortal, *amor*," Kenna replied. She held Trysta there, kissed her hard and then stripped off her dress.

Slow.

Slow.

Quick-quick.

Slow.

CHAPTER FOURTEEN

Sierra Stone drove her rental car through the beast of night, her eyes scanning the rearview mirror as vigilantly as they did the road before her. She swerved once in central Montana to avoid hitting an elk, carefully guarding her speed to avoid being stopped. Exhausted by morning, she parked behind a supermarket and slept for an hour. When she awoke, she bought a prepaid phone and then abandoned the car in their parking lot. She hitched a ride with a trucker who let her off a few blocks from the Amtrak station, where she paid cash for a ticket under an assumed name. The one-way ticket would buy her some rest in her sleeper compartment on the 28 Empire Builder to Chicago.

Before leaving West Glacier, Montana, she had memorized the important numbers in her phone and then drove over the device several times, crushing it. The only number she called from her burner phone belonged to Dani, her one-night stand in New Orleans.

With any luck, the following day she would buy another ticket in Chicago under yet another name, and a day later Dani would pick her up at Amtrak in New Orleans. *When should I call Sonnenheim? Not yet. How did I get compromised?* Question upon question echoed in her mind from the time she had left West Glacier. She slept for minutes at a time on the train, with her finger curled around the trigger of her .22 beneath the shirt on her lap.

In her mind, every face she saw was a dormant assassin, like the one she'd encountered in Montana. She scrutinized every detail of her trip there.

Where did I pick up that tail? How did they find me? It had to have come from the Canadian side. Or did it? I wasn't followed from the airport! Or was I? At least I got the thumb drive away from the Russian, but now I just have to stay alive. Somewhere no one will look for me—and then I need to get this to Washington.

Now she wanted to know more than ever what was on that thumb drive that had almost cost her her life. She pulled out her laptop and found an outlet to plug it into. When she inserted the thumb drive into the USB port, the conductor entered her compartment. Slamming down the lid, she showed him her ticket and locked the door when he left. She had paid for the whole roomette and she wasn't about to let anyone in until she vacated it in Chicago.

Sierra opened the directory and read through a list of filenames, but nothing jumped out at her, so she chose a random file and hacked her way into it.

"What the hell is this?" she said when she saw a list of various US cities. She hacked into another protected file while eating a can of spaghetti she had bought at the market where she'd bought the cell phone. This file was a spreadsheet, whose columns held the details and numbers related to the cities in the first file. In the first column were dates, in the second one, some sort of timeline. For the next few hours, she attempted correlating what little information she could glean from those two files. Late into the night, as she sped through the vacant heartland, she continued trying to break the encryption of other files.

"I've got to find a way to get this to DC."

Wait a minute. Sonnenheim and her department were the only ones besides the contact who knew where I was going in Montana. What if someone in her office compromised me and almost got me killed! "I've got a *bad* feeling about this."

CHAPTER FIFTEEN

Raisa Lee was the last employee to leave Physio Dynamics, although technically the computer had logged her out twenty minutes earlier.

"Sorry, Mary," she said to the security guard who waited for her at the elevator.

"No problem, honey. You feeling okay?"

"I think I picked up a bug," said Raisa as she joined Mary in the elevator. "Thank God it's Friday."

Mary inserted the key into the elevator lock to override the system and then pressed the lobby button. "My grandkids are getting over something too. It must be going around. You rest up this weekend and I'm sure you'll feel better by Monday morning." The elevator door opened onto the sleek and softly lit marble lobby of the silicon industry behemoth. As Raisa exited the building, one of the machines upstairs in the Clean Room should have already uttered its final sigh before powering down.

When she got into her blue Prius, she breathed out a heavy sigh of relief even though her hands were still shaky when she started the car. She had managed to pull this off for the second time, and it would bring her a handsome reward. Her recently deceased husband Jiang would never have approved, but then coming from China, Jiang never really appreciated the opportunities inherent in capitalism.

Raisa had always toed the company line, almost never missed a day of work and had updated her skill set regularly. After initially grieving the loss of her husband to what the police had told her was random violence, all she'd thought about was having been passed over for two promotions. It was hard to swallow—how men to whom she had given the benefit of her expertise climbed the ladder while her diligence went grossly unrewarded.

Those VPs are inept, she thought. I know more than both of them combined! It's time for me to finally buy that BMW. And maybe take a cruise. Find a new job.

She'd never considered doing anything illegal, until that night months earlier when she'd first altered the settings on the machines. One small batch of computer chips didn't seem like any big deal compared to the millions that Physio Dynamics produced.

So some bureaucrat's computer will take longer to download porn. Besides, it can't be traced to me. The specs met the criteria and they signed off on it further up the line. I'm home free.

As she sped along the highway toward San Francisco, she listed the pros and cons of every potential purchase she might make with the pile of money she would soon have.

Traffic was slowing to a stop again. In no mood to sit on the freeway, Raisa cranked up the music and maneuvered quickly to the right, exited and took the side road in Woodside.

She checked her rearview mirror and noticed the car that had been inching along next to her on the freeway followed her lead. The black Escalade with the tinted windows rode behind her.

"Jerk! Turn off your high beams!" She accelerated to put some distance between them on the dark winding road, but the Escalade kept pace on the turns and then sped up around the switchback.

Ahead was a turnout. "Fine, I'll pull over so you can pass! Asshole. Maybe I'll just use that money to get a fancy place closer to work and shorten my commute."

Slowing her car, she turned on her right signal and veered to move aside. At over twice the weight, and more than ten times the power of the Prius, the eight-cylinder Escalade needed only two hard bumps to send Raisa's car plunging through the guardrail, down the hillside and into a tree.

* * *

The police waved Lieutenant Carly Avedon's car into the restricted area where she parked and walked over to her team.

"Detective Brennan," she said, "what do we have?"

"Hi Lieutenant. All we know so far is that the car went off the road. Crime Scene Investigations is on its way now."

Avedon nodded. "Okay." She changed into the hiking sneakers she kept in her trunk and then descended the hillside slope with a flashlight to where the Prius's front end had met with the large oak tree. She shined the light inside where she saw the massive contusion on the victim's forehead, from below which rested the inanimate expression.

Pulling on her latex gloves, she walked to the passenger side, opened the door and shined her flashlight on the interior. On the floor lay the deceased woman's purse, its contents spilled across the rubber mat. Avedon picked up the wallet, opened it to the folio of credit cards and located the driver's license. In the change purse section she felt something solid. The lights from the CSI team bounced as they lit a trail down from the road. Carly lifted the small object from the change purse and put it in her pocket. "Over here," she called out to the forensic team. "Hi, guys," she said. "Here's the driver's wallet and ID. Everything else is where I found it."

"It seems pretty straightforward to me that her forehead was no match for that tree," Detective Brennan said.

Carly scoffed. "Neither was the Prius for that matter."

The Medical Examiner pulled on his gloves and leaned into the passenger side to get a full view of the dead woman. Then he came around to the driver's side and examined the head wound. "We'll do a tox screen, of course, but like you said, Lieutenant, she was no match for this kind of force. She would have had to fly through that guardrail to hit this tree with the kind of speed it would have taken to kill her." He leaned back out of the car and stood upright. "Unless she was trying to kill herself, I don't know why she would have been moving that fast on this road."

"Lieutenant," the CSI investigator called out from behind the car. "Have a look at this."

Avedon moved to the rear of the car and focused on the bumper in the investigator's beam. She shined her flashlight along it. "I want photos of every angle and measurements of the black scrapes, scuffs and dents on that bumper before they tow it away," she said. "Based on the paint transfer and height, it looks like a black pickup truck or an SUV hit her."

The investigator nodded. "It looks fresh, Lieutenant."

"Doctor," she said to the medical examiner, "I believe this just became either a manslaughter or a homicide case."

"I'll let you know what I find," he replied.

Carly removed her gloves as she climbed back up the hill and drove away in her unmarked cruiser. A mile from the accident site, she pulled over and looked at the thumb drive she had taken from the victim's wallet. She placed it in the hidden compartment of her briefcase and headed back into the city.

CHAPTER SIXTEEN

Hunter van Bourgeade picked up his phone on the third ring. "I've heard of radio silence but this is ridiculous."

"I'm sorry, Hunt, but I couldn't take a chance until now," said Kenna.

"Are you okay?"

"Well, I didn't get dead, if that's what you mean. I need to ask you about something important. Have you ever heard any code name references like *Le Gros Chat*?"

Hunt sighed. "Uncle told you, huh?"

"You knew?"

"Actually, not until after he told you. I'm already working on it. I want to know his identity too."

"I know," she said.

"I heard through the grapevine that it didn't go as smoothly as you'd planned in Buenos Aires."

"Other than some bad targeting on my part, which I swiftly corrected, it worked out fine. I'm calling to let you know I'm about to go into Vince Zwarnick's office." Kenna could tell Hunter was smiling.

"Remind him he owes me a pair of Lakers tickets—courtside."

Kenna glanced up to see the aide for the Secretary of Homeland Security approaching. "I have to go, Hunt, I'll speak with you later."

"You can go right in, he's expecting you," said the secretary.

"Kenna, thank you so much for coming," said Vincent Zwarnick as he rose and walked around his desk.

"It's good to see you, Vince." They hugged as his secretary left and closed the door.

"I can't begin to thank you for the immense risk you just took on our behalf," he said.

Kenna nodded. "I've owed you one since Turkey. Though I can't help noticing all that gray hair. When did that happen?"

"I swear it was black a week ago, like yours is now. When did *that* happen?"

She chuckled. "It's my cover."

"This whole mess has turned our department upside down. How did you make out in Buenos Aires?"

Kenna flashed on Trysta. "Made out like a bandit down there," she said. "Although for a few seconds at the Chinese Embassy, I thought I was going to miss my window to extract the Chinese source code. But by some miracle I got it done."

"Why? What transpired?"

"I chose the one terminal that was immune to the RFID chip."

"That shouldn't have happened."

"Well, in all fairness it was a catering computer and obviously a poor choice on my part."

Zwarnick exhaled hard. "I was up half the night worrying what you'd say when you got here."

"Take a breath, Vince, we're right on track. Your guys have already extracted the code from my arm."

"I know. They've been working around the clock to stop the bleeding."

"Hey, have you ever heard of a code name like *Le Gros Chat*?"

Zwarnick appeared to be staring into space as he thought about it. "No. It sounds like the James Bond era. Maybe you should track down some of the Cold War guys. Like Uncle. Doesn't he know?"

She shook her head.

"What's this about, Kenna?"

"It's the only lead I have in my parents' assassination."

He looked at her warmly. "I'll make you a deal. When we get our security back under control, I'll see what I can find out."

"Thanks. So, we're done and you owe me lunch. And Hunt said something about Lakers tickets?"

He squinted at her.

"I know that look. I've never been fond of that look—it usually accompanies bad news," she said. "Please tell me that uncertainty is about the Lakers tickets."

"Yeah, I wish," he said, gesturing to the chair. "Have a seat."

"Oh, no. The look *and* the chair?" She sat. "What's wrong?"

"I need your help, Kenna. I've trusted you with my life and now with my country—"

"*Our* country, Vince. I *am* an American. And it's not as if I haven't put my life on the line before for Old Glory—like in Buenos Aires."

"Yes, but your agency is in Israel."

"We're beyond agencies, Vince. We're friends."

He smiled. "We're friends who fight the good fight. I still think about how many more people would have lost their lives that day were it not for your brains and my brawn."

Kenna shook her head. "Can you believe it's been almost two years since 9/11? What do you need?"

"You already know that the reason I called you in is because we're only using off-book operatives for this. We're running out of personnel."

"And?"

Vince sat in the guest chair next to her. "And the thumb drive containing the names of compromised personnel has disappeared, along with Sierra Stone, the asset we sent to retrieve it. To make matters more hellish, we don't know the identity of the woman who was killed in her place at the exchange. Right now, it's clear that Sierra had something go very wrong with whoever the dead woman was. Frankly, we don't yet know if she's gone rogue, or if she's been compromised, or worse."

"You didn't have a contingency plan, or thumb drive?"

"Stone *was* the contingency plan—our Plan B, and Plan C for that matter. We had another agent on it, but I had to call him in because I'd found out he'd already been compromised. This situation is getting worse by the minute."

"I'm not quite sure where you're going with this."

"Are you familiar with computer chip maker Physio Dynamics?"

"I met their CEO at the embassy soirée in Buenos Aires. That's a Chinese company."

"They bid on our government manufacturing contracts out of their Silicon Valley facility."

"Our?"

"FBI, CIA…"

"Okay…"

"Several weeks ago, the body of one of the Project Managers on our contract was found in a dump in Silicon Valley. His name was Jiang Lee." He reached across to the file on his desk and placed some photographs on the coffee table between them. "Everything points to a professional hit. Then, last night, while driving home from her job at Physio Dynamics, his wife Raisa's car was pushed off the road and into a tree, killing her. They both had pretty high security clearances and we're trying to find out if their deaths had anything to do with the Chinese hacking us. Physio Dynamics made the chips that went into our computers."

"Your people are pretty good at analysis. Once they run the code matching programs against the information from my implanted chip, you'll know where and how the code was altered."

Zwarnick scoffed. "The code may be only one of the factors. I need to know every moving part and who was involved.

It's the only way I can get to the systemic bleeding and shut it down. The wife's autopsy briefing is tomorrow and I want you there. NSA, CIA, FBI—we're all on the same page, but we have a skeleton crew because we don't know the extent of our compromised personnel. I want you to partner with the FBI consultant who's investigating Sierra Stone's disappearance, and to find that thumb drive. If you can connect the Lees' deaths to the missing thumb drive, that would be a bonus. But we have top people who will handle that. You'll meet them tomorrow."

"Who is the consultant?"

"Elana West. Do you know her?"

"No," said Kenna.

"She started out as an FBI informant. Deputy Director Sonnenheim from Special Cases brought her in. West really earned her stripes with the Bureau in a Russian sex trafficking sting that she worked with Stone. I have a plane ready to take you to meet up with West in San Francisco if you say yes." Zwarnick stood, walked behind his desk and picked up the phone receiver. He pointed it at her. "Anyone you want to clear this with?"

"Uncle already gave me the green light to help you in any way we can, with the provision that if I need Hunter, I can get to him."

Zwarnick put down the phone. "I might've known. Uncle is usually six steps ahead of the rest of us."

Kenna nodded. "It's an art form for him. Any chance this was a ruse on the missing asset's part?"

"We don't know how deep this goes. What we do know is this." Zwarnick exhaled a hard sigh and started at the beginning.

CHAPTER SEVENTEEN

Kenna's government jet touched down in San Francisco on time, followed by a traffic delay on the 101 North coming into the city. When the taxi dropped her off at the morgue on Bryant Street, she was already twenty minutes late.

Secretary Zwarnick had said that the people who would be in attendance were 'need-to-know,' and what *she* needed to know was that there would be four key people awaiting her. Among them, her new partner, Elana West—FBI consultant. The corpse around which they would convene was Raisa Lee, former Physio Dynamics computer expert—and one half of a dead married couple.

Kenna had used the long plane ride to all but memorize the files on the people who would be in the room. She and West needed to find that potentially renegade woman, the one who had the thumb drive. Still, what was so damn important about this victim that she warranted a federal trifecta at her autopsy?

"Kenna Waverly," she said to the uniformed policeman when she entered.

He glanced down at his list and then held up an electronic wand. "You can place your weapons in this locker," he said, pointing next to him.

"Okay," Kenna said. "But just so I'm clear, who would I need protection from in a morgue?" She placed her handgun in a locker and took the key.

"No one, ma'am, that's why you have me. Arms away from your body, please." He swiped the wand along her outline. "Go through the double doors at the end of the hall." He motioned.

Kenna took a surgical mask from the stack outside the door to the autopsy room and put it on. Compared to the comfort of anonymity that her cobalt Steel Eyes mask had provided, the surgical mask left her feeling exposed. For a decade, her face had been covered from her hairline to the tip of her nose, and out beyond her cheekbones. Never once had she thought of making *this* tradeoff—a surgical mask that only covered the bottom half of her face.

She pushed back the door and entered. "Sorry I'm late, I just arrived from DC."

"I'm Dr. Rayburn. We've already begun," said the medical examiner. His tone was that of a man who didn't exert himself courting the living.

Positioned around the corpse stood the four 'need-to-knowers.' Like her, these four people had been plucked from the ranks based on expertise, and a reasonable certainty that they hadn't been compromised by the hack of personnel files.

While Dr. Rayburn continued to review the preliminary information of age and cause of death, Kenna tuned him out. Instead, she identified the other spectators behind their surgical masks.

The former Special Forces in the suit across from her was Dixon Chase. Lean and broad-shouldered with a crisp appearance, his sandy-colored temples were streaked with gray. Furrows etched between his brows revealed a consistent state of burden, made more dramatic by his widow's peak hairline. According to Vince Zwarnick, Chase would take the lead on gathering and disseminating information, particularly that which connected Raisa and Jiang Lee to the cyber intrusion.

To Kenna's right, standing at shoulder height, was Specialist Nadia Pavlichenko, PhD, a CIA guru in science and technology. The daughter of Soviet defectors from the Cold War, Nadia's scientific papers had been published in nine languages. Her job was to oversee the technical components to the breach.

All eyes but Kenna's were trained on the doctor and the former Raisa Lee. Next, she observed the two women who stood opposite her across the body. The taller, androgynous-looking woman with the spiky hair and eye makeup was San Francisco Police Lieutenant Carly Avedon—the one who had signed off on the Raisa Lee crime scene. While Avedon's file read impressively, and demonstrated an ambitious cop who had ascended the ranks, Kenna quickly read her body language. *Reactive. Controlling.*

The other woman had no picture in her file because technically she didn't exist. This Elana West, the one with whom Kenna would be working, was a little harder to get behind.

Kenna wasn't fond of the idea—being paired up with someone she didn't know; someone she had no real history on. Then again, she and Vince Zwarnick had been thrown together during 9/11, before he held a place in the President's cabinet, and a place in her heart.

Elana swiped back honey-colored tendrils that escaped from her ponytail and lay against her cheekbones. She looked at Kenna with intelligent, soft blue eyes and nodded.

Not exactly the law enforcement type, Kenna thought. There was no real background on her other than she'd been recruited by the FBI as an informant, after which she'd obtained her degree in criminology from UC Irvine and become a consultant.

Focusing back on the corpse, Kenna felt West's eyes trained on her.

Dr. Rayburn continued. "The chemical residue found on the victim is consistent with those who work in technology. In fact, all the chemicals I found are those normally correlated with microchip and wafer production. Except for one anomaly."

"What's that, Doc?" asked Lieutenant Avedon.

He looked up. "It's actually something that should have been there that wasn't. Solvents."

"Why is that important?" said Avedon.

"Allow me, Doctor," said Nadia Pavlichenko. "Solvents help reduce chip failures, which improves microchip production. What's missing are the solvents that cut down the chip failure rate."

Kenna felt West's eyes on her again.

"Couldn't have said it better," said Rayburn.

Dixon Chase looked at Pavlichenko. "Nadia, are you saying it's possible that the microchips Physio Dynamics made for the US government contracts were manufactured to fail?"

"It's possible. Or they could have been treated for latency."

"What's that?" Elana asked, and then glanced at Kenna.

"Something in the chip can be altered to activate at a designated future time," Nadia began. "Programmed to do something it wasn't supposed to do, like interfere with an electric grid."

"But how could that have passed the manufacturing specs and security inspections?" said Chase.

Pavlichenko smirked. "If a chemical treatment caused latency, then the chip would test normal unless they knew specifically what to test it for."

"Still," Chase began, "somebody up the line would have to be in on the change to sign off on it."

West is staring at me again.

"I can tell you from my security experience," Avedon added, "that companies like Physio are always on the lookout for spies trying to sabotage the process."

When Kenna glanced up to find Elana staring at her again, Elana's gaze darted to the corpse. It was the fifth time in as many minutes.

What is it about her? Have I met her before?

Avedon continued. "Forensics has confirmed that the victim's car was pushed off the road by a black vehicle with a bumper the height of an SUV."

"What kind?" Elana said.

Avedon ignored her and her question.

Kenna clocked the lieutenant's attitude and reposed the question. "Lieutenant, when will your people have the make and model of the SUV?"

"They're working on that now," she answered readily.

When Kenna glanced at Elana, the woman's eyes were smiling. Kenna's eyes subtly acknowledged her.

Those eyes. How the hell do I know her? Kenna ran through every scenario she could think of.

"In the interest of making sure we all have the same information," Elana began, "you need to know that Raisa Lee was the daughter of Russian mob kingpin Vladimir Sergeyev. In New York's Little Odessa, Sergeyev is known as the badass of Brighton Beach. In LA, he owns an adult entertainment empire."

"And you know that *how?*" Avedon snapped in a dismissive tone.

Kenna watched the dynamic. *Avedon is bad-blood hostile.* She enjoyed watching West handle the reactive Avedon with calm restraint, which appeared to her only to piss Avedon off.

"When I went undercover for a sex trafficking sting years ago in LA," said Elana, "I worked in one of Sergeyev's clubs."

"One of his *strip* clubs?" Avedon asked with no small measure of assholery.

Kenna suppressed her laugh—until she almost choked on her surgical mask, because *that's* when it hit her. Her face tingled, and the visual recollections crashed down on her in a series of two-second flashbacks. *What!* She stared into Elana's eyes, and this time Elana stared back.

For that moment, they were back in the strip club's VIP room. Those gorgeous blue eyes held prisoner by heavy black eyeliner and mascara, and the woman's hair was dark, not blond.

In that vexing instant, Kenna heard only her own voice—screaming in her head. *Oh. My. God!* Although the bottom half of their faces were masked—and even though Elana was fully clothed, there wasn't a shade of doubt. Kenna had long ago sought this woman out—repeatedly. In fact, she had paid to do it.

They had never gazed into each other's eyes in the light of day, or in any real light. They had only ever met in a dark strip club in Los Angeles, where the lap dances Kenna had bought from the woman usually escalated into the private VIP room—where anything was game.

She looked so different then. Ambushed by the memory of the outrageous animal magnetism they had once shared, Kenna's heart pounded. In that moment, she felt the stripper's hot breath on her neck, and the woman's taut buttocks in her hands. All the times the dancer had asked her for a date, then enticed her with every disallowed move when they were in the back room—alone. In her mind, she heard the woman say, "I'm not supposed to do this," before she would perform some new act of seduction to entice Kenna.

"Any questions?" Dr. Rayburn asked.

Yeah, plenty! Kenna's face flushed such that she wondered if anyone noticed.

Avedon's phone rang. "Excuse me," she said as she left the room to take the call. Kenna fell deaf to the conversation between Pavlichenko, Chase and Rayburn. Instead, she peeled off her surgical mask and looked across the corpse, deep into Elana's eyes. "Alice?" she said sheepishly.

Elana peeled off her mask and smiled. "Hello, Pascale."

Pavlichenko turned to Kenna. "Aren't you Kenna Waverly?" she said.

Kenna snapped back to the present and shook Nadia's hand. "Y-yes, I am. Nice to meet you, Dr. Pavlichenko. Hello, Agent Chase."

Chase nodded. "Waverly."

"*Kenna Waverly?*" Elana mocked.

"Elana West?" Kenna replied.

"Okay," Rayburn interrupted. "Now that we all know each other, call me if you have any questions."

Nadia Pavlichenko handed a small sealed package to Kenna. "Your secure phone is in there and all of our numbers are programmed."

"I'm clear on my role," Kenna said, avoiding Elana's stare.

"I'll give you and West time to catch each other up," said Chase. "We'll see you later at the FBI field office. Let's get this done."

Lieutenant Avedon reentered the room as Pavlichenko, Chase and Dr. Rayburn left. She looked at Elana. "What are you doing here anyway, West? You don't belong here."

"Take it up with the FBI, Carly. We have multiple cases to connect, so I expect to hear about whatever you find when you find it."

Avedon scoffed. "That's *Lieutenant* Avedon. What's your part in this—"

"Lieutenant," Kenna intervened, "if it's more convenient, you can just call me. I'll be partnering with West on behalf of Homeland. You have your secure phone?"

Avedon looked Kenna up and down and nodded. "Yes. Let me know what you find out about the Lees, both Jiang and Raisa."

Kenna smiled. "Dixon Chase will be coordinating and then disseminating findings," she said matter-of-fact. "Where are Raisa's personal effects? I'd like to go through them. And I'd like to inspect her vehicle."

"Not a problem," the lieutenant said. "The car is at the impound lot. I'll call to let them know to expect you, but we've already been through it."

"Thanks," said Kenna.

"Okay then," Avedon nodded. "I'll be in touch," she added before leaving.

In the absolute stillness, Kenna and Elana stood opposite one another across the corpse, staring into each other's eyes.

"I'm pretty good at keeping a straight face, Alice, but—"

"Alice doesn't live here anymore," Elana quipped.

"I have no clue how to react to this," Kenna continued.

"You, Pascale? You have no clue?" Elana said. "You're not the one who was always topless in a G-string and a compromising position."

"If it helps to know, with you I wanted to be."

CHAPTER EIGHTEEN

Ivan Mikhailov tore out of Smolovsky's Market when he'd gotten the call, his bag of spilled groceries abandoned on the sidewalk. He jumped into his Land Rover and made it to Vladimir's house in half the time it should have taken.

He entered the house without knocking, only to find Vladimir and his wife huddled together on the sofa. Vladimir held Big Raisa as she sobbed, but his eyes met Ivan's with a bloodless stare. Ivan knew that icy, inanimate expression in the eyes that were blacker than any abyss he'd ever faced. He had seen it enough times since they were boys, beginning on the night Vladimir had killed his stepfather back in Vladivostok, Russia.

"No more," Ivan had heard him say quietly as he delivered the final blow that put an end to the stepfather's continual abuse. Now, that glacial glare was seasoned, perfected over time as it bore down upon the disloyal and unfortunate whom he had tortured. Then, and only if he was feeling generous, would Vladimir Sergeyev put an end to his victim's misery.

Ivan placed his hand lightly on Big Raisa's shoulder. "I'm so sorry, Raisa." Then he simply stared into Vladimir's eyes, for any show of real emotion was merely a sign of weakness for men like them.

Vladimir stood and embraced him. Ivan had never seen Vladimir cry before. When he finished sobbing on Ivan's shoulder, Vladimir pulled away. Ivan turned and walked to the door. He looked back at Vladimir with the unspoken invitation to join him in private. Vladimir led him into his study, closed the door and stared at Ivan.

"You find whoever did this, Ivan. You find who killed my little Raisa, and you bring them to me."

Ivan nodded. "I will, Vova," he said with eerie calm. He sauntered across the room and turned. His stare burned into Vladimir. "Now you will tell me what you've done, comrade. Everything."

Vladimir wiped away his tears, poured them both a shot of vodka and sat. Ivan had seen many regretful expressions on the faces of those he had brutally interrogated on behalf of the KGB, but he'd never seen this one before. He certainly never expected to see it on the visage of the man everyone feared—everyone except for Ivan.

"When the KGB needed someone tough," Vladimir began, "they came to you, Ivan." He downed the shot. "Find him."

"There's nothing you could have done that I wouldn't try to fix."

Vladimir poured and downed another shot. "I know. Without you, Ivan, I have no one."

In that moment, Ivan might as well have been back in the interrogation room on the right side of the table. He took out his pack of Sobranies, lit one and walked it over to Vladimir. He stepped away and turned to observe, to calibrate the consistency of Vladimir's body language. He pointed his stare into the black eyes. "I'll ask you one time, Vladimir Sergeyev. What did you do?"

Vladimir looked away and then back at Ivan, once again the frightened boy who had made his first kill. Back then, it was

Ivan who had said he would take care of it. And he did. Then he did so again and again.

Vladimir took a long draw off the Sobranie. "It all began when Raisa married the Chinese boy—Jiang. He put me in an uncomfortable position, and I regret that he made such a poor decision."

"Did your daughter know you had her husband killed?"

Vladimir shook his head. "No. But in retaliation, the Chinese have taken Raisa."

CHAPTER NINETEEN

The 59 City of New Orleans Southbound pulled into New Orleans Union Station at 3:23 p.m. Hiding beneath her LA Dodger ball cap and sunglasses, Sierra Stone exited onto Loyola Avenue. She spotted Dani's black Civic and tossed her suitcase into the backseat before getting in.

"Hey, Greer, welcome back," Dani said with the sparkling smile so big that it made her eyes squint.

Sierra kissed her on the lips. "Let's get out of here." She sunk down in her seat, her eyes darting around behind the dark sunglasses.

"To be honest, I didn't think I'd hear from you after you left so suddenly the other day," Dani said as she pulled away into traffic.

"I told you before I left, baby," Sierra began, "this wasn't over by a long shot."

"I'm really glad to see you, Greer. You're a florist of your word."

Sierra cringed just a little. "Dani, there are a couple of things I need to tell you."

"Like what, dahlin'?"

"For starters, I'm not a florist."

Dani glanced over at her, drove through the intersection and pulled into the first available parking space. "For *starters?*"

"And my name isn't Greer. It's Sierra. Sierra Stone."

Dani nodded in a thoughtful way—more like her head bobbed as she looked out the driver window, then slowly across the width of the windshield, and to the right, where she finally stopped bobbing when her eyes met Sierra's.

"Okay, wait, I can explain." Sierra pulled her sunglasses down her nose to meet Dani's eyes.

"So then basically, you're a liar?"

"No. Yes—but only professionally. I mean *I'm* not a liar. It's just what I do for a living."

Dani deadpanned her. "First you're a florist with a wedding emergency, and now you're a professional liar? With a fake name?"

Sierra held her breath and exhaled a resounding yes. "But now you know my real name."

"And that matters because…"

"Because I think we really had that certain something."

"We did, didn't we?" Dani said. "So what's your real job, Sierra Stone?"

"Before I tell you, I need your help, Dani. I wouldn't ask if it weren't a matter of national importance. I need a place for a couple of days where no one would ever come looking for me."

"Hmm, Not-Greer-The-Not-Florist…so that's why I was your one-night stand?"

"No, it all happened after I left. Assuming I'm alive when I finish this, I'd like us to start over—you know, the right way." Sierra placed her hand over Dani's.

"Assuming you're alive? Why wouldn't you be?"

"Because in doing something honorable and important, bad people came after me. I know for a fact no one has followed me here. I would never put you in danger, baby."

"Start over the right way? I couldn't find anything wrong with the way we did it the first time."

"First four times."

"Oh, no dahlin', that was one very, very, long time," Dani said. "Now, what's this liar gig?"

"I work undercover for the FBI."

Dani slipped her hand out from under Sierra's, gently touched her cheek and kissed her lips. She pulled away. "There. The truth. And ohmigosh you're still alive." She put the car in gear and pulled out into traffic. "We'll be at my place in a few minutes."

After Sierra showered and changed, she curled up on the oversized chair, and inserted the thumb drive into her laptop. Dani had already left for work at the tavern where they'd met. She gazed around the room. A large area rug lay over the old hardwood floor and under the coffee table in front of the sofa. On either side, softly lit faux Tiffany lamps sat on antique round end tables made of dark wood.

I like it here; it's cozy. And I like her, a lot.

The computer booted up and the list of files on the thumb drive appeared. She scrolled back to the file she had zeroed in on before getting off the train. What had originally caught her attention was even more compelling now—the repetition of the name *New Orleans.*

What the hell? The date, time and exact mechanism of the water plant contamination were staring her in the face. During the subsequent shutdown, she and Dani were asleep in her room at the Hilton. That was the day Sonnenheim had called her in to go to Montana.

Sierra used Dani's computer to check the newspaper articles in the respective cities where other listed events were to have occurred. They all correlated with the list on the thumb drive; even the three attacks elsewhere that had happened within three hours. On that day, the first was an airline, the second a stock exchange, and the third was a news outlet.

She searched more online news where she stumbled upon a statement from the FBI's cyber division. *After investigation, we've concluded that these events weren't related, nor do we believe they were cyber attacks.*

"Bullshit!" She reread what was on her laptop screen from the thumb drive. "So according to this list, our infrastructure is already under attack. Shit." Her mind raced. *I can't call Deputy Director Sonnenheim because her department was the only one that knew where I'd be in Montana. Someone in that department wanted to make sure I never got this thumb drive—which means they're already after me.* "Elana, where the hell are you when I need you most?"

By the time Dani arrived home from work, Sierra was already asleep in her bed. She awoke to watch Dani move quietly through the darkened room.

"Hi, baby. Welcome home," she said, reaching out.

Dani sat next to her on the bed and removed the bangs from Sierra's eyes, stroked back the loose black waves from her face. Sierra gently pulled her down into a kiss, then an embrace, and then she sighed when Dani stood. Dani stripped down to her panties and climbed between the sheets into Sierra's arms.

"Are you okay, Sierra? I was worried about you."

Sierra smiled. "I like how my name sounds leaving your lips."

"Get used to it." Dani leaned in and kissed her again. She turned off the accent light, lay back on her pillow and quietly scoffed. "Floral emergency."

CHAPTER TWENTY

Kenna and Elana finished searching through Raisa's Prius at the police impound lot, and then took a taxi to their hotel.

"Welcome to Stanford Court," said the woman at the front desk. "Name of the reservation?"

"West," Elana replied.

The woman tapped the computer keys. "West, party of two?"

"Uh, no. One."

"Sorry, my mistake. I see it now." The desk agent looked at Kenna. "You're Ms. Waverly?"

Kenna nodded. "Will you have our bags brought up as soon as they arrive?"

"Yes, Ms. Waverly. The rooms have already been taken care of. Here are your keys."

"They're adjoining rooms?" Elana asked.

"The rooms are next to each other but none of our rooms adjoin."

"Too bad," Kenna said.

Elana shot Kenna with her 9 mm-glare. "Thank you," she said, taking the room keys.

They entered the elevator and Kenna pressed four.

"Painfully quiet in here, Pascale."

"Alice…Elana. We need to sketch out some ground rules to work this case together."

"All right. Your room or mine?"

"Whichever one doesn't have a dance pole."

Elana raised her eyebrows. "You did not just say that to me."

Kenna grinned. "Too soon? Bad form?"

"Snarky."

The elevator door opened and Elana followed Kenna into her room and waited until the door closed.

"You can speak freely, Elana. The rooms have already been swept and there are cameras watching our doors."

Elana gave Kenna the once-over as she stood there across the room. "It's good to see you, Pascale. I've often wondered what happened to you. Although, I prefer you as a blonde."

"It's good to see you too, Alice. Your blond hair really threw me off at first. I'd never imagined you as anything but brunette." Kenna sighed. "Looks like we'd better figure us out quickly. There are some serious problems for us to solve, and distractions can be dangerous."

Elana nodded. "Or they can inspire." She sat down. "I'm inspired to get this job done and talk about the other things afterward. How about you?"

"Sure. Strictly professional." Her gaze rested just a second too long in Elana's. "Really."

"Just so you know, I have some questions about some of the things that happened between us. But how do we compartmentalize so that we can get down to business?"

Kenna took the armchair opposite her. She didn't miss this part of her former life—the compartmentalization. In one moment, allowing herself to feel something real, and in the next instant shifting to who she needed to be—Pascale, Steel Eyes, Marleen Spiker, goddamn whomever. Grit, grace and anonymity were more than just skills to her. They were a lifestyle; life-preserving actions that concealed her loneliness even from herself. Regardless, they were acquired skills that she'd once mastered, and it was time to dust them off. She took a deep breath, exhaled and settled into Elana's sexy stare. "We do it like this. Vince Zwarnick said that you know the asset we're looking for."

"Her name is Sierra Stone, but you may actually remember her from the strip club as Vouvray."

Kenna thought for a moment. "Do you have a photo? I only ever went to *Chez Oui* to see you." She clocked Elana's reaction to her admission. "I'm sorry, it wasn't my intention to make you uncomfortable."

"No. No, it's okay. I'm still a little shell-shocked. This is going to take some getting used to, that's all." She reached into her briefcase and opened the file she took from it. "Here," she said, handing Kenna Sierra's photo.

"Actually I do remember her. Isn't she the girl who did that amazing routine?"

"Yes. The pole melt—where she swung around the pole, wrapped her legs around it and turned upside down. I love that routine. We used to practice it as a duo. That's about when Sierra had recruited me for the FBI."

"Right," Kenna said, remembering, "'Vouvray…because *it's* sweet like honey, and so am I.'"

Elana laughed. "She worked on that line for a long time."

Kenna rested her forehead in her hand and massaged it. "Oh, man, I should have picked up on something. How did I miss that you were both agents?"

"You were there for one reason only."

"Minimize it if you must, Elana, but Alice played a key role in my life then. She saved me."

"Really. Saved you?"

"We're getting off topic."

Elana shifted and crossed her legs. "I don't believe that Sierra went rogue. I think she's laying low somewhere and that we need to find her."

"I know that Zwarnick has his doubts about her."

"He doesn't know her the way I do."

"What's your history? I'm asking because I need to know," said Kenna.

"We were close. Friends."

"Just friends?"

"Yes."

"So what makes you think she didn't go rogue?"

"I trust her. Did Zwarnick brief you about my trip to Montana to identify Sierra's body?"

Kenna nodded. "He said that the body you identified wasn't hers."

"It wasn't. We still don't have an ID on the dead woman. But the night after Sierra was there, I stayed in the same motel room. When I got out of a hot shower, I saw finger-writing on the steamy bathroom mirror."

Kenna tried not to picture it.

"Stop it, Pascale."

"What?"

Elana nicked her with another 9 mm-glance, but this time it was merely a flesh wound. "There was a series of numbers written on the mirror, but two of the digits were smudged." Elana took a scrap of paper from her wallet and handed it to Kenna. "It looks like a phone number, and the only thing we're missing is the first numeral in the area code and one in the last four digits. That last one is either a *one* or maybe a *seven*."

"Have you reported it yet? Gotten someone to run the number?"

"No. Until I know who and what are safe, I'm not going to take a chance jeopardizing Sierra. If she was the one who left this breadcrumb for me, she's missing with good reason. I don't want to turn it over to anyone until I know more. As for Secretary Zwarnick and Deputy Sonnenheim, I thought it would be best to check out the lead first. Can you live with that for now?"

"Yes. And we're not sharing this with that control freak Avedon yet either."

Elana smiled. "Well you're sure a quick judge of character."

"When we have a moment, you'll have to tell me what that little show of hers was all about."

Kenna removed her laptop from her bag, plugged into the Internet portal and began her phone number search. "Can you give me a fifteen-minute warning before we have to leave to meet Pavlichenko and Chase at the field office?"

Elana walked to the door. "Sure. I'll be in my room if you need me." Elana quickly turned away when Kenna looked up at her, and Kenna watched the door close behind her.

Once she was alone, Kenna logged into a new Internet browser. She typed in the words, '*Le Gros Chat*.'

Nadia Pavlichenko and Dixon Chase awaited Elana and Kenna in the conference room, on the eighth floor of the San Francisco FBI field office on Golden Gate Avenue. Chase removed his custom tailored suit jacket and hung it neatly on the back of a chair.

"We caught a break," he said. "We found Sierra Stone's rental car in Havre, Montana. If she was the one who ditched it there, then she's moving east."

"Any sign of foul play?" asked Elana.

Chase shook his head. "No, the car was wiped clean."

"Is there a bus station in Havre?" asked Kenna.

"No, just the train," said Pavlichenko as she took the seat opposite Kenna. "Unfortunately, there's no record of her traveling from there, and no digital print that I can find on her. So, chances are she's going about as old school as a person can in this day and age—cash."

Chase tossed a printout of his findings along with the Amtrak schedule onto the table in front of them. "The phone records are extensive, so our people will go through them and we'll get back to you when we've narrowed them down. Here's a copy of Raisa Lee's credit and debit transactions going back three months."

"Did you search Sierra's alias Greer Stabinow?" asked Elana.

Chase nodded. "Yes. Nothing so far. So—you know her, West. Where could she be going?"

Elana shook her head. "If I knew, Dixon, I'd already be on my way there. What about Deputy Director Sonnenheim? Does she have any clues?"

"No, she hasn't heard from Stone. But if she's on the move, she's either on a train, or maybe she wanted us to think she was on one. Or who knows, maybe she never even drove that car to Havre and someone else is trying to throw us off the trail."

"And the train station?" Kenna said.

Pavlichenko looked at her. "The security cameras at that station are sparse at best, but facial recognition came up with nothing. They're searching passenger records downstairs."

"Knowing Sierra," Elana began, "she could have hitched a ride with a trucker. Sierra's quite pretty and very resourceful. She's had a lot of experience manipulating the male psyche."

"What's the deal between you and Lieutenant Avedon?" Pavlichenko asked.

"She has a stick up her ass," Elana answered.

"Regardless, we need you to cooperate with her."

"I was the one who acted professionally today, so maybe you want to take that up with her."

"We will." Pavlichenko nodded. "Chase and I are staying here and working with Avedon until we have more answers about Jiang and Raisa Lee. Secretary Zwarnick called to let us know that you'll be handling the search for Sierra, so keep us apprised if you find anything significant. We need to get our hands on that drive."

"And," Chase added, "if the Lees had anything to do with the Chinese hack, we need that list to figure out who and what have already been compromised."

Kenna looked at Pavlichenko. "Whatever the reason for Jiang Lee's death, I can promise you that his wife's demise was not coincidental."

"That *would* be a mighty coincidence if the breach in our security randomly happened when the Lees' murders appeared on the radar," Chase said.

Kenna stood to leave. "Maybe there's another layer here we're not seeing."

Pavlichenko stared at her. "Like what?"

Kenna smirked. "Maybe it's a *who*, not a *what*. I'm going to start with the obvious. A Russian mobster's daughter is married to a Chinese national, with US government contracts."

"Great," Chase said, "we're right back at the beginning."

Elana looked at him. "Not necessarily."

CHAPTER TWENTY-ONE

"The Crack Shack, under the Bay Bridge please," Elana said to the cab driver.

"A late dinner?" Kenna asked. "I thought we were going back to the hotel."

"The food is great, but that's not why we're going."

"I'll bite. Why are we going?"

"Because I had to wait until we left the field office to share this with you." Elana held up a slip of paper. "I found this in Raisa's car—it's a receipt from the Crack Shack. And, if anyone knows something the cops don't, I know who it is."

"You're quite different than the person I'd have imagined Alice to be back in LA," Kenna said softly.

Elana gazed into her eyes. "That was Alice's job. To seduce you into thinking otherwise—to convince you that she wanted you."

"I don't know, Elana, I thought Pascale and Alice understood each other pretty well."

Elana turned and stared out the window. As the taxi neared the waterfront, a light fog rolled through the city, damping the sparkle of the Bay Bridge lights. It swallowed some of the beams, while others emitted a glow that diffused through the mist. None shone brightly. From underneath the bridge, at the lapping water's edge, one simply had to trust that they were knowable, that they lined up in a symmetrical manner.

As San Francisco and its waterfront had grown up, the one anachronism that remained was the small white building that jutted out over a postage stamp-size lot into the bay. Along its side and the length of the building, stretched a narrow, mostly even dock. Elana searched for the worn tugboat tied on its western flank when the cab rolled to a stop.

The old, once-white shack under the bridge always smelled like crabs in red sauce, even when the fog rolled in so thick that the blinking neon *Crack Shack* sign was barely visible. Although the word *crack* now had a different connotation, the owner, Achille Lastek, never saw fit to change the name of the landmark.

"Gravy," said Elana before exiting the cab. "Man, I've missed the gravy."

"Yeah, best red sauce in town," said the driver. "I don't know how the dot-commers missed tearing down this throwback. Hard to believe it's survived."

"Keep the change," Kenna said.

Elana led the way into the worn wooden bayside restaurant and paused to take in its visual history. Photographs from other eras lined the paneled walls; black-and-white shots of fishermen proudly displaying their prized catches. Seaworthy boats in the background, battered by salt and old men, the photos were San Francisco history from a lifestyle forgotten. From a time when a byte was a bite, and the best bites in town were cooked up fresh at The Shack.

Elana marveled at a young, strong Achille Lastek who had aged progressively with every subsequent photo of him; slowly effaced by days at sea and nights on his barstool. His hair still wavy but no longer brown, his deep-set eyes now nested between the pair of crevices beneath his unruly brows.

The old fisherman Lastek had white hair now, along with perpetual white stubble, and a smile beneath it when he and

Elana saw each other. He called out to her. "Hey, Doc! Where ya been?" He hopped off his barstool with a grimace and limped over to give her a hug.

She smiled and kissed his cheek. "Catch a big one today, Lastek?"

"I always catch the *biguns*. Where ya been, girlie?"

"Still living in LA," she answered as she slid into a booth.

Lastek didn't need an invitation, and so he grabbed his beer off the bar and slid in next to her. "Hey, who's your friend?"

"I'm Pascale, good to meet you." Kenna shook Lastek's hand. "I'll go get us a round."

Elana gathered the empty beer bottles, slid them to the front of the table to be collected, and waited until Kenna was at the bar. She looked into Lastek's eyes. "So, what do you know about the girl that was run off the road near Woodside?"

"What girl?"

Elana placed Raisa's picture on the table.

Lestak took a sudsy swig of his Budweiser and wiped his mouth on his double-layered flannel sleeve. The corner of his lip curled upward the way it did when he had made a good catch. "What makes you think I know anything, Doc?"

"I've known that look for practically my whole life, you salty dog. Your lip curled up. Spill it."

Lestak finished the beer and stacked it neatly next to the other empties. "I don't know much really. I seen her in here from time to time, you know, to say hello. Like everyone else, she's a local who had the good sense to come for the food."

Kenna returned with three beers.

"Thanks," Lestak said. "Darn shame about that girl. Good customer and always nice. I read in *The Chronicle* that they suspect her car was pushed through that guardrail into a tree." He shook his head remorsefully.

"When was the last time you saw her in here?" Kenna asked.

"Hmm, it's been a while." He nodded his head. "Yeah, a few weeks maybe."

"Did you ever see her with anyone, Achille?"

"She mostly came with her old man, the Chinese guy. I'd see them at dinnertime during the week. Sometimes they'd meet some older guy. Other times, she would just meet the older guy here alone, who always came with his bodyguard."

"How's that?"

"The bodyguard was younger than the older man, but not by much. In his forties maybe." Lestak pointed across the restaurant. "Mostly sat at that little table alone, facing the door—if you know what I mean."

"Can you describe the men?" Elana asked

"Let's see…" Lestak took a sip of beer and thought about it on the swallow. "Yeah. The bodyguard was a tall white guy, light hair, nice looking. And shoulders out to here," Lestak doubled his width using his arms like goal posts. "Beefy, like he could have played for the Niners or was a marine. The older guy was kinda stocky, in his fifties."

"Did you ever talk to the older man? Do you know if he had an accent?"

"Not really. He never stayed to eat. Like he'd meet them for a beer and then leave."

Elana pulled a grainy surveillance photo of Vladimir Sergeyev from her portfolio. "Is this him?"

Lastek studied the picture. "Maybe. I can't say for sure from that picture. He always wore one of them Brooks Brothers overcoats."

Elana chuckled. "What do you know about Brooks Brothers?"

"Hey, I ain't a fisherman from just *anywhere*. Sometimes those guys, you know, from the Financial District come down to make deals on fresh fish for their fancy parties. I seen those coats before."

"So, a tall, well-dressed, light-haired middle-aged white man," Elana said, "and a stocky older dude."

"Yeah, yeah, exactly, but they ain't no financial types, that's for sure."

"What do you mean?"

"I don't know any financial types who look tough like them. Either way, it's hard to believe those guys would be willing to get the smell of this place on those fancy suits."

"What about the husband?" asked Elana.

"One night, I saw him get all jittery when the older man showed up. It didn't look like things were going too well cause the Asian kid got up and walked out."

"How about the wife? Did she get jittery too?"

"No, no. She went outside and brought him back in. After that, everything seemed okay, but the older guy and his bodyguard left soon after."

"Did the older man ever pay the check? Like maybe there's an old credit card receipt?" Kenna said.

The fisherman thought about it. "No, either she or her husband always paid. I run the receipts at the end of the night. Lee...that was the name. The Lees."

"Thanks, Achille, that helps me a lot," said Elana.

The waitress approached with a large brown paper bag and set it on the table. "As soon as I saw you," Achille began, "I figured you were working, so I ordered for you and your friend. Got you two fish platters to go, on the house."

"Side of linguine in red sauce?" asked Elana.

Lestak laughed. "Can't believe you even asked me that, Doc!" He got up from the booth and waited for Elana to stand before he opened his arms. "Good to see you," he said when he hugged her. "Don't be a stranger."

"Achille, do you think you'd recognize those guys if you saw them again?"

"I think so."

"If I set you up with a sketch artist, would you be willing to try to describe them?"

"For you, Doc? I'd do that for you."

Elana jotted down a number on a bar napkin. "This is the number where you can leave me a message. I'll get it set up and have someone from my team get in touch with you."

"Okay. But tell me, who is he?"

"You're better off not knowing right now. But don't engage him, Achille. If you see him, call me...immediately."

He scratched his stubble. "You be safe out there. I won't be having anything happen to you, Doc."

She gave him a hug and a big kiss on the cheek, and even underneath all that stubble she could see his cheeks flush.

When she and Kenna left The Shack, the rhythmic sloshing of the night bay rippled, and the old white boat pitched a sideward dance.

* * *

Once back at the hotel, the two women devoured every bite of their Shack Specials while they worked.

"You were right, Elana. That red sauce was good enough to distract me. So how do you know Lestak and where did the nickname Doc come from?"

"I spent summers up here as a kid. My aunt and uncle lived in the city and they knew Achille, who had invited a bunch of us to go fishing with him. It was mostly guys, and a couple of women. One of the women was pregnant and went into labor three weeks early right there on the boat. We were too far offshore to get her back to a hospital. The guys became useless, so I wound up delivering the baby. Ever since that day, he's called me Doc."

"How did you know what to do?"

"I like football."

Kenna looked up from the Amtrak schedule. "What does that have to do with anything?"

"I played quarterback. Crouched down, and waited for the snap."

"Boy or girl?"

"Girl. They named her Elana," she said with a glimmer in her eyes. She hovered in front of a fold-out United States map that she had pinned to the wall. With a yellow highlighter, she traced the route from where she had investigated in Montana, to the location where Sierra's rental car was found in Havre. "So she drove just under four hours to get to Havre. It doesn't make sense."

"Why?"

If she was on the run, why waste time driving? She could've picked up a train much closer to where she started out and been farther sooner, unless she'd had a reason not to."

"What are you thinking?"

"Perhaps she was afraid the dead woman wasn't there alone and so she didn't feel safe getting on at a nearby station. Then again, someone else could have had her car. What if she was abducted?" She scraped back her hair in frustration. "Ugh!"

Across the room, Kenna sat on the bed researching area codes, specifically those whose last two numbers were oh-four. "Elana, I could use your insight to narrow down the area code list."

Elana walked over and sat on the bed. "And I could use a break," she said. "The more I think about it, the way Lestak described the older man, he basically ID'd Vladimir Sergeyev."

"So what? He's Raisa's father. Perfectly normal for them to meet for dinner."

"He's also the kingpin for the Russian mob and to Lestak it didn't look like he got along too well with his son-in-law. He and Raisa had worked on government contracts that required high levels of clearance. What if Vladimir is somehow involved in the hack?"

Kenna looked up from her list. "You mean like what if the Russians made a deal with the Chinese?"

"Maybe. Or maybe the Russians hacked the Chinese after the Chinese hacked the Americans."

"Or…perhaps the Russians hacked the US and made it look like the Chinese did it? Either way, leave that to the other Feds. Our job is to find your friend."

"Whew," Elana let out a hard sigh and flopped back on the bed. She yawned and closed her eyes.

"Sierra wouldn't be dumb enough to try to cross the Canadian border, would she?" Kenna said.

"No."

"Okay, that rules out both the two-oh-four and six-oh-four area codes. What about West Virginia or Atlanta?"

"I highly doubt it."

"Five-oh-four. How about New Orleans?"

Elana thought about it. She remembered that day in the diner, when Sonnenheim had assigned her to work with Sierra. 'Sierra won't be happy about me interrupting her weekend in New Orleans to send her to Montana,' Sonnenheim had said.

Elana's eyes popped open and she looked over at Kenna. "Yes. I wouldn't know where to look for her, but I know she was in New Orleans when Deputy Director Sonnenheim sent her to Montana. In fact, now that we're talking about it, why *hasn't* Sierra already contacted Sonnenheim?"

"You know why. Because either she can't or she isn't alive."

"Or she's holed up somewhere protecting that thumb drive. Sierra is wily. It still doesn't sit right with me that they used her as an errand girl. She's a brilliant hacker. She should have been in DC working to stop the cyber hemorrhage and then none of this would have happened."

"And we probably wouldn't have found ourselves working together. Do you think it's possible that sending Sierra to Montana was orchestrated to keep her out of DC for that very reason?"

Elana sat up. "I think we should consider it."

"That phone number is in New Orleans. We'll leave on the first flight out," Kenna said. "Unfortunately, we're going to have to find a way to search the phone numbers without alerting the agencies."

"I have someone I can call," Elana began.

Kenna grinned. "Well look at you all sneaky and everything."

"Do you want to call Chase and Pavlichenko?"

"No. Not yet. We'll let them know tomorrow, right after we throw them off the scent."

"How do we do that, Kenna?"

"We'll tell them we're going to Chicago."

"Why Chicago?"

Kenna stood and picked up the blue highlighter from the table. She walked to the wall map and traced the Amtrak train route straight across the wall from Montana to Chicago.

"But Pavlichenko said they ran facial recognition and didn't see her."

"No, Elana, she said that the cameras were sparse. Sierra could have easily boarded the Twenty-eight Empire Builder bound for Chicago without ever being spotted. It would make sense. It's a hub and she could get anywhere from there. What we won't tell them is that from there she took"—Kenna reached for the Amtrak schedule and followed the column down the page with her finger—"the Fifty-nine City of New Orleans."

"It's probably just a matter of time before Pavlichenko comes to the same conclusion we did and runs facial recognition in Chicago. Should we call the number first?"

"No. Sadly, whether your friend is alive or not, we need that thumb drive, and who knows what we're walking into. We need the element of surprise."

"Let's hope that phone number is a landline," Elana said.

"If it is, we'll find her tomorrow."

"If she's still there."

"Right now, this is our best shot at tracking her."

"Good job, Sierra," Elana said. "Hang in there." She looked into Kenna's eyes and smiled from one corner of her mouth. "So...you're *also* good at this."

* * *

Elana knocked on Kenna's door first thing the next morning.

"Come on in, breakfast is here," Kenna said when she opened the door. She hadn't yet put on any makeup and her hair was still a little wet. Wrapped in the big terry robe, she cinched it at the waist when Elana entered.

"Um, do you want me to take my breakfast to my room so you can finish up? I feel like I'm intruding."

Kenna shook her head. "Not at all. I'll be with you in a minute." She closed the bathroom door behind her and came out dressed in a soft pullover top and jeans. She pulled on her boots and took a seat at the table where Elana drank her coffee.

"I got a call from my investigator friend this morning," Elana said. "Late last night, she cross-referenced the numbers we gave her with names. She's dropping by shortly to give us the list. Elana checked her watch. "In about twenty minutes."

"Great going. We can profile the people who are on the list while we're on the flight to New Orleans." When Kenna looked up, Elana was observing her. "Everything okay?"

"You're beautiful like this. In the morning, without makeup—in jeans, with your hair still a little wet. Although I definitely do prefer you blond." Elana's cheeks flushed just a little. "Did I say all of that out loud? Sorry."

Kenna smiled and poured some coffee. "Don't be sorry, Elana. There's nothing to be sorry about."

"Okay then, I'm going downstairs to wait for my friend."

"You still have plenty of time. Finish your coffee."

"I think it's best for me to wait downstairs. Would you like me to ask about a cab to the airport?"

"Already taken care of. I have a driver here in the city who's a trusted acquaintance. I'll call and tell her to come in forty-five minutes. Will that work for you?"

Elana stood to leave. With one foot out the door, and without turning back, she said, "I'll see you downstairs, Pascale."

"Be there in a few—Alice."

CHAPTER TWENTY-TWO

Kenna pulled her hair back into a ponytail the instant she felt the pasty New Orleans humidity press against her neck. By the time Elana fetched their rental car, they had already narrowed their list of potential locations where Sierra might be down to three. Elana glanced over from the driver's seat as Kenna prioritized them and checked her watch.

"What is that thing you have going on with your watch?"

"GPS piggy-backed onto an RFID chip that's implanted in my arm."

"What does it do?"

"It tracks me, allows me to upload or download data, and it gets me into places electronically."

"Whoa. Which one of our agencies is using that?"

Kenna remained silent.

"I thought you're with Homeland, Kenna."

"It's need-to-know."

"Why is it I don't need to know?"

"You'll have to ask Secretary Zwarnick. That's really all I can say about it, Elana."

"Hmm, foreign service?"

"You might say that."

"Okay, so you're like me—an independent consultant?"

Kenna nodded as she looked back to the house that they'd been surveilling.

They ruled out the first two subjects they'd checked out on the basis of age and appearance, but it had cost them an hour and a half. At this third stop, they were parked across the street from a small remodeled Victorian in the Uptown section of the city. Fifteen minutes more had passed before a woman left the house and got into the black Civic in the driveway.

"She's cute," said Elana. "She's also Sierra's type, and there's a rainbow flag bumper sticker on her car."

"Yes, or she could be just another local lesbian."

"She fits the profile."

Kenna put her hand on Elana's arm to stop her from opening her door. "Wait. We'll approach once she's gone," Kenna said, turning back toward the house. "No need for her to know we've been there. If the house is empty, no harm, no foul."

"What if she has information for us?"

"First things first. Let's go check out the house, see who this girl is." Kenna adjusted her ankle holster, which now irritated her skin in the sticky heat. "You want the front or the back?" She glanced up when Elana hadn't answered, only to see the woman smiling at her. "What?"

"I'm still deciding if I want to enter from the front or the back," she teased.

Kenna laughed and pulled out a quarter. "Heads or tails?"

"Oooh, this just keeps getting better, Pascale."

"You're determined to torture me through all of this. Is this payback?"

"Maybe you should have taken me up on one of my offers back in the Chez Oui VIP room."

"It's not as if I didn't want to," Kenna said apologetically. "Was I part of your undercover sting?"

"Duck!"

The two women slid down low in their seats when the Civic pulled out into the street.

"You take the front door," said Kenna. "If Sierra is here, she won't be tempted to shoot without asking questions. I'll cover the backyard. You ready?"

Elana nodded and opened her door. "Let's go."

Elana rang the doorbell and waited. There was no answer. She placed her ear against the door and then rang the bell again. Nothing. She walked around to the backyard where she met Kenna on the porch.

"Someone is in there," Kenna whispered. "I saw a shadow."

"On the count of three?" Elana whispered back.

Kenna chambered her Beretta. Elana mouthed the numbers silently, counting down one finger at a time. *Three. Two...*

When she was down to the last finger, Kenna kicked open the kitchen door and Elana entered first. "Sierra? Sierra! It's Elana."

A frightfully pale Sierra opened the door to the pantry and stepped out into the kitchen clutching a .22. "Jesus, Elana, where the hell have you been? I've been trying to reach you!"

"Looking for you since the day after you left me the voice mail from Montana. All communications are secure so I don't have my normal cell phone."

"Who's she?" Sierra said, looking at Kenna.

"Believe it or not...Wonder Woman."

"What?" Kenna said as she clocked the sly smile on Elana's lips.

"No way," Sierra said.

"Wonder Woman, Elana?" Kenna said.

"It was Alice's nickname for you," Elana replied.

"Well, what's Wonder Woman doing here?" Sierra said.

"Pascale...or any other name—take your pick, but you can't be calling me Wonder Woman." Kenna holstered her Beretta.

Elana hugged Sierra. "It's okay, she's working with me. The thought of having to ID your body was insane. And when it wasn't you, I knew you'd find a way to get through to me. I found the phone number on the mirror—well most of it."

Sierra smiled. "How did you figure it out?"

"When we worked the sex sting and you had stayed with me. I remembered that game we used to play called, 'What if?' One of the situations was: Name two ways to leave a secret message. Who was the dead woman in Montana, and why haven't you called Sonnenheim?"

"Because Sonnenheim's people were the only ones who knew where I was headed and why I was going. There has to be a leak somewhere because someone tried to kill me. I'm guessing that the woman I had met with had taken the thumb drive off the real asset."

"How did you know she wasn't your contact?"

"When I met with her behind the motel, she fed me some bullshit line about a change in personnel, and then she mispronounced a word. She had placed the accent of the word 'manipulative' on the first syllable. I pegged it as Eastern European—Russian, and the hair on my arms stood up. Before I could act, she had the drop on me. She forced me at gunpoint into her pickup truck and made me drive a ways."

"She didn't take your gun?"

"She got my .38. Luckily, I had my backup piece strapped to the inside of my thigh. This nice small .22." She loosened her grip on the weapon.

"But if it was the thumb drive she was after, she already had it. Why come after you?"

"Good question, Wonder Woman."

"Thanks, *Vouvray*—because *it's* sweet like honey, and so am I."

"I'm flattered you remember."

"Sierra, focus. Why would she come after you if she already had the thumb drive?"

"Because she thought I was there to trade information for it. The Russian, or whatever she was, said that our asset had told her that on the Canadian side. She shot the asset. Once I blew her cover, she had to eliminate me. But it was so dark where she took me to kill me that I was able to reach down my pants and pull out the .22. After I shot her and grabbed the thumb drive, I took off. I picked up my gear from the hotel and wrote the phone number to this place on the mirror."

"The inside of your thigh?" Kenna said, "that's brave, and kind of hot."

"What happened to her truck?" Elana said.

"I drove it part of the way back to the motel and ditched it in a trailhead parking lot and then walked the rest of the way back to the Glacier Vista where I picked up my car."

"Who's this girl you're staying with?" Elana said.

"I met her last week so nobody knows her."

"We found your rental car in Havre. It was you who left it there, right?"

Sierra nodded. "When you get around to it, Elana, you'll have to tell me how Wonder Woman got here?"

"Pascale!" Kenna interrupted.

"I will, but you don't think I'd ever leave you in the wind, do you?"

Sierra threw her arms around Elana and hugged her again until the air was pushed out of her.

When Dani came through the front door juggling two bags of groceries, the three women were seated in her kitchen awaiting her. "What the hell happened to my back door?" she said as she placed the bags on the counter. "And who are you?"

Sierra stood and tossed her thick black hair to the side to kiss Dani. "It will be fixed before you know it, Dani. I promise. This is my friend Alice and her friend Pascale. They're Feds too. They knew about the trouble I was in so they tracked me down to help."

"Am I in jeopardy here? I mean if your friends could find you so easily…"

"No, Dani," Kenna began. "There is no way anyone can trace Sierra to your house unless you said something to someone."

"What about the security cameras at the Hilton?"

"What's that about the Hilton?" Elana asked.

"It's where Dani and I spent our first night together last week when we met."

Elana looked at Kenna. "What do you think?"

"I think that until we're certain Dani is safe, Uncle Sam needs to put her up in a hotel under an assumed name."

"Now y'all are just scaring me."

Sierra took Dani's hand. "We'll be right back. I need to speak with Dani alone."

"Don't take your time," Kenna said. "We need to move quickly."

* * *

Sierra led Dani into the bedroom and closed the door behind them. "You saved my life, Dani. And I promised you I wouldn't let any harm come to you. I'm sorry for all of this, but Pascale is right. You need to stay somewhere where I know you'll be safe. It's just a precaution, for a few days while some agent watches your house."

"What about my job?"

Sierra went to her knapsack, unzipped the inside compartment and took out an obscene wad of hundreds. "Here, baby. Whatever you do over the next few days, do it in cash, and call out sick. I'll make sure they put you up in a place with a great room service menu and plenty of good movies." Sierra kissed her and then looked deep into Dani's eyes. "When this is over, I'm coming back. I meant it, Dani, when I said I want to know you. I can't wait to wake up in those beautiful brown eyes again."

Dani dropped the wad of bills on her bed and put her arms around Sierra, then kissed her long and hard. "You'd *better* come back to me, dahlin'. Now what's this history I see between you and Alice?"

Sierra hesitated for a moment and then exhaled a hard sigh. "I promised you in bed last night that I wouldn't lie to you again unless it was a State secret. Alice and I danced together a few years ago in a government sting operation."

"Danced? As in ballet?"

Sierra shook her head.

"Twyla Tharp?"

"No."

"Ballroom? Please say 'yes.'"

Sierra shook her head again.

"Strippers?"

"Exotic dancers," Sierra corrected her.

Dani sat on the bed and looked up at Sierra. "So where are we now? An FBI stripper on the lam with a floral emergency," she said in a mocking tone. "I suppose your stripper name was Greer?"

"No."

"Well what was it?"

"Vouvray—like the wine, because *it's* sweet like honey, and so am I."

Dani raised her eyebrow. "Is there a lap dance in my future?"

Sierra smiled. "Oh, baby with all I've put you through, that's the least I could do."

"I have plenty of bills to stuff into your G-string." She flicked a glance at the wad of hundreds that had rolled across the bed.

When they came back into the kitchen, Kenna spoke up. "I just got off the phone with Secretary Zwarnick. An agent is on his way here who will introduce himself as Mike from Tulane Alumni Association. He'll take you to a safe hotel. Your door will be fixed and someone will be watching the house."

"I'm not leaving her here alone," Sierra said.

Elana moved to the counter, rinsed out the coffeepot and refilled it with water. "Then we wait."

"I bought plenty of food," Dani said. "Sandwiches, anyone?"

* * *

Kenna secured the back door with plywood and a screw gun that she found in Dani's shed.

"Thanks, Pascale," Dani said.

"It's the least I can do since I'm the one who broke through it. It'll be repaired by the time you come home."

There was a light knock on the front door. Kenna and Elana both grabbed their guns and went to the door, one of them on either side.

"Who is it?" Elana said in a singsong voice.

"Mike from Tulane Alumni Association," said the man on the other side.

Kenna holstered her weapon, but the look in her eye told Elana to not stand down. She opened the door. "Come in, Mike."

"Hi, are you Pascale or Alice?" he said when she closed the door. He turned and saw Elana's gun trained on him.

"Is that necessary?" said the young man with the military build and razor-sharp hairline who matched Zwarnick's description to a T.

Elana didn't move and Kenna opened her cell phone. With the press of two buttons, it only took one ring for the head of Homeland to pick up the phone.

"Standby to voice verify your agent," she said.

"I know him personally. Put him on."

Kenna handed Mike the phone. He cleared his throat and then straight-faced, he barked a lyric like a monotone drill instructor, until he reached the last line. "I keep forgetting to forget you. Forget your name, forget your game. I'll just forget youuuuu!" Straight-faced, he handed the phone back to Kenna.

All she could do was to close her slackened jaw and pretend that Mike had *not* just spouted the lyrics of a Steel Eyes rock and roll hit—that she'd written.

She absently put the phone to her ear. "Thanks. Got it." She nodded at Elana who then holstered her weapon.

"Okay, we're good," Kenna called out. "Stay right here, Mike." She knocked on the bedroom door, waited a second and then opened it to see tears in Dani's eyes. She glanced at Sierra and then back at Dani. "Don't worry, Dani, you're safe now and I'm certain of it."

Dani looked into Kenna's eyes. "I'm not worried for me," she began, "but are you sure Sierra will come back in one piece?"

Kenna smiled. "We've got this. Promise."

Once Dani was gone, Sierra came back into the kitchen. "I don't know all of what's involved here, but this has been some scary shit, Elana."

"Yeah," Kenna said, "scary, like all the names of compromised government personnel falling into the wrong hands."

"That's not the scariest part, Wonder Woman. That's just the beginning," Sierra said.

"What are you talking about?"

"I'm talking about the hack, Wonder Woman. It's not just Washington computers that were hacked. Our city infrastructures are under attack."

"What?" Elana said. "How do you know?"

"I hacked the password and encryption on some of the thumb drive files. And I was here in New Orleans for one of those events. I cross-referenced other cities, dates and events against news reports and they all correlated. Unfortunately, those were just the test runs...the water plant failure here, the hack of the stock exchange, an airline and a news outlet."

"Test runs for what?" said Kenna.

"I don't know."

Kenna looked to Elana. "So now, in the Russian column we have: Raisa Lee, the older man seen with Raisa at The Shack whom I presume to be her father, and now a probable Russian woman who tried to kill Sierra. What the hell do the Russians have to do with this Chinese hack of the United States? Where's that thumb drive, Sierra?"

They watched Sierra step into the pantry and reach way in the back. From the shelf of cleaning supplies, she removed the fake can of Comet cleanser and unscrewed the false bottom. "Here," she said, handing it to Elana. "I'm tired of carrying this thing around."

"How soon can we put this in Secretary Zwarnick's hand?" Elana said.

Kenna glanced at the wall clock over the doorway. "Zwarnick is bringing us in on his plane. We'll leave for the airport in half an hour which should put us there when he touches down."

"I'll gather my things," Sierra said as she left the room.

Elana poured another cup of coffee, sat at the kitchen table and looked down at her phone. "Sonnenheim's been trying to reach me. I can't return the call until I know we're safe. What do I do?"

Kenna walked to her and rested a comforting hand on her shoulder. "Don't worry. Wait until we meet with Zwarnick. Let him handle it, she's his subordinate."

Elana's fingers reached for and lightly grazed Kenna's hand as she released it from Elana's shoulder.

Kenna pulled the rental car into the side driveway of the house and drove away with the other two women. They'd been instructed to enter the airport where the freight plane hangars were located. When they arrived, two black government Escalades converged on their car at the gate. The agents verified their identities and then escorted them on foot to the hangar, where a second team escorted them onto the plane. Kenna and Sierra followed Elana up the steps into the private jet.

In the forward cabin, a team of tech people stood at the ready to analyze the thumb drive with their onboard computers. At the far end of the rear cabin, the tall man with gray hair stood and walked toward the door to greet them.

"Secretary Zwarnick," Elana said.

"Elana, Kenna," he said as they each boarded. "And you must be Sierra."

Sierra stopped and looked back at Kenna. "Wonder Woman, your name ain't really Pascale?"

CHAPTER TWENTY-THREE

Elana returned to her seat next to Kenna after twenty minutes of debriefing. Another fifteen minutes passed before Secretary Zwarnick finished up with Sierra, and the plane still had yet to take off.

"Wonder Woman, you're up," Sierra said. She moved to a computer terminal that had been reserved for her and went to work doing what she knew best—hacking.

Kenna grimaced at her, then walked to the back of the plane and sat opposite the Secretary of Homeland Security.

"Kenna, why didn't you and Elana brief Dixon Chase on where you were going?" asked Zwarnick.

"It was need-to-know."

"And you didn't think that the agent I chose to coordinate all of you was need-to-know?"

"No."

He took a long drink of water then looked into her eyes. "Want to tell me why?"

"You want my list, Vince? He stands out. He might as well have GI Joe tattooed on his forehead. And he's a red-tape kind of guy. I couldn't take that chance when, might I remind you, one of *your* people's lives was at stake. You wanted me to partner with West to find Sierra, and we managed to get it done in the time it took Chase to have his morning coffee and wonder where we were. Besides, what if we had been wrong? It would have wasted valuable time he needed to investigate Physio Dynamics and the Lees. You need this thumb drive to get that whole picture you'd told me about when you brought me on."

Zwarnick nodded and held up his hand to stop her. "Okay, okay. But remember, it's better to make friends rather than enemies in this business."

Kenna thought back to the discrimination that she had known in her young life as a rock guitarist—before Steel Eyes was born. How the male musicians would snub her, try to convince her without ever saying a word that girls weren't talented enough to be rock stars—that her presence was merely tolerated. *Chase is just like those guys.* She finally spoke. "Ask me if I care, Vince. I've known too many guys like him; the ones that think the womenfolk can't possibly be right—that we need male supervision."

"I see your point. Truth is, he's still playing in his sandbox compared to you. What would it take to get you onto our team? For good."

"Israel needs me more, and I owe that to my parents. Besides, you know I'm here for you when it counts."

"That you are." He looked beyond her to the cyber expert who stood waiting for him. "Excuse me." Zwarnick walked to where his team of cyber experts tapped away on their computers with lightning speed. He nodded his head as he listened to Sierra. Then he listened more, nodded more. He motioned for Elana to join him and Sierra as they walked back to where Kenna was waiting.

"Have a seat, ladies. You're probably wondering why we haven't yet taken off. The reason is because we weren't sure where we were headed next. Based on the information I now have from cyber, Chase and Pavlichenko, and from the three of you, if you say yes to what I'm about to ask you, we're heading to LA."

"Yay," Sierra said, "a private jet ride home for me and Elana."

Kenna stared at him. "Oh no, not again, Vince. I know that look. It's the one that landed me here. What now?"

"Right now, thanks to Sierra, there's strong evidence that the Russians have hacked the Chinese hack. I think Sierra was right. They're the ones behind the infrastructure issues we've had. This is a goddamn mess. I have people to work the Chinese angle. What I don't have is anyone who's up to speed on the Russian mob. It's no secret that most of our resources have gone to terrorism or China."

"How do you know that it wasn't the Chinese?" Elana said.

"The Chinese wouldn't take down our banking system. We owe them too much money and so do other countries whose economies would crumble in a domino effect. What *they're* after is our technology. Free Research and Development. A Senior VP from Physio Dynamics just turned, and State is in talks with the Chinese over this as we speak. The imminent challenge right now is to get inside the Russian Mafia's network to find and then stop whatever the Russians are going to do next. I believe the Russians wanted Sierra dead because they were retaliating for her part in the sex sting. It's starting to look like someone in Deputy Sonnenheim's department compromised your identity, Sierra. You and Elana are now reporting to me until further notice. Elana, they never knew that you were involved in that sting, and there's no record anywhere of you working for Sonnenheim so I'm sure you haven't been compromised."

"What are you trying to say, Mr. Secretary?"

Zwarnick leaned forward, his forearms on his thighs. He looked into Elana's eyes. "I want you to go back undercover as Alice in Vladimir Sergeyev's club."

"What? No. No, no. You're not serious."

"I'm afraid I am. In all likelihood, based on the sketch your friend described, Sergeyev was the older man who was seen with the Lees at the Crack Shack restaurant. We need someone on the inside."

"You're certain of Sergeyev's involvement in the sabotage?"

"Someone on his end got sloppy with their proxy servers on one single login out of a thousand, and Sierra nailed his IP address. Sergeyev himself just claimed Raisa's body and had it transported to LA where he's making arrangements for her burial. He's operating out of Chez Oui in LA. Please, Elana. He knows you. You left there on good terms…and with the recent loss of his daughter, my bet is he's going to take very kindly to you."

"How do you expect me to approach him?"

"All you'll need is a vulnerability. We'll set up a fake financial crisis for you and make it easy for him to get your financial records. He'll want to verify that you're telling the truth. And once he does, you'll play on his sympathy."

"What kind of fake financials?"

"We'll bankrupt you. The kind of debt only stripper money could fix. We'll set up untraceable accounts and problems he can't verify like a hospital bill for a sick relative."

"What am I supposed to do once I'm on the inside?"

"You're going to download his source code from his private computer."

"How?"

Zwarnick looked at Kenna.

"Vince, you have got to get a new look. Every time you look at me that way I go deeper down the rabbit hole."

"Once Elana is in the door, she can get you in to work there too. You can use your implanted chip to download Sergeyev's source code the same way you did it at the Chinese Embassy in Buenos Aires. Sierra will run the hack with our team."

Kenna deadpanned him. "You want me to *dance* at Chez Oui. You're out of your mind, right?"

"No, I'm not. Elana and Sierra can teach you what you need to know and they can outfit you. We'll have agents there when you're working in the event you need backup."

Elana and Kenna stared at each other speechless. No one but the three women knew the interstitial space between Alice and Pascale. And even then, Sierra never knew the depth to which their connection had swelled in the ill-lighted and private back room of Chez Oui.

Sierra laughed. "Alice in Wonder Woman Land! Man, what I wouldn't give to see this routine."

"You're going to help choreograph it," said Zwarnick. "After that, you won't be far away, Sierra. You'll be offsite in a cyber-monitoring center. I need an experienced black hat to hack Sergeyev's firewall. None of our available personnel have ever been where you've been on the dark web. You've lived it and you have connections. And no one knows that club and the people inside it better than you and Elana."

"You realize what you're asking us to do, Vince?" said Kenna.

He nodded. "I'm asking the three of you to save the world."

"What if I can't do this?" Elana said.

Kenna smiled slyly. "Come on, Alice, no government agent in history has *ever* had more skin in the game than you."

Elana stared at her with mild contempt. "And now, Wonder Woman, you'll have some skin in the game yourself."

Kenna squirmed. "Mr. Secretary, would this be a good time to ask how the Chinese code I stole for you in Buenos Aires fits into this?"

"No." Zwarnick smiled. "That was pitifully transparent and beneath you."

Elana turned to Kenna. "You got assigned to Buenos Aires? You get Buenos Aires and I score a skeezy strip club near LAX? Maybe I want to apply to *your* branch of service."

Kenna shot Zwarnick a sharpened glance. "Elana, *we* scored a skeezy strip club."

CHAPTER TWENTY-FOUR

"Agent Chase, you wanted to see me?" Carly Avedon said from the open doorway.

"Lieutenant, come in and have a seat." Chase stood at the far end of the conference room on the eighth floor of the FBI field office.

Avedon's hair was maniacally spiked in all the right places, her pantsuit androgynously law enforcement-perfected, and her lips in position to kiss whatever ass she needed to get where she wanted to go. She walked around the long table and took the first seat facing the door.

Chase smiled. "I'm happy to report that your investigation has turned up some important details. You helped uncover Physio Dynamics' part in this. That was great detective work finding the VP who signed off on Raisa Lee's altering of the settings on the chip machine. How did you find that out?"

"I have my ways, but thanks for saying so." She smiled and thought of the thumb drive she had lifted from Raisa's wallet at the accident scene.

Chase walked toward her end of the conference table and sat facing her. "I feel like I can speak freely with you, Lieutenant."

"Please, call me Carly. Feel free to speak your mind, Dixon. May I call you Dixon?"

Chase nodded. "Carly, I wasn't thrilled with the communication breakdown I experienced with Waverly and West. I also sensed some static between you and West. Did that have anything to do with the communication problem?"

"No. I dislike West for other reasons."

"What reasons?"

Avedon leaned back in her chair and crossed her arms. "She caused a killer to go free."

Chase's eyebrows arched. He sat forward. "How's that?"

"She was supposed to give testimony in a large case. My case, against a murder suspect, but she wouldn't do what needed to be done."

"And what was that?"

"Identify her confidential source."

"Would it have put an innocent life in jeopardy to do so?"

"I suppose. But she endangered a lot more lives by letting the sicko walk."

Chase pursed his lips and ran his hand through his hair while he thought about it. "I could use your help, Carly."

"What do you need, Dixon?"

"West and Waverly have been assigned to infiltrate one of Sergeyev's clubs in LA as dancers, and I would like you down there, reporting to me directly. Do you think you could handle that?"

Carly Avedon knew exactly what to think, what to handle, and she pictured how it would read on her résumé. "But my job is here in San Francisco."

"I can arrange for you to be on sabbatical for national security, as a special consultant to the FBI."

"Agent Avedon. It has a nice ring to it. What will I need to do?"

"Among other things, you'll be on rotation as a customer at Chez Oui looking for a little fun. You'll be there to back up

Waverly and West, but I also want to know of any significant activity outside the club."

"Not much of a stretch sending me in there as a gay woman."

"I'm short on personnel I can trust, your security is cleared and you're already a vital part of this case. Do you realize how many people may have already been compromised in this thing?"

"I know."

"That's why I want you to make sure everyone there is clean."

"Is there something in particular you're looking for?"

"I'll know it when I see it, Carly. Ops will set you up once you're there and you'll be providing valuable backup in case something goes sideways."

She rolled her eyes. "You're asking me if I could save West after what she did?"

"That's exactly what I'm asking you. Can you be objective here?"

"Above all else, Dixon, is the law. Yes, I can do my job."

"So then, you're in?"

She nodded and smiled. "I'm in."

"Great. Be ready to leave tomorrow evening. I want to give them time to get settled in LA. Once they do, I'll provide you with a safe house near them. Pavlichenko and I are heading back to DC in the morning. I'll be in touch from there, but in the meantime you can start with this." He handed her a portfolio. "Be careful, Carly, these dudes are *gulag*-scary."

"They're no match for naked women."

He chuckled. "Try not to enjoy the assignment too much."

Avedon stared straight at him. "I'm not the one you should be worried about."

"What do you mean?"

"Naked women don't distract me. Maybe you should save that advice for your male agents."

* * *

Two Lincoln Navigators with tinted windows waited outside the hangar in Los Angeles when Zwarnick's plane touched down. He and the women concluded their meeting before deplaning.

"Elana, you'll need to get close enough to Sergeyev to clone the security information on his badge. Sierra will take the cloner and then program the information into Kenna's implant."

"The tricky part for me," Kenna began, "is going to be getting to his personal computer."

"There's no way he could know that I'm cloning him?" Elana said.

"No. Just remember the rules. Get within a few centimeters of him and it will capture the security frequencies to gain entry. Sierra," he said, turning to her, "we'll set you up with everything you need including personnel to gain access to the actual files and source codes. Once that's in place, Kenna will run the tactical side since it all comes down to her getting inside Chez Oui."

"Sir, I'm going to need some things from my apartment," said Sierra.

"Compile a list. You too, Elana, and we'll have those things delivered to the safe house."

"Where am I staying?" Elana asked.

"We have a secure house set up for you and Kenna in West Hollywood."

"What?" Kenna said. "Do you really think it's wise to put us under the same roof?"

"Yes," Elana chimed in. "I don't think it's a good idea to—"

"Well, I do," Zwarnick interrupted. "I need to minimize risk, and it would be riskier having you two unable to communicate safely offsite from the club. It also requires more eyes on you both. Besides, Elana, you need to turn Kenna into a credible dancer."

Elana looked at Kenna. "Okay."

"Great." Kenna's eyes darted away from Elana.

"One last thing. San Francisco Police Lieutenant Carly Avedon will be working the case in the club as part of your backup team."

"Now that could turn out to be a bad idea," Kenna said. "She's got it out for Elana. Why is that, anyway?"

"Avedon had a murder case to which I uncovered information from a confidential informant. The case was no slam dunk—circumstantial mostly. It had a lot of holes in the evidence. Carly wanted me to place my CI's life in jeopardy by having him testify against the defendant. I was ninety-eight percent sure that the informant would have never lived to testify. Had Avedon's case been properly built, the CI would have never come into play. So, I refused to identify him. She credits me with putting a murder suspect back on the streets."

Kenna spoke up. "She demonstrates reactivity and someone with control issues. I can't have her getting in the way, Vince."

"Dixon Chase has already assured me that she has pledged her utmost professionalism."

Kenna stared at him straight on. "Just tell her to stay out of our way."

Zwarnick met her stare. "Are you giving me an order?"

"No, sir."

CHAPTER TWENTY-FIVE

The driver of the black Lincoln Navigator inched north on La Cienega Boulevard en route from LAX to the safe house. Zwarnick stared out the tinted passenger window, and Sierra sat sandwiched between Kenna and Elana in the backseat.

"It's awfully quiet back there," said Zwarnick.

"Yeah, maybe one of you should say something," Sierra said through teeth mildly clenched.

Kenna glanced across Sierra at Elana, who was giving Sierra the evil eye.

"What do you think they should say, Sierra?"

"Oh, Mr. Secretary, I don't know nothing."

Kenna squinted at the girl. "Okay, full disclosure. Elana and I have met before."

"How is that significant?" He paused. "Ahh. Are you saying you two were involved?"

"No," Elana said.

"Then I'll ask again. How is that relevant?"

Kenna blurted it out. "We know each other from Chez Oui. It was a long time ago. There you have it."

"Would anyone at that club recognize you, Kenna?"

"No, especially not with the black hair."

"Your hair isn't really black?" Sierra said.

Kenna ignored her.

"Is this going to be a problem?" Zwarnick said.

"No," Kenna and Elana replied in concert.

"And going forward?"

Elana looked over at Kenna. "We'll be fine."

"Need I remind you of what's at stake here?"

"No, sir, I'm clear," Elana snapped.

"Me too," said Sierra.

"How about you, Wonder Woman?" he asked with mild sarcasm.

Kenna's eyes narrowed. "I'm clear I can quit at any time, you know."

Zwarnick smiled. "But you won't. You forget I know you and your relentless sense of duty."

"Yeah, yeah." Kenna breathed out the sigh of ennui. The spy's thoughts drifted to the shimmering lapis Caribbean that surely missed her by now. She shut her eyes and tried to feel the rhythm of the waves under her sailboard. "Can't you turn on some sirens and get us out of this traffic?"

"No," said Zwarnick. "We can't draw any attention to ourselves, especially with me in the car. When we get to the house, we'll pull into the garage so that you can unload your gear and then I'm headed back to DC. Our local crew is already setting up at the Command Center in the house next door, where Sierra will be staying. Elana and Kenna, your house is ready." The secretary picked up his phone on the first ring. "Yes, I see. I'll let her know." Zwarnick hung up and turned to Elana. "Raisa Lee's funeral will be held tomorrow morning. Dixon Chase is texting you the information. I think that's your best opportunity to get to Vladimir at a more sympathetic moment."

"What about my faux financial crisis?" said Elana.

"Pavlichenko is bankrupting you as we speak."

Elana frowned. "This all goes back to normal when we're done, right?"

"As a thank-you from your government, your credit score will be as good as it gets, which will answer any questions anyone may throw at you down the road. There will also be hard documentation that the bankruptcy was due to an institutional error. A computer error."

"I have a question."

"What's that, Kenna?"

"What do we do if I'm just too old to get hired?"

"What are you talking about?" Sierra said. "You look great. With your body, I don't think anyone's going to ask your age. Right, Elana?"

"We'll choreograph a jaw-dropping routine for when you audition and you'll be a knockout."

"We've got our work cut out for us though, haven't we?" Sierra teased.

Zwarnick's eyes met Kenna's in the passenger-side visor mirror. "Why are you rolling your eyes?" he said.

"Because I'd prefer taking these guys down the old-fashioned way—with intelligence and then force."

"There's nothing more lethal than a sexy, beautiful woman," Sierra said.

Elana glanced at Kenna. "Isn't *that* the truth?"

Kenna wished they were wrong.

The Navigator turned onto the quiet residential street in West Hollywood. Palm trees outlined the block, paired like square dance partners. At the end of the block, a quaint English two-story Tudor sat next to a compact two-story bungalow.

Kenna thought of how long it had been since she'd come home to LA, land of the perpetual parking lot. She had once loved it here. All the buzz and excitement had been suitable for a younger, more restless her. Until she had experienced stardom, and later felt what it was like to breathe deeply in Jamaica, she didn't realize how intense Los Angeles was. It had been a long time.

Barely a mile away from her stood the apartment building where she and her bandmates had lived—had birthed Steel Eyes. How their fates had collided to catapult them into an unimaginable destiny, now seemed foreign. Though Mel, Rich and JJ presently lived in their fancy neighborhoods, she wished she could sneak away to see them. *Maybe when this is over.*

The automatic garage door closed once the Navigator was parked inside.

"We're doing this walk-through because I'm leaving nothing to chance," Zwarnick said as he led the way. "Kenna, your brother is here."

"Welcome home," said the handsome brown-haired man when the team entered the house. Lean and poised, at just under six-feet tall, Hunter van Bourgeade was dressed in a suit, as usual.

"Hunter, good to see you!" said Zwarnick as they shook hands.

"Hunt! What a great surprise." Kenna and he hugged and kissed on both cheeks.

"I wasn't about to let the secretary put you out there without me as your backup, Wave," said Hunt.

"Wave? That's your nickname?" Elana teased.

"Hunt, say hello to Elana aka Alice, and Sierra aka Vouvray," Kenna said.

"Vouvray? Like the wine?" Hunt asked.

The women reflexively answered, "Yes, because *it's* sweet like honey, and so am I."

Hunter laughed and then paused when he looked into Kenna's eyes. "D-did you say Alice?"

Kenna nodded.

"As in *the Alice?*"

Elana turned to Kenna. "I'm *the* Alice?"

Kenna's cheeks flushed. "Yes, Elana."

"Okay, everyone," Zwarnick interrupted, "follow me." He led them through the home that while generic on the outside, held a wealth of stealth inside its walls.

Upstairs, they spent the greatest amount of time checking their weapons cache, finally ending at the French doors in the fully stocked kitchen.

"The backyards of the two houses are conjoined so that you can all move freely," said Zwarnick. "Sierra, when we're done here, you'll come next door with me. We'll coordinate with Mardi and Joe whom you worked with on the plane." He glanced at his watch. "They should be there by now. The person who designed the software platform for Kenna's microchip implant is also coming in to train you. Except for me, you have final say on the Command Center tech ops. When I leave, you're top dog, Agent Stone."

"Sir, did you just call me *agent?*"

"You're the one who put her life on the line and safeguarded that thumb drive. You made the connection that alerted us to the Russian mob—and you did it while on the run. Not to mention the infrastructure correlation you discovered when you hacked the encryption. If that's not the work of a top agent, I don't know what is."

"Sir?"

"Yes?"

"That come with benefits?"

"I believe it does. Whatever you decide, Stone, don't let me down."

"No, sir, I won't. I'll have Elana wired and ready to go by morning."

"When this is all over with, you'll still have to jump through a few hoops, but you'll have my personal recommendation and a full-time job waiting for you."

"Thank you, Mr. Secretary. Thanks a lot."

"Vince," said Kenna, "the asset wouldn't happen to be Annaliese Dahl, would it?"

"Yes, she's the one who set you up in Curaçao, right?"

Kenna nodded. "You could say that." She felt her stomach tighten into a sailor's knot.

Elana turned to her. "So you got Buenos Aires *and* Curaçao? Sheesh."

"Annaliese will be staying next door?" Kenna asked.

"Yes, she'll be here tomorrow to work with Sierra on the frequencies and download capabilities. Wait, we almost forgot the living room."

They followed him in but Kenna stopped cold when she saw the centerpiece in front of the mirrored wall. She sneered. "This day just keeps getting better. Are you serious?"

Sierra answered on his behalf. "How can we turn you into a believable pole dance partner without a pole, Wonder Woman?"

Hunt snickered. "Wonder Woman?"

"It's a long story, Hunt."

"A *duo?*" he teased.

Kenna glared at him. "You know what? Just shut up."

"Yeah, Hunt," Sierra interjected. "She and Elana. You know, Alice in Wonder Woman Land. Catchy, right?"

Hunt couldn't suppress his laugh until Kenna grimaced. "Okay, Wave, shutting up now. I swear."

Even Vince Zwarnick had to turn away when he smiled.

* * *

Late that night, Elana found Kenna on the living room sofa staring into the fire. The flames' spikes danced on, and reflected off the metal pole in the middle of the room.

"May I join you?" Elana said.

"Sure." Kenna did a double take of the woman dressed in yoga pants and a sweatshirt, and then refocused on the fire.

Elana's medium-length blond hair was pulled back into a ponytail, more reminiscent of a yoga instructor than an Alice. She sat on the opposite end of the sofa tailor style, silent until Kenna let out a sigh not plagued with ennui.

"It will be okay, Kenna."

"What will?"

"The pole routine."

Kenna turned to her. "How did you know that's what I was thinking about?"

"Because you're wondering how we're going to do it, and how you're going to do it with *me*. One little hitch in our plan is to get you confident on that pole."

"I'd never have guessed that my weapons cache would be a G-string and three-inch heels."

Elana chuckled. "Five-inch heels are the better weapon."

"That would be a suicide attempt."

"You can wear three inch."

"If it's a weapon I need, I'd prefer my Beretta."

"Illusion is your weapon. It's all about the fantasy, and that, you create with attitude."

"Yes, Alice taught me all about illusion."

"Not all of it was an illusion, you know. Are you nervous about dancing almost naked?"

"*Almost* is preferable to the alternative, though I'm not happy about it. When I think of all the rights we women have had to fight for…"

"Wait a sec, that's a bit of a double standard considering why you had come to Chez Oui in the first place; why you repeatedly sought out Alice."

"That was different."

"Oh?"

"You can drop the sarcasm, Elana. I'm a woman and I wasn't there to subjugate women."

"Regardless, Alice was still an object to you."

"No, she wasn't. She was a lifeline."

"A lifeline," Elana deadpanned her.

"Yes. Damn, you're cynical. Was there ever a time that I disrespected Alice? That I did something she didn't want me to do?"

"No. What was it about Alice that drew you in?"

Kenna didn't have to think about it. "There wasn't anything that *didn't* draw me in."

"That's the illusion. You mirror the customer's fantasy."

"So that's what Alice did with Pascale?"

"No, that was different."

"How so?"

"You were there. You know."

"Maybe we'd better stick to business right now."

Elana stared at the fire. "Secretary Zwarnick told me you're a brilliant tactician, Kenna. So why not see the dancing for what it is?"

"What's that?"

"Just another tactical component."

Kenna gazed into her eyes as she listened. "I know we agreed to wait until this op was over before we sorted out our past, but you just asked me a question and I dodged the answer."

"How?"

"You asked me what it was about Alice that kept me coming back."

"And?"

"Out of all those steamy nights, something happened once that stopped me in my tracks."

"What was it?" Elana asked.

"No, I can't go there until this op is over."

"Why?"

"It's too personal," Kenna admitted.

"Tell me," Elana whispered.

"All I'll say about it for now is, during that week I came back to Chez Oui at least three times. When Alice did her routine, every time I felt her—felt *your* hot breath on my neck, I imagined feeling it for days afterward."

Elana remained silent.

"I'm sorry. Should I not have said anything?"

"No, it's okay," Elana said softly. "I remember it. And I remember thinking, 'I wish she'd kiss me already.'"

Kenna looked at her dumbfounded. "You're serious."

"I am."

"Wow, I wonder how differently things might have gone had I known that."

Elana leaned over and jabbed Kenna playfully. "I hope you're more intuitive than that in the field," she teased.

Kenna finally smiled. "I'm only clueless when it comes to women. I know this isn't the easiest partnership, but honestly if I have to dance in a strip club, there isn't anyone I'd rather do it with than Alice."

They stared into each other's eyes the way they had long ago, in that darkened room, with unspoken needs that words would have betrayed. They had never needed any words—until now.

"It's getting late and you have a funeral to attend in the morning, Elana. Are you nervous about walking into that hornet's nest?"

"Yes. I have to ingratiate myself to Vladimir Sergeyev, and somehow persuade him to hire Alice again or the entire op is blown."

"Stay the course. I can't imagine anyone turning Alice down."

"You did."

"Huh. Imagine that. Me, an idiot."

CHAPTER TWENTY-SIX

The next morning, Elana arrived on time at the bulbous, onion-domed Russian Orthodox church. Clothed in an appropriate black dress, she wore light makeup, and her straight blond hair framed her face. She took stock of the mourners while she waited in a line to offer her condolences to Vladimir Sergeyev and his wife.

"Video and sound?" she whispered.

"Check." Sierra's voice was so clear that Elana felt like it was coming from inside her own head. The two women directly in line behind her talked softly. She moved half a step closer to eavesdrop.

The older woman was nearest, with a face that was round like a Russian nesting doll. "It was a *bad* death," she said to the younger woman.

"Don't say that, Mama."

"It's true, and you know what that means. Surely death and destruction always follows."

What does that mean? A bad *death. Aren't they all pretty bad?* Elana continued moving up in line. *Death and destruction always follows*, she repeated to herself. She could see Sergeyev standing while his wife sat in the pew next to him.

Elana surveyed the ornate church with its flat Byzantine-style icons that offered no real perspective of their subject, except for that which the gold leaf halos provided. A few steps farther she was able to see the crew seated in the first row. Even from behind, the bodyguards looked like a Russian wrestling team, sitting shoulder to shoulder in their black suits. Every few seconds, Elana casually looked around, turning her head slightly while wearing the glasses whose frames transmitted the video.

Immediately to Vladimir's left stood an older man roughly his same age, of medium height with broad shoulders. When she was five people away, Vladimir's eyes locked on hers. He nodded and thanked the people ahead of her in line, his glance darting back to hers between the greetings. As she neared, she pretended to adjust her glasses, tapping twice to deactivate the zoom lens.

"Hello, Vladimir. It's been a long time. May her memory be eternal," Elana said, according to the Russian tradition. She gazed at his wife, "I'm very sorry for your loss, Mrs. Sergeyev."

Raisa Sergeyev looked up at her with eyes red from crying, and nodded.

It took the man a moment to react. "Alice." He held her hand and squeezed it warmly. "I didn't recognize you with the blond hair. Thank you for coming, it *has* been a long time."

"I wish we were reuniting under better circumstances. I didn't believe it when I'd heard this terrible news. Let me know if there's anything I can do."

"You will come to the memorial dinner tonight." Vladimir voiced it as a statement rather than a question.

"Of course." She took her leave and followed the other mourners to the casket, knowing she was expected to bow and kiss the deceased's ribbon. She took a deep breath and pretended to do so solemnly.

The man who stood to Vladimir's left watched their exchange with quiet intensity and said nothing. Elana felt his eyes locked on her the whole time.

She walked toward the back of the church and heard Sierra in her left ear. "You go, Alice! Video came through perfectly. You got the whole row."

Elana stood among the mourners in the back of the sanctuary, hypnotized by the priest's continual swinging of the censer. For an hour, she listened to psalms, hymns and prayers in Russian—and then ditched the burial.

When she returned to the safe house, Elana entered the gym, where she found Kenna throwing a roundhouse kick at Hunter's head. He caught her leg midair and used his leverage to flip her off her other foot and onto the mat.

Kenna landed with a thud and a grunt. "Oh, hey, Elana," she said, glancing up from the floor. Hunt pulled her back to her feet before reaching for his towel.

"Remind me never to take on either one of you," said Elana.

Hunt smiled. "We've been doing this since we were little kids."

"Are we done, Hunt?"

"I need to clean up and get to Mom's for dinner," he answered. "She said she'll make you whatever you want when this op is over."

"I don't know what I'll want for dinner, but I already know what's on the dessert menu."

"Let me guess," he said sarcastically. "French plum cake."

"I heard the funeral was a success," Kenna said.

"Yeah."

"You okay?"

"It's just sad when someone dies so young. I'd met Raisa, you know."

"No, I didn't know."

"She was a nice girl actually. Vladimir invited me to the memorial dinner, so I think tonight is my 'in.' I'm going to change into something comfortable and then head next door before I leave again."

"I'll grab a quick shower and be right over."

Elana nodded and closed the door when she left the room.

"You like her, Wave," Hunt said while gathering his gear.

"What?"

"You *like* her."

"I do like her, Hunt. But I'm a little conflicted about our history, not to mention becoming a pole dancer. I need to keep my head clear."

"Understandable. I can't even imagine what you're feeling, going from rock star to undercover exotic dancer, of all things."

She looked into his eyes with disbelief. "Every time I think I've found myself, it turns out I'm someone else."

He shook his head. "It's the nature of our business. But if you don't ask that woman for a date when this is over, I will lose all respect for you."

"Why?"

He smiled. "Because she really likes you too."

"In the meantime, how am I supposed to focus with Annaliese Dahl next door? Your mother and Uncle did everything but set a wedding date for us. And Annaliese did everything to try to make something happen from the moment I swam to her yacht and stayed the night in her mansion."

Hunt laughed. "You let Mom and Uncle fix you up?"

"No! I didn't *let* them."

"Well, were you interested in her? Did anything happen that night?"

"I didn't feel any spark. You're going to think I'm crazy when you meet her. Honestly, the woman has it all going for her. I mean in every way. But I just wasn't there, you know?"

He smirked. "Elana is a different story, and you know it."

"Unfortunately, I do."

"Wave, you can't still be thinking about Alex Winthrop. That relationship was like a hundred-thousand years ago."

"I'm not. At least not like I used to. My breakup with her is what turned me into Steel Eyes though."

"Yeah, a couple of decades ago!"

"She was a hard act to follow, that's all."

"I'm putting my money on Elana. It's obvious to me that there's something between you."

"You'd better get out of here. Your mother hates it when you're late for dinner. And if—"

"I know," he interrupted, "if she made French plum cake, I'll bring you some."

* * *

"Hey, girls," Sierra said. "You remember Mardi and Joe from Secretary Zwarnick's cyber team?"

"Welcome aboard," said Elana.

"Thanks," said Mardi before she and Joe swiveled back to their keyboard mad-skills.

"Hello, Kenna," Annaliese said coolly when she made her entrance from the far side of the room.

Kenna swallowed hard. "Annaliese, nice to see you. Thanks for your help on this."

"I never expected you to still be stateside," the woman replied.

"Me either."

"*Ahem*," Elana said.

"Excuse me." Kenna turned to Elana. "Annaliese this is Elana—code name Alice, my partner on this team. Elana, Annaliese programmed my chip implant in Curaçao."

"So *you're* Curaçao." When they shook hands, Kenna pretended to ignore the laser-like Alice-stare that Elana gave the woman. "It's nice to meet you, Annaliese. I've heard you're quite the expert, but I should warn you that Sierra is dark web gritty-good."

Annaliese nodded. "So I've already learned. We're among the few who even understand the dark web."

"I take it Secretary Zwarnick has filled you in?" Kenna said.

"Yes, I'll check your calibration as soon as I have all the information I need. I really thought you'd be back in Jamaica by now."

"I thought so, too, but I'm a sucker for a good cause."

Annaliese glanced at Elana. "Apparently."

Kenna continued. "Everything went pretty smoothly in Buenos Aires, except for a slight miscalculation on my part."

Annaliese burned a stare into her. "I heard."

"Oh?" said Kenna.

"From Trysta actually."

"We're quite the network, aren't we?" Kenna countered.

Annaliese smiled. "Is it me or are *gay-gents* the only off-book agents left?"

"Jamaica too, Kenna?" Elana interjected.

"No, Elana, that and New Jersey are home."

Annaliese looked at Sierra. "I need to know more about the club and what equipment is there. Who is cloning the security?"

"I am," said Elana. "I'm trying to find a way to get into the club—though I haven't a clue yet how and when. Hopefully, I'll have the answer to that in a few hours when I return from a memorial dinner with the owner."

"Vladimir Sergeyev, right?"

"Yes. You know of him?"

Annaliese nodded. "Many major European players have had dealings with him at some point. Sex trafficking was his big deal years ago."

"Yes, Sierra and I worked on one of those stings. Unfortunately, the only people who went down for it were the guys under him. But maybe we'll get him this time. How will I clone his security?" Elana asked.

"Our intelligence shows that Sergeyev is using electronic readers for his secure locations. You'll need to target an upper level employee, or Sergeyev himself would be ideal. I'll have you wired to clone it, but you'll need to be within a few centimeters of the person for it to clone automatically."

"Sounds complicated," Elana said.

"Shake hands, bump into someone, or just get really close to them. In the time it takes to say hello or apologize, I'll have the information from their badge. You'll bring the device back here afterward and I'll use it to program access into Kenna's implant and make you a duplicate card."

"Okay."

Annaliese smiled. "Good. Tonight while you're gone, Sierra and I will work on the software end."

Sierra opened a new window on her computer. "Elana, I want to tweak your comms devices while we have Annaliese here."

"Why, did we lose anything?"

"No. In fact, the first facial recognition is coming in now. We're analyzing the rest so that we can identify all the players." Sierra tapped the keyboard and transferred the image to the wall screen.

"Who is that guy?" Elana said. "He hovers over Vladimir, and he had his eyes on my every move."

"Ladies, meet Ivan Mikhailov," said Sierra.

"Never heard of him," Kenna said.

"Hold that thought." Sierra tapped more keys and placed a call.

"Zwarnick here," he said through the speakers.

"We're all here, sir," Sierra said. "We're secure and the video should be connecting now."

"I can see you fine," Zwarnick said. "I heard you did well today, Elana, and that you've been invited to the memorial dinner."

"Yes."

"That's not a small thing when the father of the deceased invites you, you know."

"Yes sir."

"Annaliese, thanks for coming on such short notice. The man you see on your other screen is Ivan Mikhailov. He entered the US six months ago. According to my sources in Moscow, Ivan is one badass dude. He's former KGB, and he and Sergeyev grew up together in the city of Vladivostok."

"How bad is he, Vince?"

"Let's put it this way, Kenna, when the KGB lacked the stomach for something, they brought in Mikhailov."

"Great. I don't like the idea of Elana going in alone. It's too dangerous," Kenna said.

"If everything goes as planned, you'll be in there with her soon enough."

"So how do you want me to play this?" Elana asked.

"Play it easy and slow. Now that we know Ivan is Vladimir's right hand, I promise you he's already checking you out. Nadia Pavlichenko is notified every time someone gains access to your records. She said at the rate he's going, Ivan will know everything we want him to know by dinnertime. We have his IP address. With a little bit of luck, he'll use his extensive Cold War spy training to clock all your weaknesses and then he'll use them against you. I wouldn't be surprised if he recruits you before dessert."

"Okay then. Slow and steady wins the race," Elana said with finality.

"Anything else?" Zwarnick asked.

"No sir."

"Call me afterward."

"Yes sir."

Zwarnick disconnected.

"Elana, let me drive you there. I'll park off site just in case you need backup."

"No, Kenna. We can't take a chance of anyone spotting you just yet. There's no danger there tonight."

"No danger you'll be able to see coming."

Elana smiled at Kenna sweetly. "It will be fine. I'm going to rest for a while before I go. See you all later." Elana left the Command Center.

"Sierra," said Kenna, "are you sure her comms are working right?"

"Don't worry, Wonder Woman, I got this."

Kenna nodded. "Make sure you do."

"I care about her too, you know."

"Hmm," said Annaliese.

CHAPTER TWENTY-SEVEN

The formal wrought-iron gates to the Van Bourgeade estate peeled away when Hunt entered the access code, and then placed his thumb on the pad. Neither oversized nor garish as far as Bel Air mansions went, he was thankful that his parents had had the good taste to not buy the mausoleum-style, or the comically turreted estates that plagued the well-moneyed neighborhood. Although his father had been gone for years now, Maurice van Bourgeade's famous photographs and solid appreciation for aesthetics still colored the place. Hunt coasted along the semicircular drive and parked the car at the grand front entrance.

"Hi, Maman." His voice echoed between the marble floor and high ceiling. She descended the grand double staircase and greeted him with a kiss on both cheeks.

"I'm so glad you could make it tonight," she said, smiling.

"I thought Uncle would be here too."

"He'll be downstairs in a few minutes. He's finishing up a communication with France."

"So, how are you, Mom?" He followed her through the foyer and into the kitchen.

"I'm fine, except that I'm a little worried."

Hunter lifted the wine bottle from the counter. "What are you worried about?" He poured a glass from Uncle's French vineyard and inhaled its bouquet.

Phyllis busied herself with a tray of hors d'oeuvres. "Namely, Kenna, and you, and your sister Chantal."

Hunt chuckled and sat on a barstool. "Is that all? Why are you worried about me? Let's start there."

"Who is this girl you're seeing?"

"What girl?"

"Hunter!"

"Mother, that tone hasn't worked since I was six and in trouble. What about her?"

"Are you ever going to bring her around for me to meet her? I assume that she is the reason why I've seen so little of you lately."

"Maybe when this op is over and done." He thought of Kenna and used her proven expertise at what she'd termed, *Fending off the Phyllis.* "Right now I'm focused on the seriousness of this operation and keeping Kenna safe, so can we revisit this when that's over?"

"Fine, but don't think just because I'm dropping it for now that I'm dropping the subject for good, mister. And you could at least tell me her name."

"I won't forget. Her name is Devon."

"Hunter, I heard that they're bringing in Annaliese Dahl to help with Kenna's electronics. Have you met her?"

"No, I haven't yet had the pleasure."

"Well, has Kenna told you all about her?"

The woman is relentless. "She mentioned her."

"That's it? She *mentioned* her?"

"Uh-huh. Why?"

"I don't know what is wrong with that girl."

"Who? Kenna?"

"Yes Kenna!"

"What do you mean?"

"She's been alone on that island for years now—doing God knows what. Honestly, since she gave up her music and her Steel Eyes identity, she's been aimless. I finally find the perfect woman for her and is there anything going on? I don't know. And why don't I know? Because Kenna won't tell me a damn thing. You need to find out for me."

Hunt laughed. "Have you ever thought that maybe you're pushing her a little too hard?"

"No! She needs direction."

"Mom, Kenna's not a kid anymore. The woman has been a global rock star, and a spy to be reckoned with. I'm sure if she's interested in Annaliese, she'll pursue it. Have you ever thought that maybe it's Kenna's business and not yours?"

"Don't be ridiculous. Who else is working this job with her?"

"Elana West, an FBI consultant, and a soon-to-be full agent for Vince Zwarnick by the name of Sierra Stone."

"Are they good?" Phyllis's tone reeked of protective mama.

"Yes, they're both excellent at their jobs."

"What are their jobs?" Phyllis uncovered a fruit plate and placed it in front of her son.

Hunt stopped breathing for a moment. "I guess Kenna hasn't told you about the op?"

"No, but if you know what's good for you, you'll tell me right now."

"Well, Sierra is a dark web prodigy who discovered that the Russians are somehow involved."

"And this Elana person?"

"Her expertise is the Russian mob and exotic dancing."

"Exotic dancing?"

"Yes, she and Kenna will be infiltrating a club owned by the man that the Feds are targeting."

"How is Kenna supposed to infiltrate? What's her cover?"

I cannot believe that Kenna left the dirty work for me! "Elana is training her to be an exotic dancer."

"What! You mean a stripper?"

"Yes."

"No wonder she keeps avoiding me."

"Hello, Hunter," the man said as he entered.

"Uncle." Hunter raced to greet him. "I am so glad to see you."

"Me too." Uncle hugged him.

It took but one sympathetic look from Hunter for Uncle to laugh.

"Phyllis," he said, "are you interrogating your son?"

"No, I'm simply having a conversation with him."

"Yeah," said Hunt, "the kind of conversation that sounds *nothing* like interrogation."

"Now, Phyllis, I told you, if you're going to extract information from the boy, you should at least feed him first."

"Let's adjourn to the patio. We're dining al fresco," Phyllis said.

Hunter extended his arm toward the dining patio. "After you, Mom."

They took their seats at the table on the brick patio, aside the waterfall and overflowing bougainvillea. Phyllis's server placed the hors d'oeuvres on the table and poured the wine.

Uncle followed her with his eyes until she was out of range. "You need to watch over Kenna, Hunter."

"That's why I'm in on this op, Uncle."

Uncle stared into Hunter's eyes. "What I mean is, you need to know her every move. If it looks like the Americans are screwing it up, you need to get her out of there."

Hunter studied the man. "I'll have to leave right after dinner to do a stakeout of one of the team members. But there's something you're not saying, Uncle."

"There's a tidbit that's come to light about the assassination of Sam and Dalia Waverly."

"What?"

"I'm really not certain yet. If the intelligence proves true, I'll let you know."

"Have you read Kenna in on this news about her parents?"

Uncle glanced at Phyllis before answering. "No. Your mother feels it would compromise her focus and therefore her safety. And I agree."

"Why, Maman?"

"Because you know her. She'll go after them with blind vengeance—and she'd have no qualms about putting her life on the line to do so. When we've accumulated more information, and verified it, then we can plan to do something about it."

"Until then," Uncle began, "she needs to focus on the job at hand. Understood?"

"I don't like keeping things from her, but yes I understand,"

Uncle smiled. "Good. Now who is this young lady you've been seeing?"

Hunter rolled his eyes, and while he answered Uncle's question, he stared right at his mother. "She's a nice girl. A librarian actually."

"Don't be so modest, Hunter, I'll bet she's quite a bit more than that," Phyllis said.

"I knew it! You're already having her vetted, aren't you? How did you find her?"

Phyllis opened her eyes wide, and replied straight-faced, "I haven't a clue what you're talking about."

"Uncle, help me out here."

"Of course." Uncle lifted the wine bottle. "Here you are," he said while he poured Hunt a tall glass.

"That's not what I meant."

"Give me a break," Uncle replied, "it's Phyllis we're dealing with here."

Hunt looked at her and scoffed. "The terrorists could learn a lot from you, Mom."

"Nonsense, *mon chou*." She held up the plate of appetizers. "Hors d'oeuvres?"

CHAPTER TWENTY-EIGHT

Elana surveyed the restaurant from the entry before stopping at the bar. "I'll have a white wine, please," she said. She tapped the frame of her glasses to activate the video.

"I've got you, Alice," Sierra said in her ear.

Elana paid for the wine and walked to the private back room where the Sergeyevs hosted their daughter's memorial. She panned the room slowly.

"Running recognition now," Sierra said. "Two tables up on your right, there's an empty seat next to Ivan Mikhailov. By design, I'm sure."

Elana advanced, pretending not to notice Ivan until he stood to greet her.

"Alice," he said, holding out his hand. "I am Ivan," he said in his thick Russian accent. "Mr. Sergeyev asked me to welcome you. Please join us."

Alice smiled and shook his hand. "Very nice to meet you, Ivan. Thank you." She took the seat next to him.

"I would like to introduce you to Crystal, Diamond and Chastity." He pointed as he named them. "They work at Chez Oui. Ladies, this is Alice. Alice used to work there too."

She smiled back at each of them as they were introduced. "Hi, nice to meet you."

"Likewise," said Diamond.

"I see you already have something to drink," Ivan said. He pointed to the serving dishes filled with hors d'oeuvres in the center of the table. "Please, help yourself to the *zakuski*."

"Yeah," said Chastity as she pointed to one of the dishes. "Those *peroskees* are delish."

Ivan shook his head and chuckled. *Pirozhki*, Chastity, *pirozhki*.

Chastity rolled her eyes. "What he said."

Alice put some hors d'oeuvres on a small plate. "So you all work at Chez Oui. How is it these days?"

"I'm pulling in a small fortune on the weekends," said Crystal, "so I guess it's pretty good."

"Wow. I miss *those* days," said Alice.

"How long ago did you work there?" asked Diamond.

"It's been a few years. Now I only dance for exercise." She glanced at Ivan. "Chez Oui is the most upscale club I've ever worked in. Mr. Sergeyev was always fair and his guys made me feel very safe."

Ivan smiled a satisfied smile. "I always take care of you girls, don't I?"

"You sure do, Ivan," Crystal replied. "I don't know what I'd have done without you two Saturday nights ago."

"Don't worry, Crystal. That man disrespected you, and he will *never* bother you again."

"So, do you ever think of coming back?" Diamond asked.

"I've thought about it. But if I ever danced again, I wouldn't want to do it anywhere else. I've been out of the game for so long, I wouldn't even know where to buy costumes now."

"That's easy, girl," Diamond said, "I'll show you."

From the corner of her eye, Alice saw Vladimir making his rounds to the tables. Ivan stood when he arrived at theirs.

"Sit, Ivan, sit," Vladimir said. "I want to thank you all for showing me the respect of coming to my daughter Raisa's memorial dinner. It's nice to see you again, Alice."

"However unfortunate the circumstance," Alice said kindly.

"Tell me, how did you hear about Raisa's passing?"

Alice could feel Ivan's eyes clocking her every expression. She used the opportunity to lean in closer to him, hoping to be near enough to clone his security. "Do you remember Margo?"

"Hmm. No I don't remember her."

"I'm not surprised. She only danced for a few weeks. Anyway, I ran into Margo and she told me about it. I don't know how she knew."

Vladimir nodded. "It's not important now." In a daze he finished his shot of vodka and panned her tablemates. "I'm touched that you are all here today…" he said, his voice trailing off.

"Thank you for inviting me, Vladimir," Alice offered in sympathy. "Raisa was a nice girl, and smart too. I remember when she was in college and came to visit you. You held that little luncheon for her at your home. I'm glad I got to know her."

Diamond fidgeted in her chair.

He smiled. "Ah, yes, I remember that now. She liked you too."

Alice raised her glass. "To Raisa, may her memory be eternal."

"Thank you," Vladimir said through his somber smile.

Ivan and the girls raised their glasses.

"I will leave you to Ivan, Alice. But watch yourself, he's a real playboy."

"Oh?"

Vladimir left and the waiters served the meat and potatoes dinner. She could still feel Ivan's stare even while he conversed with the other women. He waited until Alice was halfway through her meal before he made his move.

"Alice, you said earlier that you might want to dance again?"

Zwarnick was spot-on about being recruited tonight. "I don't know. Maybe."

"I've heard you were very good, and one of our top earners. You could make a lot of money. Does that interest you? Making a lot of money?"

She stared him squarely in the eye. "Yes, Ivan, that does interest me."

"Good. Tomorrow you will come by the club and we will talk."

"What time?"

"Let's say four o'clock?"

Alice smiled. "Four it is."

"But right now, let's take a little walk," he said. "I would like to continue our conversation."

Alice felt a chill down her spine, and then from the periphery, she saw Crystal and Diamond wink at each other.

* * *

Kenna snoozed on the living room sofa with one eye open, and awoke when she heard the kitchen door from the garage open.

"Hey," Elana said, "what are you doing in here?"

Kenna sat up slowly and rubbed her tired eyes. "I couldn't really sleep until I knew you were safe. How did it go?"

Elana smiled. "Alice is going back to Chez Oui."

"I don't know whether to congratulate you or kidnap you. By the way, you look very pretty, Elana."

"You like my Republican look?" She sat on the sofa and exhaled a hard sigh.

"So, give me the highlights."

"You weren't listening in with Sierra?"

"No."

Elana pulled off her earrings. "Vince Zwarnick was right on the money. Ivan Mikhailov was on me from the moment I arrived. He started off with flattery and went downhill from there. I played the damsel in distress. You know, 'a big strong man like you could save me.'"

"Be careful, Elana. You can't play this loose. He's a very dangerous man."

"I know. He made me take a walk with him where he asked me why I had stopped dancing, and how things had gone since I left Chez Oui. So transparent. But I let him lead me in the direction where we want him to go." Elana imitated the Russian accent. 'You could make a lot of money. Does making a lot of money interest you?' Then he told me how much Vladimir liked me and thought I should come back to work at the club and on and on. Frankly, it was exhausting. I think my cheeks hurt from fake smiling. In the end, I told him if I came back, I'd need to make a lot of money, and to do that I need to separate myself from all the other acts. He asked what I had in mind, and I asked him if he'd be receptive to a two-girl pole routine."

"What did he say?"

"He told me to come by the club tomorrow at four to talk business."

Kenna exhaled hard. "I guess we'd better get started on that routine first thing in the morning, huh?"

"Yes."

"While you were in transit to the dinner, Sierra gave me a couple of moves to practice. I think I got a few of the basics down. She said she'll have some music for us to try out by tonight or tomorrow."

Elana lifted an eyebrow. "Did you practice your moves on Annaliese?"

Kenna chuckled. "Snarky, Elana. Very snarky."

"Then I suppose we're even from that remark you made in the hotel elevator in San Francisco."

"Now what was it I said?"

"When deciding which room we should work in, I believe you said, 'Whichever one doesn't have a dance pole.'"

Kenna laughed. "I wasn't involved with Annaliese personally."

"Does she know that?"

"I'm afraid so."

"Oh, so that was the attitude that she splashed all over you."

"If *you're* interested in her…"

"No, I'm not."

"You might want to reserve judgment. Annaliese is not only beautiful and smart, she's also exceedingly wealthy."

"Kenna, the only thing on my mind is saving the world from a meltdown and coming through this with both of us unharmed."

"Don't be a buzzkill, Alice."

Elana laughed. "Right now I owe the secretary a phone call and I need to give Annaliese the gadget she stuck on me so that she can program you."

Kenna stood. "Come on, I'll go over to Ops with you."

"No, you should turn in for the night. It's late back east so I'm sure it won't be a long call. If anything important comes up, I'll let you know."

"If you'd rather be alone with Annaliese, just say so."

Elana winced at Kenna and left through the French doors.

Kenna watched her leave and then waited for her to return.

"Everything go okay?" Kenna said.

"What are you still doing here? I thought you were going to bed."

"I wanted to wait until you spoke with Zwarnick."

"It's all good. Annaliese and Sierra are working on your software now. *She* said she'll see you tomorrow."

"Who?"

"Not Sierra." Elana placed a CD on the coffee table. "Sierra made us a music mix to try out to see what works for us." She flopped down on the sofa. "We'll go over it in the morning."

Kenna remained silent.

"So your brother is not staying here with us?"

"No. Hunt lives out by the beach, where I used to live, but that was a long time ago for me. We're still very close."

"Is that where you lived back when I met Pascale?"

"Come to think of it, yes," Kenna answered.

"Were you in undercover work back then?"

Kenna thought of the Steel Eyes heyday and smiled. "You could say that."

"I don't mean to pry, but you and Hunter don't look anything alike."

"Actually, I'm adopted. I was orphaned as a teenager and my family and the Van Bourgeades were very close friends, so they inherited me. I've known them my whole life."

Elana reached out and placed her hand on Kenna's. "I'm so sorry."

"Why? You didn't assassinate my parents."

Elana's eyebrows arched, her eyes wide with surprise. "Your folks were assassinated?"

Kenna nodded.

"So you're in the family business."

"I am."

"Who killed them? And why?"

"I don't know who did it. The 'why' requires a complex answer that I just don't have the energy for right now. What about you, Elana?"

"From Orange County. But as I told you, I got to spend part of my summers in San Francisco. My family pretty much disowned me when I came out, and then they doubled down when I became a dancer."

"Why?"

"There would have been a scandal at the country club."

"And then Sierra recruited you."

"My parents cut off my college funding when I told them I was gay. So, I danced until I had enough money to quit and finish at UC Irvine. That's where I earned my criminology degree. By the way, thanks for all your help."

"My help?"

Elana smiled. "Yes, your very generous help. You were a great tipper. You alone probably covered a whole semester of living expenses. Huh, I didn't know the Feds paid that well."

Kenna chuckled. "Good to know it went for a high-quality education. So, you put yourself through school and that didn't earn your parents' respect?"

"It earned me holiday invitations. Christmas, Thanksgiving, but with the understanding that I never bring home a woman as a date."

"Wow. It must be hard for them to breathe in that tiny box. From what I can tell, you're pretty good at this work. You should be proud."

"Thank you. Are you involved with someone? I mean other than with Annaliese?"

"Stop it. Committed."

"Oh."

"Committed to my aimlessness." Kenna laughed. "I'm laughing because it's true. What's your status, Elana?"

"Independently owned and operated."

"Maybe you'll get lucky with Annaliese. She's quite a woman, you know. She has a gorgeous yacht and mansion on the water in Curaçao. And rumor has it there's a sex dungeon." Kenna could barely keep a straight face.

"Maybe I'm not interested in all of that."

"What are you interested in, Elana?"

"Forget it. You'd have a better chance of catching fish with that bait."

They both laughed.

"Is this getting easier, or is it just me?" Kenna said.

"I get that no one would ever use the word 'easy' to describe you. You're a bit of a mystery."

Kenna yawned. "It's no mystery that I'm tired."

"I hear you. I can't wait for my head to hit the pillow."

"Come on, let's go to bed," Kenna said. She flushed when she heard the words leave her lips. "I meant…"

"I know what you meant."

They climbed the stairs to their bedrooms across the hall from one another. Kenna turned the handle, opened her door and glanced over her shoulder to see Elana entering her room. Once inside, she turned to close the door and caught Elana stealing a glance.

Elana smiled. "Goodnight, Pascale."

"Sweet dreams, Alice."

* * *

At three a.m., in the house next door, a series of electronic dings woke Sierra who then knocked on Annaliese's door. "Wake up, we've got something," she said bleary-eyed.

They dashed into the computer room and activated the screens to watch the jumble of code scrolling faster than they could read it. Sierra logged them into her master file and ran simultaneous backups. Annaliese turned on the computer next to Sierra and started typing.

"Great work on your device, Annaliese. I can track every file Ivan is running on Alice. And now...hey, there's porn."

"Whoa," Annaliese said, "I like kink, but what the hell is this guy into? We could spoof the site."

"Not a bad idea. That way he thinks he's on his porn site, only it'll be us hacking him. On second thought, let's stick to our plan." She watched the screen. "I'd say that Ivan just graduated from badass dude to sick sonofabitch."

"We're in with our virtual private network, Sierra. Now, tunnel right through the bastard's firewall."

Sierra fervently tapped her keyboard, typing for two straight minutes. When she finished, she sat back in her chair with a Cheshire grin. "Boom! Take *that*, bitch! I have your backdoor."

Annaliese chuckled. "You just nailed him. By morning we should have what we need to install a little malware and begin infecting his files."

"Hmm."

"Something wrong, Sierra?"

"I set filters for bank codes but we're not getting anything."

"You mean like account numbers, names?"

"Yes."

"Maybe the Russians don't have it on their computer. Perhaps it's on a separate drive," said Annaliese.

"Not another fucking thumb drive! I almost got killed tracking down the last one."

"I think this time it's Pascale's job."

Sierra stood and turned. "Annaliese, you're brilliant. And the sexiest geek I've ever met."

"Thank you. You're pretty hot yourself, Sierra Stone."

"Stone is my stage name. It's Sanchez actually. Sierra Sanchez."

Annaliese smiled. "Sierra Sanchez, I'm having fun. How about you?"

"Are you kidding? That was—hot."

Annaliese yawned. "I have a sense that morning will be here in about five minutes."

Sierra scoffed. "Better catch some winks while you can."

Annaliese winked at Sierra. "Throwing an extra one your way. Goodnight."

"Night." Sierra watched her leave, waited a respectable minute, and then went to bed.

CHAPTER TWENTY-NINE

Later that morning at the safe house, Kenna poured a cup of coffee and brought it into the living room to face off against enemy number one—the pole. When she arrived, Elana was already using it to stretch and practice her choreography. She held the pole at full arm's length and rotated around it, her weight pulling against it and creating momentum as she flew into a fast spin.

Kenna watched her turn upside down, clutching the pole with only one bent knee. Then, Elana hooked her elbows around it behind her and spun faster, giving the impression that her flowing hair couldn't catch up to her.

"Good morning," said Elana. "You can't practice in those clothes."

Kenna looked down at herself. "What's wrong with them?"

"No long pants. You could slip off the pole and hurt yourself." Elana turned upright, dismounted and stepped toward her water bottle. "Same thing for your arms and armpits." She took a swig of water and with her towel, wiped the sweat from the metal. "Oh and no lotion on your skin—anywhere."

"I guess I'll be right back."

When Kenna returned, she was wearing the skimpy bikini that Annaliese had given to her on the yacht. Elana choked then coughed at the sight of her, causing her to have to spit out her water midswallow.

"You okay, Elana?"

Elana looked her up and down. And then she did it again. "Yeah I don't think we'll have any trouble getting you hired." Her eyes moved to the scars that landscaped Kenna's left shoulder. "Is your shoulder okay?"

"It's fine."

"Surgery?"

"Shot. Almost died. Okay, where do you want me?"

"How can you say that so casually?"

"I'm fine."

"Why do I get the feeling that there's an awful lot more to that story?"

Kenna stared at her to ward off the questions. *What am I supposed to say? Remember the assassination attempt on Steel Eyes's life?*

Elana walked to the CD player. "For your audition you're going to need a couple of songs. One medium tempo. And one slow should suffice."

"Which one are you playing?" asked Kenna.

"To give you an idea of tempo, this would be the slow one. You can preview them after I teach you some basic moves, but I think it's best to start with the slow songs to help you get the moves down and become confident. The one I'm about to play is definitely your best bet. Whatever we choose, you're going to need to know the music in your sleep."

Kenna bent forward from her waist to stretch her hamstrings. "What song is it?"

"'She's Outta Control,' by the Steel Eyes Band."

Kenna dropped to the floor and looked up at Elana with an expression of disbelief. "No. No Steel Eyes music."

"Yes, Kenna. It's slow, sultry and has that sexy bass line for an intro. It pounds like a heartbeat and it's very sensuous. Trust me, it's perfect for you."

Damn you, Mel for being such a great bassist! Oh shut up, you only have yourself to blame for writing the damn song. Kenna breathed out the first sigh of ennui of the day. "Great. Fine, Elana."

"And I think it's a good idea if from now on we only call each other by our club names so that it becomes reflex."

Kenna scoffed. "You can't be calling me Wonder Woman around the house."

"Okay. Pascale will suffice until we're at the club."

"Wonderful, Alice. Anything else?"

"What's with you?"

"Nothing. I've complained enough."

Alice smiled. "Hit your quota?"

"Where do I start?" Pascale asked.

"First you have to learn how to do a basic wraparound move. Start behind the pole like this." Alice stood behind the pole, grabbed it and let her weight hang away from it. "Then swing this leg out to the side while you pivot on the foot on the ground." Alice demonstrated and then stepped away from the pole. "You try it."

Pascale grabbed the pole with her right hand and performed her first wraparound move. "That's kind of fun."

Alice chuckled. "It is fun. All right, next let's see you climb the pole like this." Alice grabbed onto the pole, hooked her ankle around it and reached hand over hand as her bent legs clenched the pole and propelled her upward.

Pascale mimicked her and made it to the top with little effort.

"You're going to be really good at this, Pascale. What do you do to stay in such great shape?"

"I'm an ocean swimmer and I windsurf."

"In Jamaica."

"Yes."

"Now just learn to relax and reach out. Smile. Remember, there's no personal space to protect in a strip club because you'll have little to none. Get used to it."

Pascale nodded. "I've never been so motivated to get an op over with."

"Just wait until we get into the doubles routines."

"Actually, Alice, that's the part I'm looking forward to."

While they worked diligently on their routine, Sierra and Annaliese came in to watch.

"I see you're getting good use out of that bikini," Annaliese said to Kenna.

"It's a good thing you gave it to me because according to Alice, it's the only thing I own that's suitable for the pole."

"That's not all it was good for," Annaliese replied.

Kenna pretended not to notice the famous 9 mm-glance that Elana tossed at the woman.

"Elana, you almost ready for a break?" said Sierra.

"I could definitely use some fresh air. Why?"

"The secretary wants a video call in half an hour. Everything is going according to plan. Late last night Ivan was checking out all your online information."

"Well, yours and the S&M porn websites," Annaliese added.

"Get any new ideas for your sex dungeon, Annaliese?" Kenna said dryly.

"Nice, Pascale," Elana said. "Let's try that last spin, the Flying Fox, one more time before we take a break."

"Jesus, Elana, you have her doing a Layback Spin already?" Sierra asked.

"Well, it's rudimentary, but she can do it. Go figure!"

"Balancing is a little like windsurfing." Kenna stepped up to the pole, grabbed it at head height. She swung forward with enough momentum to grab the pole with her other hand behind her.

"Wow," said Sierra. "It's easier if you position your top hand a little higher and step into it. That will let you grab the pole with your other hand behind you with less effort. Here, like this." Kenna stepped away from the pole and watched Sierra perform a perfect Flying Fox.

Kenna tried again.

"Yes!" said Elana and Sierra.

"Being here is like a slice of heaven," Annaliese said. "The only thing missing is a Bloody Mary and a wad of single dollars."

Kenna smiled as she dismounted. "I see what you mean. That *is* easier."

"This is the best op ever," said Annaliese.

Kenna laughed. "You mean as long as it's our asses up here instead of yours."

"Personally, I had as good a time watching you swim the ocean."

"You watched Wonder Woman swim the ocean?" Sierra said.

"Yes, she swam to my yacht."

"And you have a yacht? Who do *you* work for?"

Annaliese grinned. "At the moment, I'm working for the three of you."

Elana's eyes narrowed and she gulped down enough water to drown her reaction. "Okay, I want to try some basic moves to the song, see if they fit," she said. She hit the Play button on the sound system and Kenna sat next to Sierra to watch.

Mel's bass started out sultry and slow; it pulsated like the heartbeat Steel Eyes had felt when she wrote the hit song, "She's Outta Control." She had written the tune after meeting Alice. It was every heartbeat she'd felt the night Alice had given her a lap dance for the very first time.

Kenna felt her cheeks get warm as she blocked out Sierra, Annaliese and the rest of the world. *Just swallow the irony.* She fixated on Alice conquering the pole, to music she had written for the woman. *Alice can make* any *pole her bitch.*

Elana dismounted and pressed the Stop button on the player. "So what do you think, Sierra?"

"It looks good."

Annaliese smiled at her. "Do I get a vote?"

"Sure, why not," Elana answered.

Annaliese glanced at Kenna. "I can't wait to see *Pascale* do it."

Kenna stood and grabbed a bottle of water from the table.

"I'm going to grab a quick shower before we call the secretary," Elana said.

"Me too." Kenna wiped the sweat from her forehead.

"A shame you two can't shower together to save time," Sierra teased.

Kenna laughed. "But it would take so much longer that way." She draped her towel over her head, and didn't look back to clock their reactions when she left the room.

CHAPTER THIRTY

Lieutenant Carly Avedon coasted through the parking lot of Chez Oui a little before midnight. She noticed security cameras mounted high on some of the light poles, but not all areas were well lit. Cruising toward the parking spaces at the end of a row, she pointed her motor-driven camera at the license plates of high-end vehicles as she passed them and then pulled into a spot. Dressed in black slacks and a pinstriped shirt, she put on red lipstick and adjusted her easily concealed Beretta Tomcat that was strapped to her right ankle.

"Hi." She smiled at the doorman.

"You alone tonight, babe?"

"Yep."

"No charge for ladies tonight."

"Awesome, dude. Can you get me a table not too far from a stage?"

He took the twenty she held out to him. "Sure. Follow me."

Carly took note of the floor plan as she entered the club. "Wow, this is a nice place."

"How's this?" said the doorman, holding out her chair.

"Great, thanks." She smiled. "What's back there?" She flicked a glance at a darkened passageway toward the back of the room.

"That's *the back*. You know, the VIP rooms."

"What does it take to get into the VIP room?"

"A dancer and a pile of cash."

"How much?"

He smiled. "Depends on what you're looking for. If you're interested, just ask whichever dancer you like."

She smiled back. "Okay. I'm here to have a good time." She sat at her own table and gazed around the joint. Young women danced topless on the men at the bar and at the tables. The few dancers who met her stare, quickly averted their eyes.

"Hi, welcome to Chez Oui." The voice came from her blind side. "What would you like to drink?"

"Grey Goose and soda."

While the beefy men who walked through the club vigilantly surveyed the patrons to ensure the women's safety, Carly watched the woman dance on the stage in front of her. She peeled some singles from the roll in her pocket. Standing at the edge of the platform, she reached out toward the dancer and held out the bills until the woman came to retrieve them. Carly tucked the bills into the band on her G-string and smiled.

"Thanks, honey," said the dancer as she wound her way around the stage for the other spectators to reward her talent.

From the corner of her eye, Carly watched the waitress set her drink down on the table. She made her wait an extra beat to get paid and then tipped her the cost of the drink.

"Oh," the girl said, "thank you very much."

Now it would only be a matter of time until the waitress made Carly's tipping habits known. As she predicted, it only took another minute for a dancer to approach her.

"I'm sorry for staring at you when you came in," said the busty blonde. "I thought you were my ex. Thank God you're not my ex."

"Oh, I don't know, I've always thought I've made a pretty decent ex."

"Had a lot of practice?"

Carly smiled. "How are you tonight?"

"I'd feel much better if I was on your lap."

"What's your name?"

"I'm Diamond, like the gemstone, because I sparkle," the girl replied. "What's your name?"

Carly hesitated for an instant. Having an alias was the one thing she had forgotten about. She went with the first name that popped into her head. "I'm Jane." *As in Jane Doe.*

Carly threw some cash on the table and sat back in her chair with her arms open. "Well, come feel better, Diamond."

The girl smiled, and while looking into Carly's eyes, she bent forward at the waist and moved closer until their personal spaces fused. She placed both her hands on Carly's thighs and locked her elbows to brace herself, then leaned in closer.

"Beautiful, Diamond. Are those real?" she asked, referring to the woman's breasts.

"That's all me," the dancer replied.

Diamond bent her elbows and slowly slid her way down Carly's body. The move ended with Diamond's breasts gliding along Carly's thighs until the dancer was on her knees looking up into the lieutenant's eyes. The stripper stood and then straddled her.

Carly felt her face get warm.

Diamond looked into her eyes. "You really do remind me of my ex, except that you're cuter," she said before contorting into a rubbery tantric backbend. "Would you like to do this somewhere more private?" she said, using her taut abdomen to pull herself upright.

"I would. Next time. I can't stay long tonight. When are you here?"

"Every night except Monday and Tuesday."

Carly looked into Diamond's eyes. "So if I want to do this privately, what's the deal?"

"The house mother can tell you all about it when you come back. But right now, Jane, why not sit back and enjoy the dance?"

Carly let the girl fawn over her and tease her, keeping her hands to herself the whole time. When the dance was over, she paid for another one and then a third. If there was one thing Carly had come to do, it was to make a connection with a female employee.

I love my job.

With each dance, Diamond got a little more personal, stroking the sides of Carly's thighs, leaning in so that her naked breasts got closer and closer to Carly's face. "I'd let you touch them in the VIP room, Jane."

"I'll look forward to that."

Diamond took the cash when Carly paid her and smiled when she saw the generous tip. "I'll be looking forward to it too, Jane."

The vodka soda remained on the table untouched when Carly left the club.

"Leaving so soon?" said the doorman.

"I have an early day tomorrow." Carly started her car, and in her side mirror she noticed the blond doorman follow her with his eyes. She watched her rearview mirror and took a circuitous route for the first half mile. Once she was certain she hadn't been followed, she drove onto the 405 North and headed back toward her safe house. She placed her evening call to report to Dixon Chase. "All's quiet."

"There's something else I need you to do for me, Carly."

"What is it?"

"I want surveillance inside Waverly and West's safe house, and another in the operation center."

"So why not just have your guys install it?"

Chase paused. "This is just between us. It's for an extra layer of safety."

"Does Secretary Zwarnick know?"

"It's my job to make sure everyone on this op is safe. The secretary has more important things to tend to right now."

"But doesn't this open us up to another breach? Especially if the devices aren't secured?"

"I'll see you at your safe house," he added before the line went dead.

* * *

About the time that Carly Avedon left Chez Oui, Ivan swiped his card in front of the electronic reader and entered the office.

Vladimir looked up from his computer screen. "Ivan, come look at this."

Ivan walked around the desk and leaned on the back of Vladimir's chair.

"What is that?"

Vladimir drew a breath. "It's the information that came from Raisa."

"How did you get it?"

"She had this thumb drive sent to me the day she died."

"What does all of that mean?" Ivan asked, staring at the screen.

"It means, that I don't care that the Chinese are going after the Americans' deep space satellites. It also means, as far as we're concerned, whatever the Chinese are doing to the Americans is meaningless to us. Politics is useless. If you want to know the politics of *anything*, simply follow the money." Vladimir downed a shot of vodka and then stood staring at Ivan. "What is important is that right here I have banking transfer codes, account numbers, and passwords to hundreds of thousands of bank accounts. We'll be ready soon enough."

Vladimir had never guessed when this began that it would cost him his daughter. Although he'd never admit it, he should never have had Jiang killed. It haunted him—woke him in the night. Once the Chinese had figured it out, they took Raisa in retaliation. Now he *had* to move forward with his plan or Raisa's death would have been in vain.

"With this kind of information we can siphon money from those accounts directly into our offshore bank accounts," said Ivan.

"We could." Vladimir turned and grinned.

Ivan stared at him and waited.

"Or we can bring the whole banking system to its knees."

"I like my idea better. We get rich, and by the time anyone figures it out, the money is gone forever. Nice and neat."

Vladimir's head swayed from side to side as he mulled it over. "Okay, we start slow. A little at a time. We take small amounts that won't set off any alarms." He handed Ivan a printout. "Here is a list of random accounts to start with. All you need to do is use those passwords for the account numbers on the left. See?" He pointed to the columns.

"Looks easy enough. So then, once we know we're safe, we transfer more from other accounts?"

"Yes. Did you meet with Alice?"

"Yes, she auditioned and she's bringing us another girl that she's going to do pole routines with."

Vladimir looked at him. "*Two* girls on the pole?"

"*Da.*"

"At the same time?"

"Yes."

"Hmm. You must let me know when they start. This I would like to see. When?"

"In a couple of days. Alice said she has the girl and they're working on the routine."

"Who is this other girl?"

"I don't know, but Alice said that she's very reliable. I'll meet her tomorrow when she auditions at the other club."

"Good. We don't want any drug addicts like the girls you fired. Will they work the back rooms? It's good business for them and we make more money."

"I don't know, but I'll ask them."

"You know, Ivan, when this is over, you should take a little vacation to the Cayman Islands to follow up with our banker. Bring one of the girls with you." He chuckled. "Or bring a few."

"Hmm. I already know who I would invite."

"Who?"

"Alice." Ivan smiled.

"Maybe you should start out slower. You're not so young anymore, Ivan. A girl like that could kill you."

Ivan laughed. "And then I would die a happy man."

"A happy, rich man."

"Yes, Vova, maybe you're right. That girl may be too much for me."

"I never thought the day would come when the *leopard* thought a girl was much of anything! So, old friend, who will you bring instead?"

"Chastity, Diamond…"

"Maybe the new girl?"

"Which girl?"

"The one you told me Alice will be dancing with."

"Perhaps I need to give this greater thought."

"Don't think too much, Ivan. It's never been your strong suit."

Ivan nodded. "That's why I have you, Vova."

"Yes, that is exactly why. When I meet the new girl, I'll tell you if she's for you or not."

Ivan opened the bottle of vodka on Vladimir's desk and poured them each a shot. "I know it's no consolation for losing Raisa, but just think about how rich we are about to become. May her memory be eternal," he said when he clinked Vladimir's glass with his own.

Vladimir sighed. "To Raisa, Ivan."

CHAPTER THIRTY-ONE

The following morning, Hunter waited in his rental car, three houses east of Carly Avedon's residence. For two days, he'd followed her at random times, always in a different car. He wondered if Vince Zwarnick knew every detail about the lieutenant. That she shopped at natural markets and liked to sleep late was not significant. What was relevant to him, was that he didn't have a good feeling about her. Something was off, and he didn't know what it was—yet.

That gut feeling had saved him many times, but his greater concern was that starting tonight, Kenna would be nearly naked in the belly of the beast. It bothered him to not be the one calling the shots to protect her. Then he worried about Elana's experience, or lack of it, leading Kenna through the world of Chez Oui. If something wasn't right, he needed to find it—now.

Vince Zwarnick had virtually given him carte blanche when it came to making adjustments during the operation. Like Hunt, Zwarnick knew from experience that all too often, no plan ever went according to plan. As such, Hunt planned contingencies for his contingencies.

'We may work for different countries, but we're brothers in the cause,' Zwarnick had told him. And then they shook on it. They had accomplished much together after 9/11, even when the politics of the day didn't translate verbatim. Hunt had once trusted Zwarnick with his life, and he thought that now might be a good time to return the favor.

Today, instead of following Avedon, he would let the GPS he had planted under her bumper do its job, while he would break into the home to see what else he could find out about her.

"Come on, Lieutenant, if you don't leave soon, I'm going to have to pee in a cup." He set his coffee cup back in the holder. A few minutes later, Carly drove away in the green Chevy. According to his intel, tomorrow it would be a black Ford. Hunt reached for his set of lockpicks on the passenger seat and got out of the car. As he casually stepped off the curb to cross the street, he saw the front door to the house open again. He dove behind his car and watched Dixon Chase get into a white Toyota one house away.

"What are you doing here, Dixon, and why didn't I know about it?"

He waited for Chase to drive away, and then quickly made his way to and through the back door. He took two steps at a time to the upper level, and searched the agent's room. Chase's belongings yielded a stunning commentary on how militaristically, how orderly, he functioned. Hunt opened the folder on Chase's dresser, and slid out a sketch of a man. He studied the face, thinking it looked vaguely familiar, and then photographed it before replacing it on the dresser.

Next, he entered Carly's bedroom and found a file in the false bottom of her suitcase. After he photographed the contents, he placed a bug behind a picture on the wall over her bed, and on the way out, positioned another one in the living room.

Once back in the car, Hunt checked his stopwatch. "Not bad. Four minutes and forty-six seconds, including breaking and entering, and a pit stop."

He drove to Kenna's safe house with the thought that it was time for them to speak, alone. On the ride, he thought it through, and knew there had to be a reason that Chase was here. But that didn't mean the reason was viable, or that it was a good idea. And whose idea was it anyway? He needed Sierra to set him up with a private call to the secretary of homeland security.

* * *

Sierra entered ops and set her coffee mug next to the keyboard. "Good morning. What's new since my shift?"

Joe looked away from his screen. "Not much. These guys sleep mostly in the morning, so you get all the good stuff. Mardi, give Sierra the message."

"Right. We routed a personal call to you but you were asleep."

"Who called me?"

"A woman named Dani," said Mardi. She held out a phone and slip of paper with the number on it. "You can call back using this. It's untraceable."

Sierra grabbed the no-frills flip phone and number, then picked up her coffee. "I'll take it out back."

Grinning, she raced to the wooden gazebo at the far corner of the yard, put her mug on the table, and placed the call. The number rang four times.

"Hello?"

"Hi Dani. I'm so glad to hear from you."

"Hi Sierra. You said to call that number you gave me if I needed to reach you."

"Are you okay, baby?"

Dani fell silent. Then she said, "No. Not really."

"What's wrong? You sound different."

"I'm okay but…"

"But what?"

"Sierra, honey, I'm struggling because I don't know how to say this."

Sierra felt an uncomfortable tightening in her gut. "Just say it," she said softly.

"I really like you. I do. But I don't think I'm cut out for all of this."

"Cut out for what, Dani?"

"Whatever you call this dangerous undercover stuff. Now that I've had a few days to think about what happened when you were here, I realize I can't do it. I mean, like, I want to do it, to be okay with all of this. But the truth is, I'm not. I've been looking over my shoulder wherever I go, and I've been worried to death about you. I'm not sleeping. I can only imagine how I'd feel if we were in a long-term relationship. Honestly, dahlin', I'm not handling this all too well."

"Dani, don't do this. We can work it out. I want to work it out."

"Are you planning to leave this job anytime soon?"

"Ironic. I just got the promotion of my dreams. Why don't we wait until this op is over? I'll come back to New Orleans first thing, and then we can talk about it face-to-face."

"When will it be over?"

"I-I don't know."

Dani sighed.

"Okay," Sierra said, her stare fixed on the ground. "I understand. And I can't fault you. But I was hoping for more. I was really hoping."

"Me too, Sierra. I'm sorry but I have to go—before I change my mind."

"Then stay, and change your mind."

"Stay safe, Sierra," Dani said before the line went dead.

"Dammit," Sierra said under her breath. Coffee splashed onto the table when she dumped the phone into her cup.

She sat there and wondered if she wasn't cut out for something real—something like true love. The women in her past had *told* her they loved her, and then for whatever reason, one day they didn't anymore. In retrospect, none of those women had ever actually shown their love beyond words.

I thought this time was different.

With Dani, for a brief moment, she knew what it meant to be completely vulnerable and to have to trust someone. And

Dani came through for her; had put herself in danger to help Sierra out when she was on the run. Dani had somehow made her feel safe, had shown her caring and affection—for all the good *that* did.

When Sierra finally reentered the computer room, she did her best to avoid eye contact.

"Good morning, Sierra," said Annaliese.

Sierra nodded at her and looked away.

"Are you okay?"

"Yeah, why?"

"No reason."

Sierra pulled a second chair to her computer for Annaliese, and then sat staring at her screen. "Okay, where did we leave off last night?"

"Give me the keyboard, Sierra, I'll begin. Why don't you pour yourself a cup of coffee? I brewed a new pot."

Sierra smirked. "Not a bad idea. Mine has a phone in it," she said as she left the room.

"Mardi, who was Sierra talking to on the phone?" Annaliese asked casually.

"Some woman named Dani. From New Orleans."

Annaliese opened their software program and began typing. "Joe, do you have the audio link ready to go for Secretary Zwarnick?"

"Ready and waiting," Joe replied. "When are our people getting inside?"

"Tonight."

Sierra returned and set a hot cup of coffee next to her software co-conspirator. "Here's a fresh one for you."

Annaliese looked up at her and smiled. "Thank you. Have a seat, stripper-stud. We have a problem."

"That's exotic dancer, *and* agent." Sierra smiled from the corner of her lips and sat. "I already don't like this day."

"So it seems." Annaliese pulled up the code Sierra had written the night before. "How does this last section look to you?"

Sierra focused as she scrolled down the screen. "No. No! This isn't right."

"Exactly," Annaliese said. "I believe you were right about the actual banking information not being on Sergeyev's computer. He must have some kind of external or portable drive."

"Which he probably has under lock and key somewhere," Sierra added.

Mardi shook her head. "Without that portable drive, we fail. We can infect the Russian's computers, but unless we know when he's going to send that information, we're in the dark."

"Not entirely true," said Annaliese. "Anyone else smell a RAT?"

"Explain," said Joe.

"Wherever they're keeping the banking information, they're going to have to send it at some point."

Sierra interrupted. "Last night we found the Remote Access Trojan that Sergeyev used on the domestic financial clearing houses. He got someone to open one of their email attachments, and that's how they penetrated the banking sector with their malware."

Annaliese continued, "If we could get those account numbers that he's stolen, we could infect the information. But that's a lot of accounts. So, I found the original email sent from Ivan's computer—when he wasn't watching porn, that is, and used it to infect his computer."

"Ahh," said Mardi. "So you're saying we should track the infected emails from Ivan's Sent file?"

"There's not enough time," said Sierra. "We need Ivan's list."

Mardi shook her head. "If he was able to get an infected email into the financial network, it won't take long for it to spread and control other computers."

Sierra looked at her. "Except, now it's our turn to beat them at their own game. And I'm in just the right mood to take them down."

"Good," Joe said. "This kind of malware can do a lot of damage. Especially if someone keeps a webcam in their bedroom."

"Why?" asked Mardi.

"Because in addition to collecting sensitive information, and gaining full control over the victim machine, it can also turn on webcams."

Mardi's speaker beeped. "Ivan Mikhailov just logged on," she said.

Sierra looked away from her screen. "From where?"

"Getting the GPS coordinates and sending them to you now."

A few seconds later, a map popped up on Sierra's screen, with a pin at the location. "He's in Malibu. Is that his residence, Mardi?"

"Stand by." She tapped more keys. "The house is owned by Vladimir Sergeyev, but this isn't the address I show for Ivan. In fact, this location isn't even on our list."

Annaliese took a sip of coffee. "Sierra, send those coordinates to our GPS file, just in case we need them later."

"Doing it now," Sierra replied. "I'm going to find a way to get those accounts. Joe, what do you have?"

"That Remote Access Trojan you found? It came from the IP address that Ivan is using right now, so maybe this is where they're operating from."

"How long until our conference call with the secretary?" asked Mardi.

"An hour," Sierra answered.

Mardi removed her glasses and rubbed her tired-looking eyes. "After Joe and I outfit Hunt and Lieutenant Avedon with their communications for the club, is it okay with you if we get some sleep, Sierra?"

"Unless the secretary has other plans for you two, I'd highly recommend it. I need everyone at their best by the time Alice and Wonder Woman leave for Chez Oui. Annaliese and I will continue where you left off. Great work, guys."

CHAPTER THIRTY-TWO

Hunt arrived at the safe house and watched Kenna and Elana put the final touches on their pole dance. He applauded from the living room threshold as the music faded.

"Hey, that routine is looking great," he said, entering the room.

"Hi Hunt. You think I'll pass for a pole dancer?" Kenna said.

"You're really good at this, Wave. No joke."

She grabbed a towel and wiped the sweat from her forehead. "It's fun, and a great workout. I'm actually considering putting one of these poles in my house."

"Don't tell my mom. She's already pissed that you've avoided telling her about becoming an exotic dancer."

Elana looked at Hunter. "You shouldn't be telling her anything about our op."

"Trust me, she's more menacing as a mother than she is as a spy. Besides, she's cleared."

Elana shook her head. "How many spies are in your family, anyway?"

"It's easier to count those who aren't. So, are you ready for your big debut?" Hunt asked.

"Not really," said Kenna. "This is daunting."

"Come on, Wave, how hard could it be? You've done some harrowing ops in your career."

"True. I've just never done one this naked."

Hunt laughed. "You mean with an audience greater than one. Besides, how is what you're wearing right now any different from the bikinis you wore on Zuma Beach when we were teenagers?"

"The surfers weren't a bunch of lechers throwing money at me hoping for sex."

"That's because the surfers didn't have any money. I'm pretty sure they still held out their hopes for sex."

Elana gave her the once-over. "Surfer dudes? Well now, that's just a waste for the rest of us."

"Surfer *girls*, Elana. Oh, I'm sorry, *Alice*."

Elana smiled. "No need to be testy, Pascale. It's time to lighten up, girl. From here on out, it's all about the show, not the tell."

"I didn't mean to interrupt," Hunt began. "I actually came by to check in with Sierra before the video conference. But I'll be there tonight for your debut—in disguise, of course."

"Do you always wear a suit?" Elana asked.

"Yes, but not when I'm in disguise."

"Why don't *you* wear a G-string tonight, Hunt?" Kenna said.

"No time to wax, babe. I promise I'll be the first to volunteer when they need male strippers."

"Oh, brother!" Kenna rolled her eyes.

"Yes?" Hunt answered.

"Go! Go see Sierra and stop pestering me."

Hunt smiled. "The team briefing is in an hour. I'll see you there." He left through the French doors.

Elana chuckled. "You even argue like brother and sister, Kenna."

"We're brother, sister, best friends, confidants, and intelligence team all rolled into one."

Elana gathered her towel and water bottle. "I bet he'd do anything for you."

"Just like I would do for him."

Elana placed her hand on Kenna's shoulder and looked into her eyes. "You're going to do fine tonight. I know it." She massaged Kenna's shoulder. "Relax and have fun. While we're on that stage, that's our only job."

"It's what comes afterward that has me concerned."

"You mean breaking into Vladimir Sergeyev's office, or fending off Sergeyev and Ivan's advances?"

"Yes."

"You'll feel better after you get a shower and some food, Pascale."

"I'm headed to the shower now, but I'm going to wait until after the conference call with Zwarnick to get something to eat."

"Same here, but I'm pretty hungry right now." Elana bit into her apple as they left the living room.

"Alice, have you ever considered teaching pole dancing? As exercise. You're a great teacher," Kenna said as they climbed the stairs to their rooms.

"Thanks. See you at Ops?"

Kenna nodded. "Sounds good."

* * *

Hunt entered Ops from the yard. "Hi, Sierra."

She glanced up from her computer screen. "Oh hey, Hunt. You're early."

"Yes, I wanted to meet Annaliese before the briefing, and to have a word with you. Is now good?"

"Ah, so you're Phyllis's son. I'm Annaliese." She smiled and shook his hand.

"Nice to finally meet you in person, Annaliese. Mother and Uncle speak so highly of you. I'm glad you're here and working with Sierra. From what I hear, you two have mad, mad skills."

Sierra and Annaliese exchanged a micro-glance.

"We are pretty good together," Annaliese said.

"Am I interrupting?" said Carly when she entered from the hallway.

"No, not at all, Lieutenant," Sierra said. "What was it you wanted to talk about, Hunt?"

"It can hold. Lieutenant Avedon," Hunt said, offering her his hand. "Hunt van Bourgeade."

She shook it. "Call me Carly. You're Waverly's partner?"

"Yes. I hope you ate your Wheaties today. We have a busy night ahead with a lot at stake."

"Namely our banking system," Carly said.

Hunt corrected her. "Two women operatives on the inside, nearly naked, and at the mercy of the Russian mob."

Carly hesitated a millisecond. "W-well of course. That goes without saying."

He stared at her. "Yet, it bears repeating."

"Where are Kenna and Elana?" Sierra asked.

"I was just there while they finished working on their routine," Hunt replied. "I'm sure they'll be over soon."

"Excuse me," Carly began as she headed toward the door. "I think I'll use the bathroom before we get started on the communications training."

When Carly left the room, Hunt watched Annaliese do what she reportedly did best. Her computer screen listed a host of Ports that the Internet used in the transport of information. Each one on the Russians' system signified a different connectivity. Beneath the FBI seal at the top of the page, Hunt read the following:

{Hacking sequence: Port scan/Avail

Port Scan 22...Closed

Port Scan 23...Closed

Port Scan 25...Closed

Port Scan 53...Closed

Port Scan 80...Closed

Port Scan 135...Open

"Hello, boys!" Annaliese said to her screen.

"What does all that mean?" asked Hunt.

"See this?" Annaliese pointed to: Port Scan 135...Open.

"What about it?"

"This port shouldn't be anywhere near the Internet, but it's our malware that made it possible." Annaliese started typing again. "This open port also happens to be an anonymity network."

"Meaning?" Hunt said.

"It's probably how they're communicating with whomever it is they'll be routing the bank funds to. They'll use this port for Onion Routing."

"What's that?"

"Onion routing allows them to obscure their IP address and encrypt the data when they send it. So, wherever they send their money, the information goes through several relay stations or routers. No one can read the data, and each station can only unwrap one layer. That layer tells them where to send the data next."

"So you're saying that the process keeps repeating until the information reaches its final destination—and only those people can read the data?"

"Exactly. What we can't locate are the numbers of the accounts where the money is coming from. Chances are, we'll be able to see where it's gone. But by then, it will be too late to recover the funds. Sergeyev hasn't put that information on his computer, which leads us to believe he has some sort of external hard drive with the transfer codes ready to go. We need to get our hands on that ASAP."

Hunt watched Annaliese type.

Access Port # 135

Please provide login for remote access.

*Password * * ****

Access granted.

"Sierra, I'm in Sergeyev's network," said Annaliese.

"What's the password?"

"RaisaVladivostok."

"Upload the rest of the malware," Sierra said.

"Already on it."

"Sierra," Hunt said casually, "can you step out back with me for a moment? I'd like to review a few things with you." When she looked over at him, he stared into her eyes.

She nodded. "Sure. Give me one minute."

"Now is better," he said evenly.

She picked up her coffee cup and followed him to the far end of the yard, where they sat in the small gazebo beside the coffee with the drowned burner phone.

"Something wrong, Hunt?"

"I'm not sure, but I think it's a question worth asking."

"Everything checks out on my end," she said.

"Are you certain?"

"Yes. Why?"

"Because I've discovered a deviation."

"A deviation?"

"Do you know anything about Dixon Chase being in LA?"

"No. I thought he was traveling between DC and San Francisco, after Elana and Kenna tracked me down. I haven't heard much from him except in the briefings since he's mostly following the Chinese involvement. He's now sure the Lees compromised the computer chips that were installed into the government computers. But my job is to hack the Russians."

"So then, Secretary Zwarnick didn't change protocol as far as you know?"

"No, he didn't."

"What's your take on Avedon?" he asked.

"She's cocky, a little rough around the edges. So far, she's done everything according to the rules."

"Think, Sierra. Is there anything, however minor, that seems off to you? Anything at all."

Sierra took a sip of coffee and thought about it. "Yesterday, she stopped by and asked me about our communications tools. She had me walk her through the whole routine. I didn't make anything of it because she only wanted to know how the final parts would come together. You know, the timing and where everyone would be."

"That's it?"

"Yeah. Except that later on, she called me to ask about the frequencies we were using. She said that Chase had wanted her to ask me, so I told her."

"Why would they need that information?"

Sierra stared into Hunt's eyes. "Good question. I see what you mean. I've been so wrapped up in hacking Sergeyev's computer, I hadn't really thought about that. Do you want me to hook you up to a private call with the secretary?"

"Not yet. What about Annaliese?"

"What about her?"

"Anything unusual there?"

"No! The woman is a cyber goddess. If it wasn't for her, we wouldn't be ready to go into Chez Oui tonight. She has the software reprogrammed and ready to download onto Wonder Woman's, I mean, Kenna's implant. The system checks out, and once Kenna downloads files and finds the portable drive with those bank codes, we're golden. Elana's communication is set to go. I think we're ready."

"How is Kenna supposed to find some portable drive?"

"My guess is it's under lock and key. My suggestion is to look for a safe in Sergeyev's office."

Hunt nodded. "This op just got exponentially more dangerous."

"I know Elana well. Trust me, she'll make sure Kenna's safe once they're inside."

"I hope you're right. But in the event that something goes wrong, I'm going to be right there."

"So will Avedon."

"Before you go, I have a small favor to ask."

"What do you need, Hunt?"

"About the lieutenant."

* * *

While Hunt and Sierra talked outside, Carly roamed around the room eyeing the equipment. She picked up a few items and studied them before putting them back on the shelf. Her cell phone dropped to the floor when she pulled it from her pocket, and as she bent down to retrieve it, she left a small black device behind a cache of boxes on the floor.

She meandered across the room and sat in the chair next to Annaliese. "So, Annaliese, which branch of the Fed are you?"

Annaliese smiled and continued working.

"Oh. Probably need-to-know, huh? Are you local?"

Annaliese turned to her. "Why so curious?"

"*Cop-upational* hazard, I guess. I'm a San Francisco Bay girl myself."

"What a great place to live."

"You speak the truth. Is everything working right and are we ready to go for tonight?"

"Yes, we are. Once we're certain that all the logistics and communications go smoothly then the rest is up to Kenna and Elana. Until we get what we came for, can you keep them safe while they're in there?"

"I can and I will. You seem pretty confident that it will go smoothly."

"Why should anything go wrong?" Annaliese asked, wide-eyed.

"Why indeed," Carly answered. "I've worked scarier locations than Chez Oui. As strip clubs go, it's pretty swanky."

"Try not to have too good a time."

"I'll be there for one reason only."

"Make sure it's the right reason."

Carly chuckled. "Oh, come on, I'm just playing."

Annaliese remained quiet.

"Do you have any coffee?"

Annaliese smiled. "There's always a fresh pot on. Help yourself."

Carly left and didn't return until Joe called for her.

CHAPTER THIRTY-THREE

Kenna and Elana arrived at Ops while Joe finished answering Carly's questions about her communications devices.

"Thanks, Joe. I think I've got it down," said Carly. "With my hair over my ears, you can't see the earpiece, can you?"

A flurry of "No," came from everyone in the room.

"Secretary Zwarnick will be calling in five minutes," Sierra called out over the a cappella clacking of keyboards. She leaned toward Annaliese when she noticed her staring across the room at Kenna instead of working. "So, Wonder Woman is your type?" she whispered.

"I thought so when we met. But I'm partial to someone else."

Sierra stopped typing and looked at her. "Who is she?"

Annaliese reached for Sierra's keyboard and typed between two lines of code on Sierra's screen: *'A sweet, beautiful woman who has very sexy hacking skills!'*

Sierra typed back. *'Do I know her?'*

Annaliese tapped out, *'You are her!'*

Sierra deleted the exchange when the video call connected.

"Hello, everyone," Vince Zwarnick said. His usual even demeanor was replaced with sober focus. "Sierra, where are we?"

"We're on schedule, sir. Annaliese and I have penetrated Sergeyev's network and uploaded our malware. We're ready to transfer the club's entry codes to Kenna's implant, and then all we need is for Kenna to get into his office and download his protected files. Although, we've encountered our first real wrinkle."

"What is it?"

"We can't find the banking codes on Sergeyev's computer. We believe all of that information may be on a separate hard drive in his possession."

"That's some wrinkle," Zwarnick said.

"Mr. Secretary?"

"Yes, Elana."

"I know that Vladimir has a safe in his office. It's where he puts the cash when the house collects more than a certain amount."

"Kenna, do you think you can crack a safe you know nothing about?"

"Doubtful," she replied. "Tonight will be our dress rehearsal. The goal is for me to get into that room and see what I'm up against."

"I don't like the idea of having to break in a second time. It's too risky." Zwarnick shook his head.

She stared into the camera. "What other option do we have?"

"Once we know what's going on inside that place," Zwarnick began, "we could stage a break-in when the place is closed."

Kenna shook her head. "That would only give them warning that we're onto them. Besides, we don't have the luxury of that much time."

"Mr. Secretary, if I may interrupt."

"Yes, Lieutenant?"

"I've made contact with one of the dancers. I'll see what I can find out from her—like what she knows about the boss's routine and whereabouts."

He nodded. "Tread lightly."

"Yes sir."

"So then, if everything goes as planned tonight, tomorrow you'll go for the takedown. Elana and Kenna, is that routine ready to play in public?"

"Yes," Elana answered.

"Kenna?"

"Right here."

"Are you completely confident in your tactical approach?"

"Not yet, but I will be once we get ready for tonight."

"What are you waiting for, Waverly?"

"For this call to end so that Annaliese can program my chip," she answered without affect. "And I'd like a copy of the blueprints for the building."

"Annaliese, can you get that and load it onto Kenna's watch?"

"Yes, Mr. Secretary."

"I know that look, Vince," Kenna said. "What is it?"

"Stay safe, both of you. Vladimir's bodyguards are his private army. Lieutenant Avedon and Hunter, do you have your signals worked out?"

"Yes," Hunt answered.

"Contingency plans in place as well?"

"Yes," answered Carly.

"Mardi, Joe and Sierra," Zwarnick continued, "all of your equipment checks out?"

"All communications are working," Sierra began, "and Annaliese will be running point on getting Kenna through anything that shows up while she's in the club."

Zwarnick nodded. "Good. Elana, Nadia Pavlichenko wanted you to know that Ivan has been making inquiries into your cover story."

"He likes me, sir."

"How's that?"

"He *likes* me."

"Good, you have a weakness to exploit. Watch yourself in there tonight—he's a seasoned psychopath. I can't have two of my best hurt in any way. Avedon and Hunt—I'm counting on you both to keep them safe."

"You can take that to the bank, Mr. Secretary," Carly said.

Zwarnick squinted at her. "Not the time for jokes, Avedon. I'm deferring to Dixon Chase here. He seems to have confidence in you."

"Thank you."

Zwarnick's image grew larger as he leaned toward his screen. "I want you all to remember that if we don't get what we need tonight, then we'll get it tomorrow. If any part of this op develops a snag, I want you to abort. We live to fight another day only if you're *all* alive. What time do you ladies go to work?"

"About seven o'clock, Pacific time."

The secretary nodded. "Sierra, you'll update me as we go."

"Already have your channel set up, sir. You'll be able to listen to communications in a live feed. I've already connected you to the live link."

The secretary sighed. "While the Chinese don't yet know that the Russians have hacked them…or that we've hacked the Russians, it's critical that your part goes smoothly. The whole world is counting on you to save the financial systems. You're all clear on that?"

"We know," Sierra said, glancing at Annaliese.

"You should know we've found the Chinese hacker who initiated this whole thing."

"Were you able to debrief him?" asked Hunt.

"I'm afraid not. He's dead. But, what we now know is that the infrastructure hacks weren't the target the Chinese were after. We think the water plant breakdown, electric grids and the banks were a diversion."

"What? Well, what are they after?" Kenna said.

"We're working on that. Stay safe everyone, especially Kenna and Elana."

"Thank you. We will," Elana said.

The large screen turned blue when the call ended, and silence crashed the party.

Kenna searched Elana's eyes for solace—for a soft place to land for a fraction of time. In the aftermath of Zwarnick's call, she heard no clacking of keyboards, no playful remarks to break the tension. Instead, she surveyed her small pieced-together team of uncompromised agents, not all from the same government, on whose shoulders rested the world's financial systems.

She met each of their eyes as a sort of final confirmation. When she nodded, any expressions of doubt and fear in the room morphed into those of certitude, issued by comrades, in a war playing out on a binary battlefield.

Emotions, allegiances, individual expertise were all binary minefields to her. They were *yesses* or *nos*. Or in the Boolean tradition, they were simply 'True' or 'False.'

Annaliese looked over at Kenna. "It's time for us to program your chip—Wonder Woman."

Kenna raised her eyebrow. "We've played this little game before."

"I'll bet," Elana muttered.

CHAPTER THIRTY-FOUR

When Elana pulled into the employee parking space behind Chez Oui, Kenna's stomach pitched like a boat on a choppy sea.

"This is it, Pascale."

Kenna exhaled hard. "Lead the way, Alice."

"Maksim," Alice called out as she swept toward the entrance. "It's good to see you!"

The blondish bouncer smiled wide and held out his wrestler arms. "Alice!" He enveloped her in his meaty embrace and swayed from side to side. "I heard you were coming back." He pulled back and looked at Kenna. "Is this the new girl?"

"Yes, say hi to Pascale. She's my pole dance partner."

Maksim shook Pascale's hand. "Nice to meet you, Pascale. Doubles. Wow, no one has done that here. I'll look forward to seeing it. You have your electronic ID, Alice?"

"Yes, let's catch up later." She smiled. "Follow me, Pascale."

Kenna panned the club when they entered. Black leather. Flattering dim lighting. Girls. Joan Jett singing "I Wanna Be Your Dog"—the metal guitar solo stinging Steel Eyes's ears.

The club still looked pretty much the way Kenna remembered it. The reason she had originally chosen Chez Oui was its spaciousness. Other clubs had made her feel claustrophobic; made her feel too close to the other patrons, who consisted overwhelmingly of men. Chez Oui on the other hand, had four small but adequate-size stages in addition to the main stage. And while each stage had its own pit for the minions, the customers sat a comfortable distance apart.

Beyond the small stage to the left was the wide oblong bar. Recessed in shadows on the opposite wall, leather partitions separated high-back private lap dance chairs. The discreet bank of stations made for a veritable assembly line of faux fantasy.

Kenna stared at the chair on the end—where Alice had given Pascale her first lap dance. Through a small hallway at the end of the row, the VIP room and the private cubicles awaited those with money—real money. And intention. This time, Pascale's intentions couldn't have been more disparate than on every other visit, distracted though she was by the syndicate of night workers. How they glided and gyrated with such confidence, without fear or shame, had always intrigued her. Tonight, she had to stay focused on her own routine. Here, she would portray an unabashedly confident stripper, or so she kept telling herself.

Alice and Pascale moved through the club toward the right, past an unbroken contour of undulating bodies. Pascale glimpsed the door to the VIP room as she moved beyond it, and tried to forget those steamy nights with Alice—tried to un-know the way Alice had made her feel.

Give it up, she thought. Once you know something, you can't un-know it.

Her only other unpalatable option was to forget the memory she still held close, so instead, she succumbed to un-remembering it. It was the best she could do. Once again, Alice fell victim to the compartmentalization that comprised the real estate in Pascale's spy brain.

When they reached the employee door, a tall, short-haired woman clad in a costume of long straps made to look like chains, stepped in front of the door and blocked it.

"Hi, Alice."

"Hello, Shay," Alice said coldly.

Pascale watched the exchange, smelled the sewer-full of disdain in Alice's tone.

Shay gave Pascale the once-over. "Did you miss me, Alice?"

Alice laughed. "How could I miss you after who you turned out to be?"

Shay smiled. "Oh come on, you know you love me. Besides, you never know what's over the horizon."

"Honey, that's not a horizon—it's a cliff."

"I'm sure I'll see you and your friend later."

Alice rolled her eyes, and moved beyond Shay to unlock the employee's door. "Excuse us."

Pascale waited and watched Shay saunter away before letting the door close behind them. "So, what's her story?" she said, elongating her stride to catch up.

Alice sneered. "She's not a story. She's barely a footnote."

Pascale followed her down the long hallway with the rose-colored walls. "What did you ever see in that girl?"

Alice shook her head. "I knew the instant our eyes met that she was bad news. But the first time I saw her, she took my breath away. It took me a while to realize she was really just trying to asphyxiate me."

"How?"

"I was happy keeping it casual. But she pushed it, manipulated me. She's a dangerous, satan-y type. First it was, 'Elana, I know you don't want to hear this, but I love you.' Then, 'I'm in love with you and I'm calling this a relationship.' The truth is, she's a user. And once she gets whatever her user-brain drums up, you're history."

"What did she want from you?"

"What all vampires want—to suck the life out of their victims."

"Been there. But you size people up very well. How did you misjudge her?"

"I didn't misjudge her at all. I knew who she was the instant our eyes met. I just didn't listen to myself. She ran a brilliant campaign and I drank the Kool-Aid. The good news is I only made two mistakes. The first was believing her; the second was believing *in* her."

"Is that all?" Pascale smiled.

They passed a corridor on the left and took the first right into a long hallway, at the end of which was the dressing room.

"This is pretty nice," Pascale said, laying her duffel bag onto a chair.

"I can't believe we're the only ones in here," Alice said. "That means it's a good night on the floor."

Pascale rolled her eyes. "Oh, I'm so happy."

Alice unzipped her jeans and reached for the costume in her case. "Attitude, Pascale, attitude."

"Yeah, yeah, attitude, blah blah, attitude."

Alice moved toward the lockers and whispered into Pascale's ear as she passed her. "We're probably not alone."

They changed into the outfits that Sierra had ordered for them. Until that moment, Pascale never would have thought to wonder how quickly the Feds could get their hands on *four* two-piece, rhinestone-studded, double-strapped bikinis with matching fringe halter tops. All in white, she gleamed and glittered atop the high heels that placed her over six feet.

Alice glanced at her in the mirror and then turned to look directly at her.

Their eyes met with the same adoration they had known on that night so long ago in the VIP room, where Alice's slender and muscular thighs straddled Pascale. Wordless. Grinding. Pascale pushed away the memory.

They said nothing.

Alice pulled on her fishnet bodysuit and then stepped into the G-string that covered her. Two dots of cloth hid her nipples. Pascale watched her. *This is Elana, not Alice. Alice isn't real! Alice was never real*, she repeated silently. *Damn. She was real to me.*

"Take your time warming up," Alice said, "I'll be back after my solo number. Wish me luck, Pascale."

"Good luck. I'll see you when you get back." Pascale smiled and gazed into her eyes. "Quite a different story this time around," she whispered.

Alice smiled slyly. "Well, it is, and then again it isn't. We're just going to have a different kind of fun tonight."

While Pascale stretched, she subtly scanned the room for surveillance, noting two spots that would be perfect for hiding cameras. Then, she spotted a pinhole next to the full-length mirror hanging on the wall. Behind it would be a miniature camera. If she could somehow get onto that transmission frequency, she might be able to get Sierra to trace the feed and hack into other cameras. She spied a hook next to the mirror, and casually hung her towel on it to blind whoever was watching her.

Take that, asshole!

CHAPTER THIRTY-FIVE

Carly waited until dark. After the women had left the safe house for Chez Oui, she slipped through the French doors into their living room, and headed for the second floor. First she stepped into the bedroom on the left, turned on her flashlight, and kept the beam low to the floor.

The bed sheets were rumpled on only one side of the bed. "I thought they'd be sleeping together by now," she mumbled. She flipped through the file Elana had left in the night table drawer. The pages within included one devoted to Carly, along with Elana's handwritten notes on the team. "So, you're checking up on me, huh?" When she read Annaliese's page, one item piqued her interest. *Home Agency: Dutch Intelligence*

"What the hell? She's not even American?"

What fascinated her most however, like the file given to her, there were no pages or notes on Waverly or Hunter van Bourgeade—with whom she'd be partnering at Chez Oui.

"They must be CIA."

She returned the file to the drawer and moved across the hall to Kenna's room. Other than an old family picture of her, standing between two adults who Carly assumed were her parents, she found nothing.

"You look like your mother." She laid the photo back onto the bureau, searched the dresser drawers, and placed a bug in the floor lamp. "Now we'll find out who you really are, Ms. Waverly."

* * *

Hunt slid down in the driver's seat of his rental car when Carly exited onto the sidewalk. Thanks to the GPS tracker he had placed under her bumper, he knew just where to find her. She had only been in the house for eight minutes before he watched her leave.

He thought about the dossier he'd found in her suitcase. It contained background information on everyone except him and Kenna. Even still, she had a page with both of their names, under which he'd read words like: *Agency, Pascale, Affiliation, Past? Adopted, Highly trained, Brief DC.*

That last entry puzzled him most. What was being sent to or received from Washington, DC, about him and Kenna? Did Zwarnick ask her to report on them? If so, he thought, they should have at least taught her some basic tradecraft—for instance— like false-bottom suitcases were the place to hide something you *want* someone else to find. Based on what he'd seen of her thus far, his biggest issue was her lack of sophistication.

Hunt gave her time to get to her car before he started out for Chez Oui, thinking the whole time about what he didn't know. Why was Carly sneaking into the safe house? Why hadn't he and the team been informed of Chase's presence? He hit the gas and cut off every car that tried to get in his way. Why hadn't Vince briefed him? *Could it be that Zwarnick doesn't know?* His questions would have to wait. Right now, he had two agents to protect—one of them, his sister.

When he parked at Chez Oui, Hunt adjusted the prosthetic belly that added a gelatinous twenty pounds of girth to his buff midsection. His handgun lay snug inside the false fat. He checked his fake beard and mustache once more in the visor mirror then put on a pair of horn-rimmed glasses. Dressed in a cheap short-sleeve shirt and khakis, he'd mastered the overall countenance of a paunchy, middle-aged mathlete. He switched out his wallet with that of his alias, ready to engage the nodus of the operation as Michael Hardy.

Inside the club, he took a seat near the steps of the main stage, on the side facing the velvet roped section, and ordered a Corona. He recognized four of the bouncers from the briefing that contained the video Elana had filmed at Raisa Lee's funeral. He watched employees part like the Red Sea when the two block-like older men in suits walked through the club. Their bodyguard unhooked the burgundy velvet rope, and Vladimir Sergeyev and Ivan Mikhailov sat in the alcove with the plush sofas.

"Xena," he whispered into his wristband. "Do you read me?" Carly didn't respond. "Vouvray?" he said to Sierra. "Do you copy? This is Big Papa. Come in." Low-level static made him wonder if there was interference at his location.

"Hang on to my seat, would you, honey?" he said to the waitress. "I gotta use the can." He handed her a five spot and left for the men's room holding his beer. Once he was certain he was alone, he entered a stall and quietly tried again. "Vouvray, come in."

"I'm here, Big Papa."

"I must have been in a dead zone. Xena, do you copy?"

"I'm near the bar. You're cutting out."

"I'm wearing a mustache and beard, short-sleeve blue shirt, main stage."

Hunt exited and again took his seat. This time he casually surveyed the crowd until he saw Carly Avedon. He trailed her with his eyes until she acknowledged him with a subtle nod and sat two seats away. He listened to her conversation with the dancer who solicited her.

"Good evening, Jane," the girl said.

"Hi, Diamond. You're sparkling as usual."

"How about a lap dance tonight, Jane?"

"How about it? Lead the way," Carly replied. She followed the woman to the darkened tunnel of lap dance recliners.

Carly chose a lap dance chair and Diamond straddled her. "You really do look like my ex, you know."

"Want to make me your ex, Diamond?"

"No thanks, been there. I'm looking to make my future."

"Would asking you out qualify—you know, because we'd have to do it in the future?"

"You really are very cute, Jane."

"Cute enough to share your secrets with?"

Diamond looked around, leaned in close and placed her mouth to Carly's ear. "What is it you want to know?" she whispered.

CHAPTER THIRTY-SIX

Alice sauntered back through the club in her fishnet body stocking and the white fringe two-piece. She smiled at the bouncers, surveyed the dancers, and scoped out the clientele as she worked her way across the room to the DJ's booth. Of the four men she spotted, she recognized two from the front row of Raisa Lee's funeral.

"Hi, I'm Alice," she said to the DJ.

"Hey, Alice, I'm NastDJay."

"Great name." She laughed and handed him her CD. "Here are my songs for tonight. The first is my solo act. The next is for my doubles routine. Do you have the introduction scripts?"

"Got it right here." He slid the disc out from its sleeve and read the titles. "Oldies. I haven't played these…hell I haven't even heard this first one since the eighties."

"Hot is hot, and my act isn't like anyone else's so why should my music be?"

"I like your style, Alice. You ready?"

Alice nodded.

NastD turned on his mic. "We have a special treat tonight as we welcome the amazing Alice back to the main stage!"

Alice took her place at the foot of the stairs to the stage during the ass-wiggling drum intro to the song "Nasty Girl" by Vanity 6. Her streamlined shape and softly sculpted body commanded everyone's attention, including the working girls. Some of the lap dancers positioned themselves so their clients couldn't see the stage beyond them. But the men looked past them to give Alice the attention she garnered so naturally.

Her long legs balanced perfectly on the stiletto heels when she climbed the steps and took her place onstage. The front-woman Vanity sang the first line of the Prince song: *"Tonight don't you want to come with me, do you think I'm a nasty girl?"* Alice grabbed the pole with both hands and lifted off the ground, wrapping her legs around it and spinning a full 360 degrees before landing on her feet. Above her head she clasped the pole, launching into a spin, and changing momentum to turn upside down while Vanity sang about being in the fantasy of her own nasty world.

She thought of Pascale, and swung her legs sensually upward, flexing her feet and tightening her thighs and buttocks, her blond hair hanging freely. Equal parts sensual and acrobatic, she next performed a transition move up and down the pole; a combination of inversion and upright, of legs clenching the pole before spreading them out in a V.

A patchwork of men hastened toward the main stage, tossing five-dollar bills, tens, twenties. Couples abandoned the lesser stages in favor of watching Alice, drawn to the seasoned temptress dancing the flawless routine. A round-faced man in a suit fanned out a wad of cash before her. She smiled, ripped off her Velcro bikini bottom to reveal her G-string, and inverted on the pole. He climbed onto the stage and let the cash rain down on Alice's upside down, fishnet ass. The sonofabitch made it rain! Alice loved the rain.

When the song ended, Alice scooped up the piles of cash. The audience applauded as she left the stage drenched in rainmaker currency. She passed Shay, who stood there and watched her with an expression that Alice remembered all too well—envy.

"Nice job, Alice!" said Ray, one of the bouncers. They kissed on the cheek as she passed him and reached for the employee's door.

"Good to see you, Ray!" she said before the door closed behind her. When she returned to the dressing room, Pascale stood from her chair.

"How did it go?"

"I was actually nervous when I got out there, but then I just let it all fly."

Pascale glanced at the wad of cash tucked into Alice's G-string, then at the stacks of bills in her hands. "Wow, how much did you get for those three minutes of work?"

Alice dropped the bills onto the vanity and then yanked out the rest of her bounty from her G-string. "Haven't a clue. But there was a rainmaker, so it's probably a lot." Alice gulped down a bottle of water and wiped the sweat from her body, then sat down in front of the mirror to touch up her makeup.

"A rainmaker?"

"Some guy fanned out a wad of cash and let it rain down all over my ass."

"Oh, I don't know if I can do this."

Alice glanced up at her in the mirror. "You'll know in five minutes."

"Five minutes? We're on in five?"

"Stop thinking, Pascale, it'll be fine. You have the routine down cold. And you're doing it with me."

"That doesn't help."

* * *

Pascale thought of Steel Eyes and how many times her drummer JJ had called out, "We're on in five, sweetie." *How can I be more nervous right now than playing guitar for a stadium full of die-hard rockers!*

Alice stood and downed the last of her water. She smiled at Pascale. "You ready?"

Pascale exhaled hard and laughed nervously. "Win, lose or draw, Alice, it's too late to turn back now."

They had entered the dressing room as two agents in the fight for good, and exited as sexy amazon hunters of money, bad men and cyber sabotage.

Pascale stared at Alice's body. *Sexy. Amazon hunter.*

Even with her cover-up over her costume, Pascale shivered from the air-conditioned chill in the club. Although she was on her way to make her exotic dancing debut, she realized that this would be the first time she had gotten anywhere near a stage since the night that Steel Eyes had been shot at Madison Square Garden. Then she thought perhaps the chill wasn't from the air-conditioning at all.

Diamond and Crystal walked toward them, headed for the dressing room.

"Hey, Alice, great routine!" Diamond called out.

"Wonder Woman, good luck!" said Crystal as they passed by.

"Thanks," said Alice. "Are you okay, Pascale? You look a little pale."

"I can't believe I'm about to do this."

"Stay on purpose. We've practiced this. If you draw a blank on any move, go into a transitional move like the backward wiggle. Trust me, it's sexy and the crowds like it."

"Okay. Backward wiggle. Got it." Pascale's breathing was shallow.

"Vladimir and Ivan are in the audience for our debut."

"You just had to tell me that right now, Alice?"

"We need to sell it, baby!"

"Alice, did you just call me *baby*?"

"*That's* what you're focused on? When we're done, we'll sit with them, and then you'll excuse yourself and do your thing."

"You think you can keep them occupied long enough for me to break in and download what we need while searching for that hard drive?"

"Ivan has a thing for me. So if I ignore him and flirt with Vladimir, he'll spend his time trying to win my attention. We'll be fine. His pathetic ego is really that big."

"You read me, Sierra?"

"I read you but there's static, Wonder Woman. Alice isn't coming through at all."

"Then fix it!" Pascale said under her breath.

"I'm working on it!"

"Alice," Pascale whispered. "There's a problem with your comms. Sierra can't hear you," she said as they opened the door from the hallway and entered the club.

NastDJay flipped the switch to the transition music when they neared the main stage, and then lowered the volume. "Gentlemen and ladies," he said into the mic in his whispered baritone, "for all of you hardcore pole lovers, we have a Doubles debut. Welcome Alice and Wonder Woman to the main stage, as they take you on the journey of, Alice in Wonder Woman Land—to the tune, 'She's Outta Control.'"

The bass thumped like a collective tribal heartbeat. Stage lights surfed through the spectrum and landed on back alley blue. Alice and Wonder Woman took the stage and performed their first revolution to the provocative beat that Kenna had written for Alice so long ago. The Steel Eyes song had topped the charts for fourteen weeks straight before it lost the number one spot.

As Alice did a Body Wave, undulating against the pole like a snake imitating a wave, Steel Eyes's fellow guitar player Rich sang the lyrics:

In the lights,
When the bass pounds soft and low
And the girl's someone you know
She wraps her legs around it
You wrap your mind around her

The women performed a modified wraparound move, spinning around the pole, their faces only inches apart. Each with one knee bent around the pole and hooked to their mirror images, they arched backward. When they came upright, their thighs pressed hard against each other. Alice stepped back to allow Wonder Woman to climb to the top position on the pole.

Wonder Woman's sculpted thighs gripped it, her flexed foot on one side of the pole and her knee hooked around the opposite side. When she reached the top, she extended into a seated position, with her legs straight out in front of her, and hooked her elbow around the pole. Her sparkly high heels rested just above Alice's head.

Two octaves above the bass, Steel Eyes's watery metal guitar strings pushed and pulled the music through the first chorus. Alice clutched the pole with one hand, and as she stepped with forward momentum into a fast rotation, she pushed Wonder Woman's foot, sending her into a spin around the pole above her. As Alice spun faster, she kicked her legs out horizontally.

Rich sang the second verse:
Don't you know
When you reach and climb that pole
There's a heartbeat in my soul
And my body catches fire
I'm outta control!

The electric guitars wailed as the tempo sped up. Customers stood three deep by the stage to tip them. This time, the rain escalated to a deluge. Fives, tens, twenties, fifties. Alice dismounted to let Wonder Woman turn upside down. In a sleek and slow transition, Wonder Woman inverted and held the pole with only her legs, her long black hair hanging toward the floor. She and Alice grabbed each other's forearms, and Alice placed the flat of her foot along the pole. With a forward push from her other foot, Alice stretched out perpendicular, her momentum spinning them both like whirligigs.

You tease me with your eyes
You move against my thighs
Then you climb into my soul
We're both
So outta control.

Wonder Woman turned upright and slid down onto her feet, then pressed the length of her body against the pole. Alice mirrored Wonder Woman's pose, and they ended the routine with Alice pressing her whole body up against Wonder Woman, with only the pole between them.

By the time the Steel Eyes song faded and they disengaged, the stage was a veritable green magic carpet ride. Enough for rent *and* a vacation—or as Pascale thought of it, funding the animal shelter's spay and neuter program. She wondered if there was a program to neuter Russian criminals.

"Alice in Wonder Woman Land!" NastD called out. They left the stage to whistles and hollers.

The women donned their silk robes before walking behind the velvet rope to Vladimir's table. Ivan stood and applauded, then held out a chair for each of them.

"Didn't I tell you, Vova?" Ivan said.

Vladimir nodded and smiled. "You girls are going to pull in a fortune. And look at the crowd ordering drinks and women."

"I know," said Ivan. "Just wait until word gets out about them. We'll have all the customers coming here instead of that shithole down the street."

Pascale heard Sierra's voice. "Say something, Alice."

Alice didn't respond.

Sierra tried again to no avail.

Pascale looked at the men. "Thank you, Ivan. We're working to make the routine even better."

"Pascale, if you can hear me," Sierra said, "clear your throat."

Pascale cleared her throat.

"If something is wrong with Alice's comms, cough."

Pascale coughed. She heard Sierra say, "Fuck."

"I hope you're not catching a cold," Vladimir said to Pascale.

"I'm fine. My throat is dry."

"I can fix that," said Vladimir. A casual glance from Vladimir made his personal server appear.

"More champagne, Mr. Sergeyev?" she said.

"*Da.*" He nodded.

Vladimir smiled at Alice. "You have not lost your touch, Alice. The routine was good. Very good."

"So you did like it?" she replied excitedly.

"Yes, and I'm not the only one! Look at all that cash. The bartenders and waitresses are going to be happy too tonight."

Pascale laughed. "Make no mistake, sir, we want everyone happy!"

"Now that's the right attitude," said Ivan.

"Would you gentlemen excuse me? I need to use the ladies' room," Pascale began, "or I won't have room for that champagne."

Ivan was glued to Alice. "Okay, Pascale. Hurry back before we drink it all."

She looked into Vladimir's eyes. "Excuse me, Mr. Sergeyev?"

He nodded.

Vladimir waited until Pascale left. "I like your friend, Alice. She shows respect."

Alice smiled. "Of course she does, Vladimir. Pascale is top-notch."

"There's something familiar about her," he said.

"Oh?"

"Yes, I could swear I've seen her before. Very unusual—the gray eyes." He smiled and followed Pascale with his gaze. "Will she work the VIP room?"

"I haven't asked her yet. This is her first real gig."

"Perhaps with the right—motivation," Ivan said, staring at the pile of cash on the table.

"Perhaps," said Alice.

* * *

Pascale entered the dark hallway and passed the VIP rooms. She swiped her entry card in the locked door, turned right toward the dressing room and passed it. She removed the decorative watch face cover that hid her computer screen, and headed for Vladimir's office. As she approached the door, she heard the latch click when the RFID reader picked up her chip frequency.

Waiting for the download of Vladimir's computer, Pascale stared at the watch's face waiting for the icon to appear. Nothing.

Just wait. Nothing!

She was losing her window of opportunity, and Vladimir could be back at any moment. Her eyes methodically scanned the room and then her gaze dropped to the floor. She bent down behind the desk and lifted the corner of the area rug.

The floor safe showed a drill-resistant hard plate atop the solid steel door. Even if the external hard drive containing the vital banking codes was in there, she needed time she didn't have, and tools that weren't available. Still, it was up to her to get those codes.

But how, she wondered.

"Sierra, the chip isn't working. Do you read me? Come in." Sierra didn't respond. Pascale pushed a button on her watch that turned it into a camera and took a photo of the safe. She hit the button again to return to the download screen but it was blank. The mission protocol was to abort if any *one* thing didn't work perfectly—and as of now the only thing that *was* working was Alice's spell on Ivan.

It was time to get out of there. She listened at the door, then opened it an inch, saw nothing and stepped out. As Pascale rounded the corner near the dressing room, she ran smack into Diamond.

"What are you doing down that way, Pascale?" the blond stripper said.

"I got turned around. I think I passed the dressing room?"

"Yep, it's straight ahead. Hey, how did you girls do?"

"I think it went pretty well, but Alice is probably a better judge. Well, Mr. Sergeyev is waiting for me."

"Then you'd better go, girl. Don't keep him waiting, he gets cranky."

"Ivan too?" Pascale said.

"Ivan's more laid-back about those things."

"Then what's Vladimir's deal?"

Diamond looked her in the eye, and Pascale held steady. She knew Diamond was sizing her up, and her best bet right now was to become *one of the girls*.

Diamond looked behind her, then turned to Pascale and whispered. "Don't piss him off. I've heard that some girls who supposedly quit suddenly, didn't really quit. And nobody heard from them afterward. Just stay clean and don't piss the dude off."

Pascale hugged her. "Thanks, honey."

Diamond held on a little longer. "So, what's your story, Pascale? You single?"

"I don't want to be rude, but after what you just told me…"

"Come on, I'll walk you out. What about the dressing room?"

"It can wait." Pascale smiled, and threw a thimble-full of Steel Eyes seduction at the girl.

"Um, yummy," Diamond said. "You free tomorrow?"

* * *

Pascale reentered the club and smiled at Vladimir when she took her seat.

"So, Pascale," Vladimir began, "Alice tells me that you're new to dancing."

"Yes." She took a sip of champagne.

"What made you want to dance?"

"Alice said the money is great, and it's certainly keeping me in shape."

Vladimir chuckled. "That it is. You're a practical girl."

"How so?" she asked.

He laughed. "You're getting paid to work out."

"I suppose you're right about that."

Alice and Pascale left shortly after, but Alice waited until they were alone in the hallway to the dressing room before speaking. She lifted the corners of her lips into a sly smile. "Are you okay, Pascale?" she said in a hushed tone.

"Do you think I passed the test?" asked Pascale.

"Honey, you nailed it."

"I can't believe we just pole danced together at Chez Oui. But we have a problem."

"What problem?"

"Not here," Pascale whispered.

"How do you feel having conquered the pole in front of all those people?"

"I survived it. How much did we make?"

"A lot, baby. A lot."

Pascale chuckled. "Did you just call me 'baby'? Again?"

Sierra's voice came through her earpiece. "Yes, Pascale, she called you 'baby.' I'm dizzy from spinning with you both. I got Sergeyev and Ivan's audio. But something isn't right."

"Where were you when I was in the office, Sierra?" Pascale asked quietly.

"I'm so sorry but our comms went down."

"I can hear you now," said Alice. "It's a shame you don't have eyes from the audience's section to see the routine."

"Ah, but I do," Sierra said. "Xena, the warrior lieutenant has a cam."

"She's here?" said Alice.

"Oh yeah. And she's funny too."

"What are you talking about?" Alice said quietly through clenched teeth.

"She tossed you a twenty."

"Forget about her, Alice," said Pascale.

Alice glared at her. "I suddenly feel like I want to put clothes on. A lot of thick winter clothes—and a big parka."

"Now, now, Alice," Sierra began, "we're all on the same team. Did you get the download?"

"Negative, I had to abort," Pascale replied. "And we have another major problem."

"Dammit!" Sierra said. "I'll see you here. Out."

CHAPTER THIRTY-SEVEN

Elana raced into the safe house and right out through the French doors to the Ops house. "What the hell, Sierra! Annaliese? Joe?" she said as she tore open the back door.

"We're working on it," Annaliese said. "I don't know what could have possibly gone wrong."

Kenna's approach was barely softer. "I found the safe in Vladimir's office. But you would have already known that had the comms been functioning."

"That's good news," Annaliese said.

"It's a floor safe—drill resistant. We're going to need another way in. We need someone with the combination."

"Unless Vladimir keeps a thumb drive on his person like I did," Sierra added. She stared at Kenna. "You mean we need Ivan or Vladimir."

"Unfortunately."

Hunt entered next, followed shortly thereafter by Carly.

Elana turned and took in Hunt's disguise. "I would have never guessed that was you, Hunt."

"Yeah, great disguise," Kenna snickered.

He gently peeled off the facial hair and took off his cheap shirt to remove the extra belly. "Tonight I suddenly found myself very sympathetic to pregnant women," he said while pulling on a black Hugo Boss t-shirt.

"What the heck happened to the communications?" Carly said. "I could barely hear Hunt most of the time, and I couldn't hear you at all, Sierra."

"We're working on it," Annaliese grumbled.

"This shouldn't have happened," Sierra began. "Give me your devices right now. All of you."

"I've got this," Joe said.

"You remember how to check the frequencies?" Annaliese asked.

"Yes. Give me a minute." Joe lined up all the earpieces on his desk and fetched the wand that Annaliese had brought with her. "I've never seen anything like this," Joe said. "They're all testing normal."

"Even mine?" said Elana. "I couldn't hear shit. If Kenna hadn't been with me, I wouldn't have known what was going on!"

Sierra stopped reading the code on her screen and looked at Kenna. "Why *did* yours work better than anyone else's?"

Annaliese looked at her. "Sierra, it has to be the implant. Kenna's implant is equipped with radio frequency."

"Radio frequency. Duh. The internal antenna must have boosted her signal."

"I'll put on a fresh pot of coffee," Mardi said. "It's going to be a long night."

Sierra looked up at her when Kenna placed her hand on the hacker's shoulder. "Take a breath. Everyone's safe. No one's cover's been blown. I'm going back to the safe house to take a shower and get some food. I'll come back in a while and see how you're doing."

Sierra sighed. "Thanks, Wonder Woman. Annaliese and I *will* resolve this."

Kenna smiled. "I know you will." She turned to Hunt. "Silly to drive back to the beach tonight. Why don't you grab your go-bag from the car and stay with us? There's an open bedroom."

"That's a good idea. Thanks."

"And Hunt, if you ever again hear me say I want to go to a strip club, just shoot me and pocket the gas money."

He laughed.

"Elana," said Kenna, "let's give the geeks a little breathing room, huh?"

"Sure. I'm sorry, Sierra."

"No, Elana. You're right. You put your life in my hands and I failed you—and everyone else."

"No. Like Kenna said, we're all here. Let's get it right next time."

"You've got it."

"Before you go," said Annaliese. "Did any of you see anything electronic at Chez Oui that resembled a black box with stubby antennas on it?"

"I didn't," said Elana.

No one else had either.

"Are you thinking there could be some kind of signal jammer at work there?" Hunt asked.

"That seems the most obvious," Sierra said.

"I'm heading back to my safe house," Carly said.

"Wait. What's the deal with you and that dancer Diamond?" Hunt asked.

"She doesn't know it, but she's been feeding me information on Sergeyev. She likes me, and she's a good cover for why I'm there. The bouncers know I'm coming to see her."

"Do you think she can be recruited?" asked Hunt.

"I do," Kenna interrupted. "She came on to me in the back hall tonight. Diamond almost caught me coming out of Sergeyev's office and I had to think fast."

"So then, don't you mean *you* came on to *her*?" Elana stared at her.

Sierra, Annaliese and Hunt glanced at Kenna and Elana, and then each turned away, Hunt suppressing a smile.

"No, El, I believe her exact words were, 'Um yummy,' when she hugged me, and then, 'You free tomorrow?'"

"What was your answer?"

"I told her Mr. Sergeyev was waiting for me and left."

Carly laughed. "This is more entertaining than Chez Oui. Call me when you have something." She stepped toward the door, then stopped when she reached Elana. "You were really great on that pole, West."

"Thanks, *Lieutenant*."

Carly laughed. "I was just giving you shit at the San Fran morgue. Call me Carly," she said and then left.

* * *

Hunt waited a few minutes before he left the safe house. He parked his car next to a large bush one house away from Carly's house and turned on his receiver. He listened through the bug he had placed behind the picture in her room as she talked on the phone. It would have been ideal to hear both sides of the conversation, but there was no chance of that with the secure line she was using. That meant the person on the other end was also secure.

She recounted the events at Chez Oui, including the failure of the communications team. She offered no name, no real sense of familiarity, and the call ended almost as quickly as it began, only with a curt: "Yes, sir. I'll keep you informed."

"Sir," Hunt repeated. His mind flooded with thoughts as he drove away. *Do I confront Zwarnick? Is the team safe? Do I pull Kenna off the op?*

His car headed in the first direction he could think of. Twenty minutes later Hunt pressed the security code on the gate's keypad, then lay his thumb on the fingerprint reader. He drove onto the Van Bourgeade estate as the gate peeled back, and then called Phyllis.

"Don't shoot, Mom, I'm coming in," he said.

As he stepped through the door, Phyllis van Bourgeade was pulling on a robe while she descended on the right side of the grand double staircase.

"What's wrong?" she asked.

"I need to speak with Uncle," Hunt said. "I'll wait in the study."

Alone in his father's study, Hunt reminisced over the family photos that still lined the perimeter. There were few pictures in which a young Kenna Waverly didn't appear. And just as often, there was a young Hunter right by her side. The pool parties, Hunter's Bar Mitzvah, the Fourth of July barbeques, the family birthdays—all seen through his late father's expert eye. Then there were the photographs of an even younger Kenna with her parents. From the age of fifteen, Hunt had shared his parents and his heart with the girl he'd already thought of as his sister. In so many ways he was still closer to her than to his real sister Chantal—the only one among them who lived a blessed life where soccer games and PTA were her only missions.

Not a day had passed in their young lives where he and Kenna didn't have each other's back. And now, Kenna was potentially in jeopardy. Although he didn't know what was wrong, he could feel it in his lizard brain—the core survival lobe of any agent who fancied living. The only thing important to him was that he *did* feel that way, and he needed Uncle's help.

Uncle stepped into the study and closed the door behind him. "Bonsoir, Hunter, *qu'est-ce qui se passe?*" he said.

"Thanks for seeing me Uncle. It's about Kenna."

"Did something happen to her?" Uncle asked concerned.

"No, and I'm trying to keep it that way. Have you had any contact with Secretary Zwarnick?"

"Yes, I'm updated daily," answered Uncle. "I trust your lives to no one but myself."

"Uncle, has Zwarnick mentioned anything about Lieutenant Carly Avedon or Dixon Chase?"

"No. Why?"

"There's been a deviation. Chase isn't supposed to be in LA. Hell, he's not even supposed to be working the Russian aspect of the case, but I saw him here."

Uncle moved to the mini bar, poured two snifters of brandy and walked one over to Hunt. "This is not the best news," he said.

"I know." Hunt took a swig of brandy.

"Do you know what Dixon Chase was doing here?"

"No, but I know he stayed in the same safe house as Avedon. She didn't say anything about it, and neither did Zwarnick. When I searched her room I found the words 'Brief DC' on a page with both mine and Kenna's names."

Uncle thought for a moment. "DC. As in Washington, DC? Or as in Dixon Chase?"

"I hadn't considered the option."

"Continue," Uncle said, swirling his brandy.

"Tonight before the op began inside Chez Oui, Avedon broke into Kenna's safe house."

"Why?"

"I assume she was doing what I did to her earlier—looking for information."

"You need to sweep that house for electronic surveillance."

"I'll have Annaliese do it."

"Yes, Hunter, see that you do. While you're here, there's something else I wanted to bring to your attention."

"What?"

"While I still don't know his real identity, I've learned that *Le Gros Chat*, the assassin who killed Kenna's parents, had ties to the KGB."

"Was he Russian?"

"No one knows."

"Do you think Vladimir Sergeyev may have known him?" asked Hunt.

"Perhaps, considering his power and reach. Besides, The Big Cat would likely be in his age group, if he's even still alive."

Hunt nodded and while he thought about it all, he picked up a photo from the mantel and stared down at it.

Uncle smiled. "Let's see what you have there."

Hunter handed him the framed photo and Uncle chuckled. "As usual, your father is missing. Always *behind* that damn camera."

"There we are," Hunt began. "The Van Bourgeade/Waverly clan. No child should lose both of their parents, let alone in the same tragic incident."

"I'm glad we were able to keep her from knowing they were assassinated until she was an adult," Uncle said.

"I need to protect her, Uncle. Especially now."

"I hate to inform you, Hunter, but she's tougher than all of us."

Hunt smirked. "Ironically, her greatest weakness is her inherent strength."

"So then, I will place a call to Secretary Zwarnick and find out why you're in the dark here. I think you should let Annaliese in on the status of things. She can use her hackery to at least keep an ear on you."

"I don't know about that. We had a communications breakdown tonight. Thankfully, going into it, we all knew it was potentially a dress rehearsal. But speaking of keeping an ear on things, I stopped on my way here to listen in on Carly Avedon. She recounted the details of the evening to someone she referred to as 'Sir.'"

"Someone in the house?"

"No, on the phone."

"We need to know who."

"Tread lightly, Uncle. If I need to blow this op and get Kenna and Elana out of there, the sooner I know, the better."

Uncle put his snifter on the bar next to Hunter's empty glass. The men hugged like father and son. "Thank you for bringing this to me, Hunt."

"I'll be at Kenna's safe house tonight if you need me. Tell Mother I said goodnight."

Hunt left the mansion and sat in his car for a moment before turning on the ignition. He needed to get Sierra and Annaliese alone, and away from anything electronic.

* * *

Kenna sat on a barstool at the kitchen island with her chin propped up on her hands. She watched the joy and ease with which Elana chopped vegetables, and admired the way she looked while doing it. "Watching you is making me hungrier."

"I'm ravenous. You don't realize how many calories you burn dancing."

"That's starting to smell really good, El."

"How are you feeling?" Elana asked.

"My muscles are sore."

Elana turned up the heat and tossed the vegetables into the sizzling wok. "If you're good, I'll give you a little massage after dinner."

"I'd be afraid I wouldn't let you stop."

Elana turned and looked at her. "That sore, huh?"

"I call dibs on that jet tub in your master bath."

"You've got it. So what do you think could have gone wrong tonight with the devices?"

"I think Annaliese is onto something about the signal jammer. I mean, she's probably the best in the world right now at what she does. And Sierra isn't all that far behind her, so when they said everything was working, I believe them."

Elana took two dinner plates from the cupboard. "I feel bad for having jumped down Sierra's throat." She dished out the food, slid one plate onto the counter in front of Kenna and took the seat next to her with a savory plate of her own.

Kenna passed her a fork and napkin and took a bite. "This is really good. Thanks for making it. Don't worry about Sierra. She knows you were freaked. Those hackers next door are our best shot at taking down Vladimir."

"Ivan asked me if I've ever been to the Cayman Islands."

"What!"

"He said he might have to take a business trip soon." She imitated his Russian accent. "Alice, perhaps you would like to go to Grand Cayman with me and work on your tan."

"And you're just getting around to telling me this?"

"Tonight, I was so caught up with getting you through Chez Oui, and then having to abort the plan, I forgot."

Kenna stood and walked to the French doors.

"Kenna, where are you going?"

"To tell Sierra and Annaliese to focus on the Caymans."

CHAPTER THIRTY-EIGHT

Kenna had come and gone by the time Hunt returned to speak with Sierra and Annaliese. Driving back from his mother's, he was anxious to know what Uncle would find out. As with most situations, he peeled this one apart like an onion—a layer at a time. What he knew was that something was off about Dixon Chase and Carly Avedon. From what he'd seen at Chez Oui, he also knew Carly was good at her job. He knew he trusted both Sierra and Annaliese, and he knew it was time to speak with them.

"Hey, Hunt." Sierra was leaning back on the couch in the dimly lit living room. He glanced into the computer room to make sure they were alone before he spoke.

"Finally getting some much needed downtime, I see."

"I needed a break while the computer searches—"

Hunt interrupted her silently by putting his index finger to his lips, and shaking his head 'no.' He smiled at her and quietly sat down on the sofa where he pulled out a small notepad and pen from his pocket.

She gave him a sidelong glance.

Hunt scribbled onto the paper: *Don't speak. Where's Annaliese?*
She pointed toward the ceiling.

Hunt wrote: *Wake her, and meet me at the gazebo.* Then he
walked back past the computers and into the backyard.

He saw the light go on in Annaliese's room and a minute
later watched the two women near until they joined him.

"I'm sorry to wake you, Annaliese."

"You didn't. Sierra did. What's wrong?"

"I need you to sweep for bugs."

"Bugs? But the ops room is continuously monitored."

"I know, but—" Hunt's phone rang. "Hold on. I have to take
this." He put the phone to his ear, said hello and then listened.
"Yes, Mr. Secretary, I saw him here with my own eyes. I'll take
the lead on this." He looked at Sierra. "I'm with her right now
and I'm passing her the phone."

Sierra took it. "Yes, Mr. Secretary." She listened for a solid
thirty seconds before responding. "I understand. I will." Sierra
disconnected the call and handed Hunt his phone.

"Would someone like to fill me in before I nod out?"
Annaliese said.

Sierra looked at her. "Secretary Zwarnick wants us to sweep
the house for bugs. As of now, all information goes to Hunt, not
Chase and"—she turned to Hunt—"can I tell her the rest?"

He nodded.

"Hunt will be interrogating Carly Avedon."

Annaliese's eyebrows arched. "Well that woke me up. Why?"

"I observed Carly entering the safe house tonight, after
Kenna and Elana left for Chez Oui. Before we infiltrated the
club, Avedon asked Sierra about transmission frequencies, and
we've had problems with our comms."

Sierra shook her head. "You really think she could be
sabotaging us, Hunt?"

"It seems that way. But as obnoxious as the lieutenant can
be, she's also a good cop, and she's a rule follower by nature.
When she left, she said she was going back to her place. Call her
and tell her we've found something and need her here."

Sierra nodded. "We'll sweep for bugs before we call her."

Annaliese stood and stretched. "I'll get my gear and sweep next door."

About an hour later, Sierra summoned Carly Avedon. When she arrived, Hunt was seated in one of the armchairs in the computer room. Annaliese and Sierra sat in their computer chairs.

Dressed in jeans and a Berkeley sweatshirt, Carly's glance darted between them. "Whatever it is must be pretty important," she said. "Where's the rest of the team?"

"This is just between us, Carly," said Hunt. "Have a seat."

She sat in the armchair opposite him. Sierra and Annaliese swiveled to face them.

Carly bristled. "I've gotta tell you, guys. Your energy is a little creepy right now."

"What was Dixon Chase doing in LA and why didn't you tell me he was here?" asked Hunt.

"He asked me not to tell anyone that he came to check on us."

"If he came to check on us, why didn't we see him?"

Carly shifted in her chair. "Look, I don't know exactly what he did while he was here. He's above me on the food chain."

Hunt looked into her eyes until she broke the silence.

"Okay, before I left San Francisco, Chase asked me to be his eyes and ears down here. He said he didn't want to chance any more leaks. So, every night I give him a status update."

"Is that it?" Hunt said.

"Pretty much, yeah."

"Pretty much? How much is pretty much, Carly!"

"I-I don't know. I suggest you change your tone."

"What exactly have you told him?"

"I told him that Waverly and West were moving ahead with the stripper covers. Then, he had me bug the house next door."

Hunt stared her down. He rose from his chair and took two small devices from his right pocket. He laid them on the coffee table in front of her. "With these?"

"Yes."

"How many did you plant?"

"Two in the house next door, and one in here."

"Here?" Sierra said. "We didn't find any in here."

"Well, the one in here isn't like those." She rose and moved to the opposite side of the room where she bent down and reached behind the boxes. "Here," she said as she stood and held up the little black box she had left there.

"Motherfu—" Sierra began.

"There's our signal jammer," Anneliese interrupted her.

Carly's face flushed red before she exploded with outrage. "That asshole told me it was a signal booster to help transmission! Shit. Are you saying Chase sabotaged us? The comms failures were my fault?" She fell back onto her chair, her face now frozen in shock. She looked up at Hunt. "I've got to make this right! What can I do?"

"It's my decision whether or not to boot you off this team."

"Don't," she said. "We can use this to our advantage. Just let me know what you want Chase to know. I tried to question him when he ordered me to do this—told him that this would increase our chances of another breach."

"How did he respond?"

"He became angry and pulled rank on me. I don't think it's a good idea for me to try to press him at this point."

"I agree," Hunt said. "Sierra, can you run a records search to see if Chase has ever had any kind of connection to Sergeyev? I want a list of where he goes, what restaurants he eats at, gas receipts—everything."

"And here I thought you were going to give me a challenge, Hunt."

Annaliese chimed in. "Do you really think Chase could be part of the breach?"

He ran his fingers through his hair. "I know that the secretary didn't like that he was in the dark about Chase's whereabouts."

"If we don't know for sure if Chase is on the level," Sierra began, "then we have to blow the op. We can't send Alice and Pascale into Chez Oui until we know. I mean what if Sergeyev is already onto them?"

Carly massaged her forehead. "I may have a way to find out the answer to that question before tomorrow night."

They all looked at her.

"How?" Sierra said.

She pulled the card with Diamond's number written on it from the back pocket of her jeans. "Maybe it's time for a booty call. What can I promise Diamond if she'll work with us?"

"First off, you can't tell her about Alice and Pascale," said Hunt.

"I wasn't going to. I was going to ask her to keep Ivan occupied tomorrow night."

"And when she asks why?" Hunt asked.

"That's where my earlier question comes in. What can I promise her?"

"A spa day," Hunt answered.

"You're going to have to do better than that. The woman makes up to a grand a night."

"A weekend in Cancun."

She continued to stare at him.

"A long weekend in Cancun."

"Okay then." She took her phone from her pocket, made the call, and stood to leave. "Let's hope I get lucky. I'll be in touch."

Sierra waited until she heard the front door close. "Hunt, you really think we can trust her now?"

"I do. Like I said earlier, as annoying as the lieutenant can be, she wants to be on the winning side—her ego won't allow for anything else. And I believe that ultimately she wants to do the right thing."

"I have an idea," Annaliese said.

"I'm open to suggestions."

"Why don't we throw Chase some wrong information and see what happens to it?"

"Like what?"

"How about we tell him we can't find hard evidence that Sergeyev is behind the bank hack."

"But he's already been briefed that we're inside."

"We'll tell him we've found another player. A bigger player, and that we're backing off Sergeyev."

Hunt mulled it over. "It could work, especially if we have Secretary Zwarnick deliver the news to him. At the very least, it will throw suspicion off Kenna and Elana being at Chez Oui. But let's hope we don't have to go that far. Place the call and I'll brief him on Plan B."

"I still don't feel right about this," Sierra said. "What if their cover has already been blown?"

Hunt thought before answering. "Carly and I will be in that club every second that Kenna and Elana are there. I won't let anything happen to them."

"Should we ask for backup?"

"No, Sierra. We can't afford taking that risk not knowing who's who. I'm sure the Russians have relationships with cops who protect their enterprises."

"But what about Vladimir and Ivan's bodyguards?" Sierra asked.

"What about them?"

"No offense, Hunt, but you don't exactly look the part to take on a Russian wrestling team."

Hunt laughed. "Looks are deceiving. After I speak with the secretary, I'm going next door to brief our dancers."

"One moment, Mr. Secretary," said Annaliese. Then she handed Hunt the phone.

CHAPTER THIRTY-NINE

Near the end of her second night at Chez Oui, Pascale sauntered past the girls giving lap dances, and moved briskly past the solo men without making eye contact. Suddenly, her pole routine with Alice was the least of her worries. If she couldn't get into Vladimir's office within the next twenty-four hours to download his personal files that Sierra needed, chances were they would be too late to stop the siphoning of funds from the banks. Still, she hadn't a clue how she was going to get into that safe. She shuddered at the distinct possibility of having to force Ivan or Vladimir to open it at gunpoint, surrounded by the Russian mob—while wearing a two-piece fringe Velcro bikini and glittered heels.

According to Sierra and Annaliese, the few accounts they'd already discovered from American banks were starting to leak money like a compulsive gambler in Vegas. Worse, within forty-eight hours, Ivan would be leaving for Grand Cayman to finalize everything with the offshore bank. Once that happened, the money would be gone for good and the widespread banking breach would cause a panic—create uncertainty in the financial markets. Currency at home and abroad would spiral into turmoil.

Pascale flaunted her body and her smile, pretending to solicit as she wended her way through the club. In actuality, she took stock of everyone, including the positions of the bouncers. She made no eye contact with Carly Avedon as she passed her, yet winked at Diamond who was on her lap. Diamond tossed her hair back from her face and blew her a kiss.

Hunt had anchored himself at a stage-side seat, facing Vladimir's table behind the velvet ropes, which sat empty until Ivan showed up. This time he was alone, and according to Carly, Diamond had told her that Vladimir wasn't at the club.

No longer the paunchy bearded frump from the previous night, Hunt was now the clean-shaven blond—the restless husband—perhaps the annoyed businessman; the alpha male with money to burn—on Alice. He cruised to another stage and threw money there too. When he passed Kenna, he blinked at her twice. She answered him with an innocent tug of her right ear.

That's my cue, she thought. She passed the fully occupied lap dance chairs, then the VIP room, and entered the employee hallway.

Hunt took another seat by the main stage where he watched Ivan drink a glass of whiskey, then pour a glass for the dancer who came to sit with him. The exchange he watched between them seemed tense. The girl shook her head 'no' several times, her hands animated as though she was explaining something to him. A few minutes passed before the girl abandoned the drink on the table and left abruptly. Ivan stood and surveyed the club before leaving his private island.

"Now," was all Hunt said.

At that moment, Diamond left Carly's lap and intercepted Ivan before he made his way across the club toward the employee door. Hunt observed how quickly Diamond turned Ivan's scowl into a smile. He escorted Diamond back to his table, where she got close enough to Ivan for him to put his arm around her. They laughed. They drank.

As Carly walked past Hunt, she whispered into her earpiece. A moment later, Alice disappeared through the employee door.

* * *

Alice moved quickly down the hallway to the dressing room. She stood vigil outside it, pretending to talk on her cell phone while she waited for Pascale. Every few seconds, she glanced in the direction of the office.

Something is wrong. Pascale should be finished by now, she thought. Then she heard Sierra in her earpiece.

"Leave now, Alice," was all she said.

CHAPTER FORTY

A minute later, Elana exited the back door and slid into the passenger seat. "Let's go, Pascale."

Kenna eased off the brake and exited through the gate at the back of the parking lot. "Sierra wants us there as soon as we can make it."

Elana looked over at her. "My earpiece cut out on me again."

"I thought all those problems went away when they disabled the signal jammer."

"They did. Evidently, it's my luck. Sierra sent Carly Avedon in to swap the last one for this new one. I had to give her a lap dance so that she could slip it to me."

Kenna laughed. "Did the good lieutenant leave you a nice tip?"

Elana sneered at her. "Don't get stopped on the way home." She opened her long coat. "I'm still in my fishnet bodysuit and fringe two-piece bikini."

"Under this t-shirt and jeans, so am I."

"Did the download work?"

"As far as I know. I suppose we'll find out when we get back to Ops."

"What about the safe?"

"I'm hoping what we need was downloaded from Vladimir's computer onto my chip. If not, we're going to have to find another way in and get that safe open."

"Why don't we just dig it out of the floor and steal it?"

"All we need is the combination."

"You make that sound like it's no big thing."

"One step at a time, Elana. Let's see what Sierra uncovers from the chip before we plan the next step."

Kenna turned onto La Cienega Boulevard and headed north toward the safe house. They rode in silence most of the way, each woman vigilant about their surroundings, checking the rearview and side mirrors. Kenna made a left onto Melrose Avenue in West Hollywood and glanced over at her passenger. "You can relax, Elana, we weren't followed. What is it with you and earpieces, anyway?"

"Would you pull over on one of these side streets and park?"

"What's wrong?"

"Just for a minute. I know the safe house has been swept but I want to talk to you—privately."

Kenna did a double take. "All right." She coasted along a tree-lined block on West Knoll, parked and turned off the lights. "We really shouldn't stay here too long."

"Could Annaliese have sabotaged my comms, Kenna?"

"No."

"How do you know?"

"Because she's on our side and I'm certain she can be trusted. Besides, it's not you she wants to get even with."

"She has been a little rough on you. Kind of cute to watch actually."

"Oh really?"

"I've never seen you squirm before."

"It's called maintaining a professional attitude, El. The woman has no reason to give me a hard time."

"Sure she does."

"How's that?"

"You rejected her. I can kind of relate."

"You and I were a different story. I didn't turn you down because I didn't want you. I turned you down because I did."

"That makes no sense."

"It did then. If I had let 'us' happen, I would have gashed open wounds that had yet to heal and…"

"So basically, I was a side dish in your broken life."

"Far from it. I needed you, Elana. I needed Alice. You were my lifeline and I needed our connection like I needed air. I couldn't have stayed sane if it hadn't been for you. For a long time, you were the only woman with whom I could feel anything at all."

"Wow." Elana exhaled hard. "I never saw that coming. That's the antithesis of the story I had told myself."

Kenna continued. "Funny thing is, more than having you…I just wanted to kiss you. I spent more time fantasizing about kissing you than any other thing we did in that back room."

Elana smiled. "So you wanted to kiss me."

Kenna fidgeted. "We should really go."

"No one knows we're here. Dancing with you tonight…"

"What about it?"

"When you were up against me on the pole, I couldn't concentrate and I don't know what to do with that."

Kenna met her stare. "What are you talking about?"

"Are you serious?" She rolled her eyes. "Never mind. Let's go."

"I felt it too."

"Y-you did?"

"When you straddled me on the pole. Your legs were wrapped around me and I held you while you leaned backward."

Elana nodded.

"I felt like we were the only people in the room. It was the most natural and sensual feeling in the world—being that close to you."

"Do you think it's clouding our judgment?"

"I think if we don't remain vigilant, we'll make one wrong move that we can't undo, Elana. And the world will pay dearly for it."

"You're right. But I still feel it—that connection we had when we first met. It was there the first time Alice gave Pascale a lap dance. And then each time after…"

"I know. Sometimes I still think of that one time we had almost kissed."

Elana placed her hand over Kenna's. "I do too. When we were on the pole tonight, I couldn't get it out of my head." She gazed deeply into Kenna's eyes, leaned an inch, maybe two, in her direction. Kenna turned toward her, her fingers stroking back the hair from Elana's cheek as their lips neared. Kenna felt her heartbeat quicken when Elana's warm breath slid across her lips; when she inhaled the scent of the woman's neck, and gazed into her soft blue eyes. Elana reached for her.

Bam! Virulent force rocked the car as hard as an earthquake. *Crash!*

An implosion of glass from the back windows scattered like a thousand shards of death. Before either woman could react, Ivan's men reached around them from behind and held sweet-smelling cloths over Kenna's and Elana's faces.

They thrashed—gasped for air. Kenna succumbed, yielding to her attacker's strength under the chloroform cologne. Elana's arms flailed behind her, hopelessly reaching for the man's eyes to disable him.

Both front doors flung open at the same instant, and two men reached into the car with their vise-like grips and pulled the women out. The blue SUV rolled up alongside the car with its lights off and back door already open.

Within seconds, Kenna felt her body thud against the vehicle floor but managed to open one eye. As the SUV pulled away, she felt Elana's body roll up against her before she lost consciousness.

* * *

Groggy, Kenna came to and tried to take inventory. Elana was still knocked out, and leaning up against her on the sofa. Standing over them, one of Ivan's bodyguards pointed his gun at her.

"What do you want? Why are we here?" Kenna mustered all the innocence she could in her twilight state. "Alice, get up," she said, nudging her.

The bodyguard called out in Russian. Seconds later, Ivan entered from a blacked-out corner—his presence even darker than his shadow. Kenna watched his sickening expression, a caricature of a villain, as he walked slowly toward her. She clocked the bulge under his jacket.

"Pascale," he said, his voice soft and the Russian accent hard. He shook his head as though expressing discontent with a child. "You know you've been a bad girl."

Kenna feigned fear. "Ivan, I have no idea what you're talking about."

"Really?" He paced across her field of view, drew closer, and eclipsed the room.

"What the hell?" Elana awoke with a jolt. "Where are we? Ivan, what's going on?"

"Alice, your friend Pascale was found somewhere she wasn't supposed to be. What are you doing with her, Alice?"

"I have no idea what you're talking about. What did she do?"

"Ask her."

"Pascale, what did you do?"

"I didn't do anything, Alice. Okay, I was poking around Chez Oui a little bit." She gazed up at Ivan. "I was curious. You European types are so mysterious."

"Mysterious," Ivan said, half question, half statement. "Tell me more."

"I figured if I could find out what makes you guys tick, I could give you what you want."

The leopard slowly paced to the stage and back—his KGB training organic and cellular. Giving his detainee time to realize who was in charge. "Or you could be working for someone who is trying to do us harm."

Elana jumped in. "Who would want to do you harm? Pascale and I are just working girls."

Ivan laughed and scratched his head. "Tonight, I was alerted electronically when you entered the office at Chez Oui. You're very photogenic, Pascale. What were you doing with the computer?"

Ivan drew his pistol and looked over at his two bodyguards. "You can both go back to Chez Oui now. Leave my SUV and take the other one. I will see you when I'm done questioning the girls."

There was something about the way he pronounced the word *questioning* that made Kenna's body tighten.

Both men holstered their weapons and one of them smirked as they left—the taunt of a sociopath.

"Get up!" Ivan said.

The women glanced at each other and rose. Kenna shivered when the Russian poked her bare back with the cold barrel of his Walther 9 mm. She stumbled on her high heels when he shoved her forward—her head still woozy from his chloroform cologne.

"On the stage now—both of you," he said.

"You don't want to do this, Ivan," Elana began, "they're going to come looking for us."

Ivan waved the Walther between them. "You'll be gone by then. I take no prisoners."

Kenna glared at him. "And here I thought we had nothing in common." Though only partly illuminated, the stage lights stung her eyes. As best she could tell, there were some low level lights back toward the bar. She and Elana stepped up onto the stage in the abandoned strip club.

Ivan tossed two pairs of handcuffs at their feet. "Cuff yourself to the pole."

"No," Elana protested, "why should I?"

"Because I can make death quick and painless, or I can make it feel like dying a hundred times. Your choice," Ivan said smugly.

Kenna put one cuff on her left wrist and slapped the other end around the pole. She looked at Elana and flexed her right eyebrow. "Do it."

Elana locked herself to the stripper pole, the handcuff scraping against the metal.

The women stared into each other's eyes, grabbed the pole with both hands and Elana followed Kenna's lead as they performed a slow and sultry spin around it.

"Yes," Ivan said. "Now you dance only for me. I am the last person who will ever see you dance." He stood at the edge of the stage and lowered the gun while he watched them spin sensually in tandem. They stopped.

"Can't dance without music, Ivan," Kenna said.

Ivan lumbered off the stage, trudged to the boom box on the dusty bar and turned it on.

"If this is where we die, Pascale, I want my kiss now."

"We're not dying, Alice. Pole Melt?"

Elana nodded.

"Dance," Ivan shouted.

"Well, turn up the volume!" Elana said.

Kenna grunted. "You've got to be kidding me."

"What?" said Elana. "'She's Outta Control' is perfect for a Pole Melt. Top or bottom?" she whispered.

Kenna gripped the pole and hid her smile. "Seriously? Top."

"Dance." Ivan yelled again over the loud music.

Kenna whispered. "Don't move until he's close."

"I said dance!" Ivan stomped back to the stage, his face now crimson with anger when the women still hadn't moved.

"Wait for it," Kenna said under her breath.

Ivan jumped up onto the stage and nudged Kenna again with his gun. She stared at him playfully, seductively as she and Elana began to rotate around the pole in their skimpy two-piece white fringe stripper costumes.

Ivan stood there smiling.

They performed two full rotations and stopped.

"Ivan, I can't hook my elbow to the pole with this handcuff on," Kenna said. "If you want us to do your favorite routine…"

He unlocked the handcuff and Kenna climbed to the top position on the pole, hooked her elbow around it and extended her legs straight out in front of her.

Elana began her Spinning Straddle, holding the pole with both hands. Below Kenna, she spun around it with her legs spread apart. Picking up momentum with each rotation, she pushed Kenna's foot sending her into a spin where she turned upside down. In one perfectly timed simultaneous strike, Elana kicked the Walther from Ivan's hand with her stilettos, and Kenna's calves locked him in a choke hold. Ivan struggled, but not for long before he collapsed on the stage.

Kenna straddled his body and stared down at the Russian. "You're right, El, that *is* the perfect song for this." Then she thought, though I never would have guessed when I wrote it— for you.

Kenna searched his pockets and tossed Elana the handcuff key while she fished out the keys to his SUV—the vehicle he had used to kidnap them.

"Is it me or is it damn cold in here?" Kenna said as she slid across the stage toward the Walther.

Elana cuffed Ivan's wrists behind his back. "Not according to the Steel Eyes song. We're so outta control that we're hot."

"Maybe that's not what the lyric really means," Kenna said a little defensively—singsong.

They both whipped around toward the clatter coming from outside.

"What was that?" said Elana.

Kenna kicked off her heels, chambered the Walther and slapped Ivan awake. "On your feet!" she commanded him.

"It's coming from the front."

"Go out the back and get that SUV. I'll use Ivan to hold them off and I'll meet you at the door."

"No—" Elana began.

"Dammit, El. Go! Now."

CHAPTER FORTY-ONE

Ivan's head bobbled when Kenna slapped his fleshy cheek. "Stay awake!"

"Where am I going?" Elana made her fifth turn onto yet another residential street rife with security bars on windows. Jets hovered above LAX, static, blinking like UFOs.

"Just keep driving. Where is he, Ivan? Where is Vladimir?"

"I don't know."

In the backseat of Ivan's SUV, Kenna pushed the Walther hard into his rib cage. "You'd better pray that Alice doesn't hit any bumps."

Ivan sneered. "Of course she'll hit bump. She drives like *woman*!" he said, his Russian accent thick and his tone defiant. "It's old Russian saying: Two things that don't go together is a Kalashnikov and a *woman*!"

"What the hell is a Kalashnikov?" Elana shouted.

"He's the inventor of the AK-47," Kenna answered.

Ivan snickered.

Kenna poked the Walther deeper. "*Aaagh!*" Ivan shirked away.

"Do you want to live, Ivan? Because, you're not acting like it. Like you said, 'I can make your death quick and painless, or I can make it feel like dying a hundred times.'" She paused— pierced him with her steel gray stare. "Or, you can live. Where is Vladimir?"

"I hate to interrupt," Elana said, "but our earpieces are gone. We can't even tell the team where we are."

"They'll track us through my GPS." Kenna felt Ivan become calm in her grip—too calm. "What? What!"

He smiled the same nauseating smile she had seen when she awoke from the chloroform stupor.

"That smile is your tell, Ivan. Tell me!"

"You can't reach your people."

"What?" Elana said. Then she thought for a moment. "Another signal jammer, Pascale. There's a signal jammer in this vehicle."

"My men will find you wherever you go. You should have stayed where you belong—on the stage and in the back room getting paid for sex."

Kenna tightened her grip. "Alice, disable the car's GPS."

"How?"

"I don't know! I thought you would know. Open the glove box."

Elana pulled the SUV over to the curb and opened the lit compartment.

"Give me that screwdriver. And feel under your seat. Is there a holster there?"

Elana handed Kenna the screwdriver, then reached down. "Yes," she said, drawing the Beretta from its nest. She checked the magazine and chambered a round.

"Point that at him," Kenna said while opening her door.

"What? Pascale, where are you going?"

"To steal that old minivan across the street."

"How about the Beemer instead?"

"No modern technology."

Kenna crossed the dark street and positioned the screwdriver in the lock, then bashed it three times with the butt of the

Walther. When she opened the door, she turned off the interior light then crouched to hotwire the ignition. She breathed a sigh of relief when it started and the gas tank read half full—then she ripped out the blasting Milli Vanilli cassette and tossed it onto the floor. Kenna ran back to the SUV, reached in and pulled Ivan out. "Come on, Boris Badenov."

Elana nudged him in the back with the Beretta. "Move it, Ivan." She shoved him into the back of the van and climbed in, her pistol still trained on him.

"Who is this Boris Badenov?" Ivan asked.

Kenna pulled away slowly and didn't turn on the headlights until they reached the end of the block. "We need a phone. Where's your phone, Ivan?"

"It's on the bar at the club we just left."

"We could blindfold him and take him to the safe house," Elana offered.

"Too risky. I think we should shoot him and dump him in Malibu Canyon. I know a secluded spot off Mulholland." Kenna wound through neighborhoods headed toward Pacific Coast Highway.

"So, what's this place in Malibu Canyon?" Elana said.

"The coyotes and hawks will find him long before a human will."

"Shouldn't we keep him alive—you know, for leverage?"

Kenna monitored Ivan's eyes in the rearview mirror as they darted between her and Elana.

"His only value is to tell us where Vladimir is, and he says he doesn't know, so…"

"Wait!" said Ivan. "If I tell you, how do I know you won't kill me anyway?"

Kenna spoke softly. "Don't worry your pretty little head, Ivan. All you need to know is what will happen if you don't."

"You will never get what you want. They'll kill you," Ivan said, defiant. Then, with a tremor in his throat, the address slipped from his lips and Kenna hit the gas.

Once on Pacific Coast Highway, Kenna took a deep whiff of the salt air, trying to satiate her longing for the turquoise

Caribbean. Then she tried even harder to ignore how base and ugly her life became when lived on land. Her mind played tricks on her, instantaneously rolling back the calendar like the tide, to the era when a drive up Pacific Coast Highway meant teenage guitar jams around beach bonfires. Next, her mind flooded with flashbacks of Alex—the love of her life. After that, she conjured the first girl she had ever kissed, and the churning waves that had surfed them back to the ocean's door—to the lifeguard stand where they had made love through the night. The spy continued up the coast toward Malibu.

"Pascale, is something wrong with the car? Why are we weaving?"

"I just got really dizzy—and nauseated."

"Maybe it's a side effect from the chloroform," Elana said. "Are you okay to drive?"

"I could drive this road unconscious if I had to." *Like now.*

They made it through Santa Monica and up to Malibu, and sat at the light before the one where they would turn into Malibu Canyon.

"It's happening again," Kenna said. She opened the driver door and puked. "Alice, do you think it's possible that someone is using my chip to sicken me?"

"I don't know."

"I do," said Ivan. "You won't last long. Your frequency wasn't hard to find after you used it a few times at the club."

The light turned green, and she drove a little farther then made a right to enter the jaws of the steep and dark canyon below Pepperdine University. Suddenly, bright lights from an SUV blinded her in the rearview mirror. She slowed down and moved to the right in the second passing zone to let the vehicle pass. Instead, it pulled up beside her and slammed into the van, causing it to swerve.

Bam!

Bam! The SUV rammed them again from the driver's side. Kenna spun the wheel trying to keep the van upright—maneuvering away from the steep drop to her right. She hit the brakes to buy a few seconds to think.

"They have your GPS frequency!" Elana yelled.

Bam!

"Stay steady, Pascale! Swerve into them when I tell you!" Elana popped open the vented window behind the side door. She leaned back, bent her knee and aimed her stiletto at the Bush-Cheney sticker on the window. With black belt force, she kicked out the window, sacrificing the stiletto to a future Hollywood archaeological dig.

"Now!" Elana yelled. When the SUV veered toward them again, she fired at the passenger window, shattering it. The driver of the SUV slammed on the brakes, and Elana leaned out the window firing continuously at the slowing wheels. The final shot blew out the right front tire, and the SUV careened into the canyon behind them.

"We've got to deactivate that chip in your arm, Pascale."

"How?"

"Cut it out? Do we have a knife somewhere in this van?"

"I'm not pulling over to look. It's only a matter of time before the next brood finds us."

Elana climbed into the rear, crushing a mound of paper bags. "Groceries!" Frantic, she tore at them, tossing aside cereal boxes, soup cans and instant potatoes. It wasn't until she ripped open the third bag that she saw it. She grabbed the box, opened it, and flew over the back of the seat toward the driver.

* * *

In the Chez Oui VIP room, Carly Avedon had positioned herself strategically beneath Diamond, such that she could monitor the coming and going between the employee area and the main club.

No matter how the dancer wiggled, the lieutenant failed to respond. Diamond straddled Carly and looked down into her eyes. "Is something wrong, Jane?" she asked.

"Diamond," Carly said in a hushed tone, "I need to whisper something in your ear."

"Ooo, that's more like it." The stripper leaned her ear to Carly's lips.

"I'll give you fifty bucks to go behind that door and tell me if Pascale and Alice are back there."

Diamond shot upright. "Are you kidding me?"

"Ssh, calm down. I need your help and it's important. Life-or-death important." She stared into Diamond's eyes. "I'm not asking because I want them, or because I don't want you. I'm asking because they may be in danger."

"Who *are* you, Jane?"

"Please, Diamond. I'm here to watch their backs. I would do the same for you if I thought you were in danger. I promise we'll pick this up at a later time."

Diamond dismounted from Carly's lap, scoffed at the fifty-dollar bill, and disappeared through the employee door. Carly pretended to adjust her clothing as a bouncer passed by and glanced at her. Seconds later, Diamond returned.

"They're not here, Jane."

"Please don't mention this to anyone. Promise me," she said, staring into Diamond's eyes.

"Okay, but—"

"I'm not kidding, Diamond. It could put you in serious danger with your Russian bosses. Do you understand what I'm telling you?"

Diamond nodded.

"I'll see you soon," Carly said.

"Promise?"

Carly smiled. "Promise."

"Are they really in danger, Jane?"

"I don't know," she said and then left.

CHAPTER FORTY-TWO

Hunt had tracked Kenna as far as the abandoned strip club barely a mile from Chez Oui—and that's where the trail went frosty cold. With his headlights off, he coasted to the side of the building and parked. Empty and eerie without vehicles in the lot, the blackness swallowed him whole. While he didn't yet know where Kenna had gone, he knew she had been here—this was where her GPS signal had led him. He steered his thoughts away from visions of some psychopathic Russian butchering her arm to get to the GPS chip—or worse. His gut churned like high tide in a tropical storm.

Hunt drew his military caliber Glock and crept into the night. The front door was, as he expected, locked. Swiftly, he dashed to the back of the building where the void of night fell blackest; where finding the rear door slightly ajar made his pulse quicken and his hearing acute. He listened for any noise before he slipped inside.

With his Glock leading the way, Hunt moved with precision stealth, padding through the back hallway toward the dim light filtering from the main room. Darkened though it was, the stage was partly illuminated, with low-level lighting along walls splashed with the stale odor of neglect. He recognized the glittered high heels tossed randomly on the dusty stage—the ones Kenna had worn earlier.

He drifted over to the sofa against the back wall, and glanced down at the table in front of it. He lifted the two tiny earpieces and cradled them in his palm. Now, he was certain that Elana had been here with Kenna, and he wondered if the Russians were monitoring the team's frequency. A faint noise filtering from the bar made him turn his head in its direction. The closer he came to it, the louder the *whir* of the machine. He pressed the Stop button on the boom box, ejected the CD and read the title. *Steel Eyes-World Tour.* When he dropped the CD onto the bar, he noticed the mobile phone that lay next to it, and flipped it open.

Eight missed calls. Six of them from the same number, he thought. He redialed the repeated number and a man answered in Russian. "Ivan where have you been!" The voice belonged to the badass of Brighton Beach. Hunt ended the call then spoke quietly into his earpiece.

"Vouvray, this is Big Papa. Activate Hawk Protocol in sixty seconds." He raced back to his car and started driving. Almost a minute later, the secondary secure mobile phone received its first call, and he pulled over to take it.

"She's gone, they're gone, Sierra. I found Kenna's and Elana's earpieces—they're together. Has the GPS started transmitting again?"

"So far, we haven't picked up Kenna's signal. It fucking disappeared," Sierra said.

"I didn't see any blood where they were being held, so for now I'm assuming they're alive. How could that signal go dark?"

"There are satellite dead zones at some of the beaches, and a few spots in the canyons—I'm guessing. We're pinging it, but so far nothing." Sierra exhaled hard. "I can't believe we lost her."

"Where is Sergeyev?" Hunt asked.

"I don't know."

Hunt scrolled to the number he had redialed from Ivan's phone, and read it to her. "Locate this number and I'll find him. Has Carly checked in?"

"Not since you activated Hawk Protocol."

"I'm going to drive by Chez Oui and look around. I'll call you from there."

"Annaliese is already running the number. Be careful, Hunt."

Hunt drove to Chez Oui looking for Avedon's car. When he couldn't find it, he parked near the back employee exit and slid low in his seat. He watched dancers come and go, but it wasn't until five minutes had passed before he saw Vladimir's armed Russian wrestlers file out of a black Escalade and enter through the back door. Neither Vladimir nor Ivan was among them.

* * *

Carly barged into Ops. "What the hell is going on? Where are Elana and Kenna, and why did Hunt activate Hawk Protocol?"

Annaliese looked over at her. "Kenna's GPS signal pinged us when she and Elana were almost home, and then, it simply ceased to exist. About half an hour later, we picked it up again, and then it stopped transmitting completely."

"Why didn't they signal me they were leaving? I had to get a dancer to go into the dressing room and tell me they'd left."

"Hunt said they gave their signal when they left. I assumed you knew."

"Wait a minute," Carly said. "Isn't the purpose of an implanted GPS to enable you to track someone?"

Sierra picked up the story from there. "Yes. Hunt tracked it to the last known location and it turned out to be an abandoned strip club near Chez Oui. He found Kenna and Elana's earpieces there…"

"Oh, shit!" Carly began, "so that's why we're on the secure phones. The last I heard from Elana is that they would be leaving Chez Oui, but then nothing. Are the comms not working again?"

"They're working fine."

"Then why didn't I hear the transmission?"

Sierra and Annaliese glanced at each other. "Good question," Annaliese said. "The only logical answer is that someone is jamming the signal."

Carly scraped back her hair. "You said they pinged when they were near here. Where?"

Annaliese pulled up the map on her computer and enlarged the location.

"That's right around the corner. I'm going to check it out," Carly said. "I'll be right back."

Two blocks away, Carly cruised down the street. When she saw the strippers' sedan, she pulled over and got out of the car. She turned on her flashlight and shone it inside the smashed back window on the driver's side. Next, she popped the trunk and examined for signs of blood, and then walked to the passenger side. Her beam settled on a piece of cloth that lay at her feet. She pulled on a latex glove, bent down to examine it and coughed from the odor. Within a few minutes she was back at Ops.

"Sierra, Annaliese, I found this at the scene, next to their car. The back windows were smashed out, so they were taken by force after this was used to knock them out. Don't breathe it in." She tossed the rag onto the desk.

"That smells sweet," Sierra said. "What the hell is that?"

Annaliese looked at her. "It's chloroform."

"Where's Hunt?" the lieutenant asked.

"He should be calling any minute," Sierra said, typing frantically. "Annaliese, the number Hunt gave us is a burner phone. I can't get a fix on its location."

Their secured phone rang. Sierra put the call on speaker while Annaliese's fingers crept across the keyboard and descended into the underground world of the dark web.

"Did you find the location?" Hunt asked.

"No," Sierra answered, "it's a burner phone and it must be off."

"Shit," said Hunt. "I'll bet Vladimir destroyed it after I called and hung up."

"Hunt, it's Avedon. I found their car with the windows smashed out. Whoever took them used chloroform to subdue them."

"Wait!" Sierra rolled her chair to the adjacent computer and pulled up her tracking program. "I just picked up Kenna's signal again. I've got it! Zooming in now." She clicked the mouse several times until the street names were visible. "It looks like she's on Pacific Coast Highway in Santa Monica. They're heading up the coast."

"Santa Monica?" Hunt repeated. "Where the hell are they taking Kenna and Elana? And who has them? I just saw Ivan's crew enter Chez Oui."

"Between the bouncers and Vladimir's crew, there are plenty of guys on that payroll," said Carly.

Sierra concentrated. "North, north, what's north? Wait a second…what was that Malibu Canyon IP address we picked up, Annaliese?"

"Yes, the house owned by Vladimir but not the one he lives in," Annaliese answered. "Ivan had logged on from there. I had Mardi send the GPS coordinates to you, Sierra. I'm searching for it now, Hunt."

Sierra gazed at Annaliese. "I could kiss you right now!"

Hunt chuckled. "Save it, Sierra, it'll give you something to look forward to when this is over."

"Found it!" Annaliese blurted out the address.

"But what if they're at Vladimir's beach house?" Sierra said.

"Isn't this address out by the beach too? " asked Hunt.

"No, it's deep in the canyon," answered Sierra. "Malibu Canyon. Maybe a few miles inland."

"Hunt?"

"Yeah, Carly?"

"How about I swing by the beach house? If he's there, I'll call you. If he's not there, I'll meet you at the house in the canyon. If anything changes, let me know."

"Okay, good plan, Carly. Thanks. Anyone have a location on Sergeyev's wife? We could use her as collateral."

"She flew back to New York after the funeral," said Sierra. "You two need to hurry. If Ivan and Vladimir have Kenna and Elana, they won't be wherever they are for very long."

"Hunt, I'm going into the safe house to get weapons," Carly said. "If it comes down to it, wait for me and don't do anything stupid, like going in alone."

Carly hastened to the house next door and returned to Ops with two Kalashnikovs, two Glocks and several clips. She slipped into her San Francisco Police Department bulletproof vest, picked up the bag of weapons, extra vests, and turned to leave.

"Stay safe, Carly," Annaliese said.

Carly nodded. "Thanks."

Carly left the house, tossed the weapons onto the seat and started the car. "Man I'd give anything for my lights and sirens right now." According to her GPS, it would take her thirty-eight minutes to get to Vladimir's beach house, which in her mind translated to twenty if she didn't get pulled over. She laid rubber as she peeled out onto La Cienega Boulevard, headed south toward the Santa Monica Freeway.

CHAPTER FORTY-THREE

Kenna pulled the van into the one-car turnout on the right side of the winding canyon road. She cut the lights and engine. Dotted with nobby greenery that bulged like horizontal bushes out of the rock wall, a hanging beard of hillside flora sheltered their presence. They sat for a stuttering instant in the calm and quiet.

"Alice, what if Vladimir's men are already here waiting? We'll walk right into an ambush."

"I vote we leave the van here, and hike up that long driveway," Elana replied. She snapped an extra rubber band around Kenna's arm. "They won't get your signal now—not through that whole roll of aluminum foil I wrapped around your chip."

Kenna's arm crinkled when she straightened her elbow. "Doubt I'll be able to sneak up on anyone."

Elana glanced at Ivan. "That's the beauty of having a valuable hostage. We're going to walk right in."

"But the only weapons we have are two handguns."

Alice held up her remaining shoe. "And a stiletto heel. I told you five-inch were the better weapon."

"I'm old-fashioned. I'll stick with the Walther." Kenna sighed. "You realize that if his men can't track us, neither can Sierra. We either go back through the canyon and call Sierra on the landline—wait for backup, or—"

"No, Pascale. Right now, we have the element of surprise, so we need to strike if we can. Let's head up the hill and check it out before we decide."

"Alice, you don't have to come with me."

"You think that I'm going to cut and run at the first sign of trouble?" Elana shot back.

"No. What I'm saying is that there's no reason for both of us to be reckless, especially while barefoot, dressed in a fishnet bodysuit and fringe two-piece bikini."

"Forget it, Pascale, *we're* saving the world from a financial meltdown—and Boris Badenov here."

"Who is this Boris Badenov you keep talking about?" asked Ivan.

Kenna sighed loudly. "Gag him please." She exited the van and trained the gun on Ivan while Elana tied the cloth around his mouth and yanked him out.

Restrained in cuffs with his hands behind him, Elana pushed Ivan forward. "Pascale, walk in his footsteps since he's the one with shoes on."

As Kenna trudged up the steep driveway, the trees framing the arc of its curve made her feel like parenthetical content—an aside; a subordinate clause about to make a powerful statement. Enveloped by lush bougainvillea and succulents, it seemed paradoxical to her that a man who cared so little for human life could even appreciate such raw beauty.

Kenna gripped Ivan's arm with one hand, and held the Walther against his spine with the other. As they neared the house, Elana stopped.

"There aren't any cars in the driveway. Take him into that brush," Elana whispered. "I'll check the perimeter—find our point of entry, and see if there's anyone here."

Kenna pushed Ivan under the primeval vines that hung from the trees in the form of a giant umbrella. She blocked out the pain from the roughened earth that tore at her bare soles; a pointed rock under her right heel, jagged fallen branches that pierced her toes. She spoke into the darkness: "You and Vladimir are about to pay the price for whatever goodness you've stolen from this world, Ivan. Count on it."

Ivan choked on his muffled grunt.

Elana returned. "He's in the great room on the opposite side—on the hill. French doors, left one is ajar. No one is here. No cars, no men. The house is quiet and dark except for Vladimir sitting at the computer."

"Okay. I'm going in. Cover me from outside the door."

Elana nodded and led the way.

Kenna waited for Elana to secure her vantage point before she nudged Ivan forward with the Walther. Not overly bright, the room might have simply appeared tidy and welcoming to the unknowing. But, to Kenna it signified the whitewashed evil of men who had bought and sold women in the sex trade; men who were about to hijack the American banking system, and lord only knew what else.

On the wall to the right, a used-brick fireplace climbed boldly to the height of the cathedral ceiling with its crisp and modern lines, and the inviting decor belied a happy home. Beyond the fireplace, Vladimir sat at his computer desk, his left side closest to her. They were two steps into the room before Vladimir shrieked.

"Show your hands!" Kenna yelled so fiercely that Ivan recoiled. "Hands! Now!" She pointed the Walther at Vladimir.

His eyes burned into her with the contemptuous stare of a cornered wolf. Slowly, his hands floated upward from the keyboard.

"On your feet, Vladimir. Away from the desk!"

He didn't move.

"Now," she growled.

Vladimir rose from his chair then moved from behind the desk onto the open floor.

"On your knees."

His face contorted. "A real man doesn't cower before a *woman*."

"You smug whacko-path." She pulled the cloth from Ivan's mouth and then with a sudden strike into the back of his knees, she dropped him to the floor. "Why do you care? Neither one of you are real men."

Vladimir stared down into Ivan's eyes with disdain. "You let a *woman* get control of you? A *woman*! Pitiful to see Leopard bow to a woman."

"Leopard?" Kenna sneered. "He's a pussy. Where are the banking codes?"

"You're too late."

"Not possible. We've tracked you. I know you haven't transferred the money yet. Alice!" Kenna called out.

Elana entered, her Beretta extended in front of her. "Right here, Pascale."

"If Ivan twitches, shoot him." She moved to Vladimir and grabbed his arm. "Hands behind your back."

"I refuse." He resisted her.

Kenna forced the Walther against his spine. "Do you? Do you refuse, Vladimir?" she said in the hushed tone of a madwoman.

Vladimir placed his hands behind his back. "You're delusional. You won't get away with this."

Elana kept the Beretta trained on Ivan while Kenna walked Vladimir to where he sat.

"On the floor with your back to Ivan, keep your hands behind you," said Kenna. She waited for him to comply, then bent down and unlocked Ivan's right cuff. Before she could handcuff the men together, Vladimir twisted and punched her face with one hand, while his opposite hand reached for her pistol. Ivan tried to tackle her.

Elana fired a round just above Vladimir's head, giving Kenna the instant she needed to pull his arm high up behind him. Ivan held his hands up in submission.

"Ow! Okay, okay," Vladimir said. Kenna's tin foil crinkled, tearing the outside layer when she sank a revenge punch into his jaw.

With the men seated back to back on the floor, she cuffed their right hands together behind them, the metal teeth ratcheting closed until the handcuff hit a wall of bone. She had deprived them of conveying visual cues to one another, and the ability to strike out together. Subduing them was barely the first step. Kenna moved to the computer and looked at the screen. "It's a mishmash of codes and numbers, Alice. We have to call Ops—get them to talk us through this."

"Not the best idea, Pascale. What if their goons are already on their way here?"

"But we need to call home and tell them what's going on."

"Not before Vladimir gives us his thumb drive," said Elana.

"I will never give it to you!" Vladimir barked.

Elana raised her eyebrow. "So it *is* a thumb drive we're looking for. Thanks."

Kenna laid the Walther down on the desk next to the keyboard and ransacked the drawers, flinging the contents out haphazardly in a paper storm.

"Leopard," Vladimir said, red-faced. "I will kill you for bringing them to my door. I still don't understand how you didn't recognize her eyes when you met her."

"She was going to kill me, Vova—dump my body in the canyon."

"That would have been kinder than what I'm going to do to you."

Kenna stopped cold and looked up. "Wait—what did you just say, Vladimir? My eyes?"

"Shut up, *girl*! I'm talking to Ivan."

Kenna picked up the pistol, moved in front of Vladimir and pointed it down at him. "Repeat it."

"I said, I will kill Ivan for bringing you here."

"My eyes! What did you say about my eyes?" Kenna panicked. "Say it again, dammit! Say it!"

The mobster went mute.

"You said you didn't know how Ivan didn't recognize my eyes."

He remained silent, save for the volumes that his black stare conveyed as it bore into her.

"Why would he recognize my eyes?" Kenna paced across the room, turned and stared at Ivan. She broke a sweat on her forehead. Suddenly, her mind flooded with evicted memories and torn puzzle pieces. She wanted to throw up again, but this time it wasn't from some sickening frequency alteration of her chip implant. First, she heard Uncle's voice echo in her mind: *'For an instant, I thought you were your mother.'* 'It's the gray eyes,' she had responded. Then she remembered Uncle telling her the code name of her parents' assassin. *Fuck!* "Alice, it was me who blew our cover—they've been onto us from the start."

"What?"

Kenna looked down at Ivan. "Leopard—the Big Cat—*Le Gros Chat*. It was you!"

Ivan smirked. "What was me?"

"You're the assassin. You killed my family, you sonofabitch!" A surge of adrenaline coursed through her, such that she lost all control and pounced on the Russians. Striking them both, pistol whipping them with the Walther and lashing out with her fist to their faces. The blood that spattered on her meant nothing to her. In that moment, she wanted to bankrupt them of life, one drop at a time.

"Pascale! Stop!" Elana pleaded. She lunged toward Kenna, pushed her off Ivan and tackled her. Elana wrestled Kenna onto her back, and straddling her, stared down into her eyes. "Stop!" she commanded; then she paused. "Stop," she said softly. "You can do whatever you want to them, but not until we get what we came for and get out of here."

Kenna hyperventilated. "Get off me!" She struggled against Elana's restraint, causing the final layers of her aluminum foil shield to rip apart from her arm.

Elana flung her arms backward releasing Kenna, and then she stood. "Okay! All right."

Kenna picked up the Walther and rose from the floor. She straightened her fringe stripper outfit now adorned with Russian blood, and stood firmly in front of Vladimir. She glared at him and aimed the Walther.

Vladimir gulped hard. "M-my men will be here any minute."

"Admit that you ordered the hit."

He remained silent.

"Karma's a bitch—and *I* have her phone number." She squeezed the trigger and put a bullet in Vladimir's thigh.

"Fuck!" Vladimir yelled.

"That one is a flesh wound, but then, we've just begun. Say it," she said coldly.

Vladimir held his leg with his free hand and growled.

Kenna took aim again.

"I *didn't* order the hit," he groaned, squeezing his now bloody thigh.

Kenna walked around to face Ivan. "Who ordered the hit, Ivan?"

Ivan's face flushed. "You think that by killing me, your vengeance will bring you peace? I'm here to say it will not."

She stared with toxic indignation. "The vengeance is for my parents. The revenge is for me."

"They're the same thing, aren't they?" Ivan countered.

"Not always. And not now. Through vengeance I gain justice for their murder. With revenge, I get a free trip to hell. But it'll be worth it if I can take you with me."

"Maybe you would rather know what I know."

"W-what are you talking about?"

"How do you know I'm the guilty party? Are you certain? Don't you want to know who ordered it?"

Kenna tried to regain her composure. In her lifetime as a spy, this was the first time she couldn't control her anger. "Forget your KGB tactics. I'm certain that I'm going to kill you very slowly."

"Don't be too sure. My men will be here any moment now that your chip frequency is transmitting again."

She put the gun to Ivan's head, her hand shaking.

"Pascale, no!" said Elana, while stepping toward her. "If you do it, you'll be no different than them. You're better than this."

"Sorry to disappoint you, Alice, I'm not." She stepped back, squeezed the trigger and hit Ivan on the outside of his thigh.

Ivan growled at her.

"You're a leopard torn apart by the evil of your self-made jungle." She took aim. "See you in hell."

"Pascale, you have to stop this!" Elana pleaded. "We need that thumb drive!"

Kenna looked away from the bloody leg to take refuge in Elana's soft blue eyes, then lowered the pistol and stepped to the sofa. Using a throw pillow, she wiped the blood from her arms and tried to normalize her breathing—still seething with rage. She focused until her breathing slowed, and she could admit to herself that Elana was right. She turned to face Vladimir. "Where's the thumb drive, Vladimir? Give me the drive."

"No."

Kenna squeezed off another shot, this one aimed at his outer shoulder.

"*Aaggh*, you crazy bitch!" Tears of pain flowed from his eyes.

"I'm just getting started." She took aim again.

"Fuck you!" Vladimir spat at her.

She fired the next shot just past his head and then took aim again.

Elana moved toward her. "No more. I can't take their moaning." She stepped in the path of the next would-be shot and looked down at Vladimir. "I can't control her, Vladimir. You'd better tell us where the thumb drive is."

"Fuck you too!" he yelled.

"Like *that's* ever gonna happen," said Elana before she punched his face with a solid hit.

"Alice, call an ambulance and I will tell you."

"I'd advise you to stop stalling while Pascale and I still have bullets. If it's where you tell me it is, we'll talk about stopping before you bleed out."

He spoke between the groans of pain. "There," he tilted his head backward. "It's behind a loose brick in the fireplace."

"Which one?" Kenna asked as she followed Elana to the fireplace.

Vladimir grunted. "The seventh brick from the bottom on the right side."

Elana set her pistol down on the mantel, next to the framed picture of Vladimir and his family. She grabbed the fireplace poker, stuck the point into the corner of the brick and began prying it out.

"Drop the weapons. Hands up." The man's voice behind them was low and calm. He stepped past the threshold from the darkened inside hallway that led to the front door.

The poker bounced off the tile floor when Elana dropped it. Kenna laid the Walther on the floor, and both women turned to stare in disbelief at Dixon Chase. His Glock was pointing straight at them.

"Get me out of this, Chase, so I can kill Ivan," said Vladimir.

"Not so fast, Sergeyev."

"What?"

Chase waved the gun toward him. "Before I free you," he glanced at the women, "and get rid of them, I think we need to renegotiate our shares in this deal."

"Are you insane?" said Ivan.

Kenna observed Chase. "You can't think you're going to get away with any of this. You may be a sociopath, but you're not stupid."

Amused, Chase smiled. "That was very entertaining, watching you and West fighting on the floor. And thanks for coaxing the location of the thumb drive out of Vlad here." He stepped deeper into the room and tossed a pair of handcuffs at Elana. "Cuff yourself to her and kick that Walther over here."

"No."

He took aim at her head.

She put on the cuffs, and Kenna kicked the Walther only halfway to where Chase stood.

Chase turned his attention to Vladimir. "That's a lot of blood, boys," he said while staring at the candy apple-red puddle that leached out of the Russians and onto the floor around them. Well then, I suppose now would be a good time to renegotiate our deal."

Vladimir sneered at Chase. "What the hell do you want?"

CHAPTER FORTY-FOUR

Hunter scrambled across the hill from the neighboring property. If Kenna and Elana were inside that house, he couldn't afford to wait for Carly a moment longer. Traversing the hillside onto the Russian kingpin's driveway, he tried to map out the parameters of the house in the dark. First, with his Glock drawn, he snuck around to the side of the house, inching his way toward the back. He heard what he thought was a man's voice and paused to listen.

"Before I unlock you, Vladimir, it's time to strike a new deal," said Dixon Chase. "I want to know what my share of the take will be now. And then I'm going to dispose of *Alice* and *Pascale*."

Hunt felt his pulse quicken. I have to get in there right now, he thought. As he advanced methodically across the last slope of the hillside, a coyote's yelp suddenly caused him to lose his footing. In his attempt to grope for a sturdy tree branch to break his fall, his Glock tumbled into the darkness. He gripped the tree branch, swung across a trench and again climbed toward the voices. When he topped the hill, he drew his backup Beretta from his ankle holster.

"Sixty percent, Chase. That's my final offer," Vladimir said. "You'll be a very rich man."

"Your men and Ivan here failed to do their job tonight. These women should be long gone, and that money should already be in the Caymans bank."

"Sixty-five!" Vladimir shouted at him.

"Okay," Chase said.

"If you unlock Vladimir, then you unlock me," Ivan said.

"What do you say, Vladimir?" Chase asked.

"Fine! I'll deal with you later, Ivan."

Hunt edged to the side of the door where he could see diagonally across the room. His strike needed to be on his terms, his timing—no matter what. He took a deep breath and waited for the precise moment. Chase turned his back and bent down to unlock Vladimir.

Hunt crept inside, closed the distance between them—his gun pointing at Chase. "Don't move!"

Chase fired a Hail Mary shot in Hunt's general direction, forcing him to dive behind a sofa.

"It's over," Chase yelled. He grabbed Elana's arm. "I have your girls right here. Give it up, Van Bourgeade."

Hunt didn't have to look to know that Chase was holding Kenna and Elana at gunpoint. He stood with his hands in the air.

Chase snickered. "This night just keeps getting better."

"I can tell you where to dump their bodies in the canyon," Ivan chimed in.

"Shut up, Boris Badenov," Kenna said.

"Who is this Boris Badenov you keep talking about!" Ivan shouted.

* * *

Carly cased Hunt's car as she rolled past it at the base of the hill. She drove midway up the long driveway and parked across it so that no one could ambush her from behind, or escape her on their way out. She slung one assault rifle over each shoulder, stuffed as many ammunition magazines as she could into her pockets and holstered her Glock. The lieutenant ducked into the brush, and waited another minute to make sure that no one was patrolling the property.

Once again certain that she was alone, Carly ascended the rest of the driveway. Pressing her ear against the front door, she listened and waited in the dark until she was sure she hadn't heard any activity inside. Silently, she turned the doorknob and found it unlocked.

She tiptoed into the darkened hall and took shelter behind the staircase. Economical and surreptitious in her stride, she crept toward the voices. When Carly reached the opposite side of the house, she hugged the wall and peeked into the room from behind the door, through the crack below the top hinge.

"Dixon, you don't have to do this," said Hunt. "Turn it around right now. Help me get these guys, and the government will go easy on you. I'll see to it."

Dixon chuckled. "Cute. Has that ever worked on *anyone*, Van Bourgeade? You think I'm stupid?"

"It's the truth. Your government needs what you know. Think about it, Dixon—you have leverage here."

Chase mulled it over in one breath. "Nah, I'd rather be rich. But I'm glad you could join the party, Hunt. It's a shame that idiot Lieutenant Avedon isn't here. Either way, you and the women here will make for a good hostage trade for Vladimir, Ivan and an airplane. We'll all go away happy."

"By happy, you mean with us maimed or dead, and the three of you long gone."

"Yeah, pretty much."

"I can tell you right now, those women won't do it," said Hunt.

Chase waved his gun. "Over there next to the girls." He circled behind Hunt, their backs now facing the hallway door. "Move." He pushed Hunt forward toward the women.

Carly used the opportunity to step across the open doorway at an angle that could only be seen from where Kenna and Elana stood.

* * *

Kenna blinked twice to get Elana's attention. She tossed a furtive glance at the doorway and waited for Elana to look in Carly's direction.

Once Elana's knowing gaze drifted back to her, Kenna lifted her eyebrow and spied the Beretta that Elana had placed on the mantel when she'd traded it for the poker.

Kenna next signaled Hunt with their own brand of silent communication—the one they'd invented and perfected since childhood. Known only to them, the symbolic shorthand had saved their lives before from overflowing gutters of human trash. The twitch of her lips signaled him to be ready when she unleashed her signature brand of stealth—the *silent overwhelm maneuver.*

Hunt blinked twice to acknowledge he understood her. Kenna then made an imperceptible nod to Carly, praying she had seen it.

As Carly stepped into the room, pointing the AK-47 at Chase's back, Chase whipped around and shielded himself with Hunter.

"I wouldn't do that, Carly."

Carly kept him in the rifle's sight. "A round from an assault rifle travels at twice the speed of your handgun, Dixon. Either way, you die," she said with steely resolve.

"I don't think so, Avedon. You really want your team's blood on your hands?"

"No, I don't."

"Then put down the rifle."

"Before I do, let's talk about it. Make me an offer, Dixon."

With the transparency of a ghost—and the focus for which Kenna Waverly was known—she reached behind her and lifted the Beretta from the mantel while Carly kept Chase talking. Inaudibly, Elana stepped in tandem with her until Kenna pressed the gun against the back of Chase's head.

"Checkmate, asshole," Kenna said.

In one swift spin, Hunt whipped around, grabbed Chase's gun and delivered an iron punch to Chase's jaw, knocking him out and dropping him to the floor. Hunt reached into Chase's pocket for the key to the handcuffs as Carly shouldered her rifle and crossed toward them.

"Gun!" Elana screamed.

Kenna pivoted the moment Ivan gripped the Walther on the floor. In the instant he pointed it at her, she fired three lethal shots with the Beretta, and watched his lifeless body fold onto the wet, red tile—his expression forever frozen, fixed on her. She looked at Hunt—stared blankly into his eyes.

Elana put her hand on Kenna's shoulder. "Are you all right?"

Kenna turned to her. "Ivan was wrong. This *will* bring me peace."

"What are you talking about?" asked Hunt as he freed the women from their handcuffs.

Kenna gazed into his eyes, unable to speak in that instant. Finally, she exhaled a hard sigh. "*Le Gros Chat* has at last paid his debt for Sam and Dalia's murders," she said quietly.

"Him? He was the assassin?"

Kenna nodded.

"When did you know?"

"I put it together after we got here."

"You okay, babe?" Hunt asked.

"For now."

Carly handed her rifle to Kenna and took the handcuffs from Elana. "Not bad, West. You too, Waverly." She smiled. "Not bad at all. Someday you'll have to fill me in on what that means— *Le Gros Chat*." She walked to Vladimir and uncuffed him from Ivan's dead body, then slapped a new set of cuffs on him.

"You have the right to remain silent, you piece of shit," said the lieutenant. She tossed Hunt her phone.

He opened it and dialed. "Sierra, we need cops and an ambulance," he said. "The team is okay. Ivan is dead, but Vladimir's badly wounded and his men could be here any second. We have Chase in custody but we need to get the hell out of here. Now."

"*Aagh!*" Vladimir cried out when Carly pulled him onto his bloody legs.

"Oh, boo-hoo, does that hurt?" Carly mocked. "Come on." She kicked his wounded leg and looked at Hunt. "I think we should all pile into a car before the thugs get here. Tell the cops to meet us at the nearest hospital."

"Good idea," Kenna said.

"Cancel that, Sierra. Have the cops meet us at Malibu Hospital."

Hunt shouldered the AK-47 that Carly had left in the hallway. Headed for the front door, Kenna picked up the other Glock from the hall floor and handed it to Elana. Together, the team dragged Vladimir and a punch drunk Dixon Chase down the driveway. As they approached Carly's sideways car, a black Escalade screeched onto the steep driveway and accelerated, broadsiding the car like a battering ram. Carly threw Vladimir into the bushes and Hunt punched Chase, knocking him out again and dropping him to the ground.

Hunt and Kenna aimed the Kalashnikovs and fired on the SUV's windshield until it shattered into a mosaic. The three men who darted out of the vehicle took refuge behind it.

"*Psst*," Carly said to get Kenna's attention from the other side of the driveway. She pointed to herself and drew a big circle in the air.

Kenna nodded and pointed down her own side of the hill to indicate their help surrounding the Russians.

With the Beretta from her ankle holster in one hand, and her Glock in the other, Carly descended the hillside.

"She's going to come up behind them," Kenna whispered to Hunt.

"I'll take this flank," he said. "You provide diversion. Where's Elana?"

Kenna strained to see into the brush. "She went with Carly."

Hunt turned to leave. "I'll use the bird call."

"Okay, strike on the count of two afterward."

He nodded and backed away from the driveway before he crept down the hill.

Time to create a diversion. Kenna pointed the rifle into the driveway toward the SUV and fired low, toward the tires. Rounds of semiautomatic gunfire answered her. She flew across the driveway under fire, continuously firing back until she rolled safely onto the ground on the opposite side.

Carly and Hunt should be in position by now. She fired at the Russians again and finally heard Hunt's bird call. *One. Two!* She ran down the drive, advancing her position toward Carly's car, firing into the night. Another burst of gunfire came toward her, echoing deceptively off the mountain. It was impossible for her to tell exactly where it was coming from.

Kenna rolled under Carly's car and then underneath the SUV. She saw one of the Russians moving down the hill toward her team. She aimed the rifle, and squeezed off the shot that hit his leg and dropped him to the ground. As he screamed in pain, Kenna fired once more to put an end to his screams.

Suddenly, Kenna's ears met with deafening silence. She held her breath in fear for her brother, for Elana and for Carly. She called their names.

"We're okay," Hunt yelled. "You got the last one. We got the others!"

Kenna rolled out from under the SUV and stood in front of the one remaining headlight on the Escalade.

Seconds later, the three champions emerged from the darkness and climbed toward her. First came Elana, Warrior Stripper of the Apocalypse, in her fishnet bodysuit and two-piece fringe stripper costume, with a Glock at her side; then Hunt, uncharacteristically filthy and ragged—butch with the Kalashnikov; and lastly Carly, marching like Sheena, Queen of the Jungle, a pistol in each hand.

Hunt opened Carly's phone and called Sierra. Pointing the Kalashnikov down at a barely conscious Chase he said, "Change of plans, Sierra. We'll take that ambulance and a shitload of cops at Vladimir's. And you'd better get Secretary Zwarnick to make a few calls—get the feds here now. It's fucking ugly. Four," he added. "We have four bodies."

* * *

At two thirty in the morning, covered in Russian blood, caked-on dirt, and scrapes from a conquered mountain, the team staggered into Ops. One by one, they collapsed in the nearest empty chair.

"*Madre de Dios!*" said Sierra. "Are you guys okay?"

"I believe this is what you're waiting for," Kenna said, holding out her arm and handing Sierra the thumb drive.

Mardi dashed toward the kitchen. "I'll be right back with water."

Annaliese grabbed the stack of towels she had waiting. "Here," she said, handing them out. "Kenna, did the paramedics examine you?"

"No, I had to get out of there. Local law enforcement and the feds were at odds. The police wanted to take us in—Feds had to pull rank to keep us anonymous. I'll be okay, but the cuts on my feet hurt like hell," she said when Mardi handed her water.

"What else can I get you guys?" asked Sierra.

Hunt wiped his face with the towel. "How about a first aid kit?"

"Sure." Sierra left the room to fetch it.

Hunter gulped down his bottle of water and reached forward to hand it to Joe. "Hey, buddy, how about you get us something a little stronger?"

"You've got it. There's some vodka around here. I'll go look for it."

When Sierra returned with the first aid kit, Hunt pointed to Kenna.

"You okay, West?" asked Carly.

Elana opened her eyes. "I can't take it all in yet. The whole night just keeps flashing back in my mind. Do you know how lucky we are to come out of this alive?"

Kenna moved to sit next to her, and took Elana's hand. "Look into my eyes."

Elana engaged her.

"It's going to be okay, El. Right now you're coming down from the adrenaline, and sometimes that makes thoughts and sensations go haywire for a little while."

"Are you sure, Pascale?"

Kenna smiled. "I'm sure," she said softly.

"Good, then I'm going next door to clean up. Have that vodka ready when I get back."

"Hunt and Carly, you're welcome to clean up next door," Kenna said.

"Or here," added Annaliese. "And there's an open bedroom if you'd care to crash here, Carly."

"Thanks, Annaliese, I have the go-bag from my trunk—the only part of the rental car that wasn't shot out or smashed. To be honest, I wouldn't mind the company, especially after Dixon Chase stayed in that other house with me."

"My stuff is already at your place," Hunt said to Kenna. "And I'll be joining you for that drink, Elana."

"Me too..." Carly's voice trailed off.

Battered and spent, each agent for good, rose and headed toward their respective remedies.

CHAPTER FORTY-FIVE

The next morning, Elana awoke with a groan, restless from what remained of a fitful night—questioning whether or not she had even slept in those few passing hours. It was over—or was it? She suspected it would take time for the intensity of her *fait accompli* to sink in; to dissect the every second of an operation where she had stared down the barrel of a gun too many times. But in this moment, she exhaled into the stillness of morning inside her darkened bedroom.

Descending into the underworld of Chez Oui had stirred her darkest memories, and now she had even more sinister moments to add to the portfolio. Pascale wasn't one of them. The woman had been her only good recollection of her time as a dancer—and the one person she had never counted on seeing again.

Then she had met Kenna Waverly, someone she wanted to know even more than Alice had wanted to know Pascale. Although Pascale and Kenna inhabited the same body, like Alice's relationship to Elana, they were each oddly dissimilar from their doppelgangers. Alice and Pascale had created a fantasy that had never been unraveled or undone. However, Elana and Kenna's journey had yet to unfold. She rose, padded across the hall to Kenna's room, and tapped lightly on the door.

"Come in," Kenna said softly.

Elana stared into the darkened room from the doorway, and then moved toward the bed. Silent, she climbed in next to Kenna and wrapped her in her warm embrace. "Those bruises still hurt as much?"

"Yes, especially now that the vodka has worn off," Kenna whispered. "This is a nice surprise—your arms around me."

Elana held her closer, tighter. "I like the scent of your hair on this pillow. And more than that, I like how you feel in my arms. I've wanted to do this since the first time we met."

Kenna sighed. "I miss this."

"What?"

"The feeling of waking up and lying in the arms of someone I trust; someone I'm crazy about—someone I'm endlessly attracted to."

"Huh. I think we just skipped right to the morning after."

Kenna smiled. "Ignored the lead-up."

"Uh-huh. You told me you had this insane attraction to me when we met, and still you wouldn't let us happen. Why?"

"I-I couldn't, El." Kenna turned over and gazed into Elana's eyes, searching for the right words—or any words. "There had been someone else."

"So you stepped out on her?"

"No. We had broken up a long time before, but it took me years to get over her. Besides, I was working nonstop at the time."

"Must have been one hell of a relationship."

"This sounds corny but, for one moment—in a sliver of time, everything had skidded to a stop. There were no sounds— no breath—and the only thing I could see was *her.* Acutely aware of every cell in my being, for the first time in my life, I had connected with someone."

"What happened to her?"

"We were young. She cheated on me the whole time we were together, and it blew my world apart."

"Did you try to get back with her?"

"No. She had washed right through me as though I was a sieve. Nevertheless, I had felt it. A sea of serenity had rolled in, all on one tide; a trillion times a gazillion droplets of serenity, in one wave. And for the first time, I knew what it meant to be in love. That's the world that got blown apart inside of me before you and I had met.

"When I met Alice, that fluid wave between us—that longing—our sensuality, made me realize that one day I would love again. You gave me that. When you and I had touched, you reached behind the wall so effortlessly and gave me back my desire. And in a way I did love again, however odd the circumstance."

"And now, Pascale?"

"Now, there's the real you and the real me, and between the two of us there are five of us in this bed—if you count Wonder Woman."

Elana's smile bordered on laughter. "You really were good up there on that pole, honey. I think you fulfilled one of *my* fantasies."

"Did you just call me honey?"

"You wanna make a federal case out of it?"

"I think, by definition, Alice, it's already a federal case."

"Do you think we'll ever get that kiss that we've wanted since the night we met?"

Kenna nestled her head into Elana's shoulder. "When the time is right."

"You were ready to do it in the car when Ivan's men kidnapped us."

"About that. I'd rather wait until we're officially on vacation."

"That has a nice ring to it—on vacation." Elana sighed. "We'd better go next door for the debriefing."

Kenna pulled the cover over her head. "I don't want to move. Have you ever heard the Jamaican phrase, '*Soon come?*'"

"No. What does it mean?"

She peeked out from the cover. "If you ask for a cup of coffee and ten minutes later, you ask your waiter where your coffee is, he'll answer, 'soon come.' That means it may be here in a minute or ten, or twenty—or never."

Elana stood, walked around to Kenna's side of the bed and took her hand. She peeled her upright from her pillow. "Yeah, I don't think Secretary Zwarnick would appreciate my telling him, soon come, when he asks where you are."

"I'm acting like a ten-year-old, aren't I?"

"I'd go with thirteen."

Kenna thought it over. "Okay, thirteen is better than I thought. I'll go with thirteen. Thirteen's not so bad—right?"

Elana rolled her eyes. "I'll go make coffee. See you downstairs."

"I'm going to miss your coffee, Alice."

"I'm so tired, I'm going to cuddle the pot until you get there."

* * *

Coffee cup in hand, Kenna led the way next door.

"Morning, guys," said Elana. "Did everyone finally get some sleep last night? Or did the celebration continue after we left?"

"Something tells me the celebration continued elsewhere," Sierra teased.

"Sorry to disappoint you, Vouvray."

Sierra laughed. "It's all good, Wonder Woman."

"Hunt is fierce on pots, pans and spoons," said Joe.

"Ha! You got my brother to play kitchen percussion? That doesn't happen until the fourth"—Kenna surveyed the empty liquor bottles scattered around the room—"or the eighth martini."

"Yeah, he was really good."

"In all fairness, I did take lessons from an excellent drummer," said Hunt.

"Oh yeah? Who?" Joe asked.

Hunt smiled. "JJ Long."

"The drummer from the Steel Eyes band?"

"Yep."

"Oh snap!" said Joe. "No wonder you're so good."

"Hey, buddy," Hunt retorted, "you were pretty damn fine on that harmonica."

"I guess the answer to my question is, all celebration, no sleep," said Elana. "What about you, Mardi?"

"I was up egging these clowns on."

"She lies," said Joe. "Mardi was on vocals."

Kenna laughed. "Was she any good, Hunt?"

"She was great," he replied.

"What songs did you do?" Kenna asked.

"You know that Steel Eyes song, 'Kiss My Ax'?" said Mardi.

"Hmm. Nope," Kenna said, straight-faced.

"Aw sure you know that one, Wave," Hunt teased.

"Where's Annaliese?" Elana asked with a smile.

"Gone," Sierra said quietly.

"What? No promise to co-hack in the future?"

Sierra lowered her tone. "Maybe. But she never said goodbye."

"You're pretty banged up, Kenna," said Carly. "Are you okay?"

"My muscles are more sore from pole dancing. That shit is hard work! Makes you really appreciate the good tippers."

Carly scoffed. "Don't you mean sore from taking out the Russian mob? You're fierce, girl. Props."

Kenna grinned. "Thanks. You're pretty tough yourself."

"Sheesh, maybe, but I'm not in your league," Carly admitted.

Elana whispered in Kenna's ear. "Alice *always* appreciated Pascale's big tips."

When the secure phone rang, Sierra pressed the button and waited for Secretary Zwarnick to appear on the big screen. "Good morning, team."

A flurry of "Good morning, Mr. Secretary" fluttered across the room.

Zwarnick chuckled. "Is it me or do you all look a little hungover?"

"It's you, sir," Elana said, holding back a smile.

"Job *incredibly* well done. All of you. I couldn't have asked for a better team, especially given everything that undermined you."

"Speaking of that," said Hunt. "What happened to Dixon Chase after we turned him over to your guys?"

"They flew him back here early this morning and he's cutting deals left and right, giving up the big players for a lighter sentence. But, Vladimir will never see the light of day. Thanks to the risk you took on our behalf in Buenos Aires, Kenna, we've finally uncovered what it was the Chinese were after when they initially hacked us."

"What was it?" Kenna asked.

"Our deep space satellite technology, and the names of personnel they thought they could recruit from our ranks," Zwarnick replied.

"So the banking, the water plant failures...and the stock market glitches, were all part of that?" said Sierra.

"Part of it," Zwarnick said. "On the other hand, breaches of federal employees made them privy to a trove of intimate details about people's lives—revealed weaknesses they could exploit. They were trolling for people they could recruit as spies.

"Kenna, what you did for us was to give us a way to track their inside moves—and we nailed them. We know who they targeted and how they did it. Best of all, we stopped it. And you all had a hand in that."

"How did the Russians get involved?" asked Hunt.

"Vladimir's daughter and son-in-law, Raisa and Jiang Lee, gave vital information to him that undermined our infrastructure and allowed him to exploit it. The Chinese only just discovered that Vladimir was going after their money, too, and now they're groveling to get the intelligence *you* so expertly obtained, Kenna. As for the compromised computer chips from Physio Dynamics, that company is toast. Your country owes you all a debt of gratitude—especially you, Sierra, for discovering this attack on our infrastructure which blew the whole thing wide open."

"Thank you, sir."

"Kenna and Hunt," Zwarnick continued, "I've already briefed your superiors, and they're waiting for you as we speak." He smiled. "I believe you know the address."

"Great," Hunt said. "Now, my mother gets a chance to grill us."

The secretary chuckled. "An unenviable task—I asked her to go easy on you. Well, I hope you're all ready for your next assignment."

Joe groaned. "Oops. Sorry, Mr. Secretary."

Zwarnick paused before speaking. "I'd like written statements of the last twenty-four hours on my desk by midnight, my time. And you can omit the party."

"You really want reports today?" Kenna said, exhaling like a leaky balloon.

"Yes, I do. One reason is because I need you and Elana ready to go in the morning."

"Go where?" asked Elana.

"You're going to the Cayman Islands to pick up documents from Vladimir's bank. The banker there is cooperating with us."

"So, I'm a courier?"

"Well, it's not like I'm asking you to be a bicycle messenger— I'm sending a plane for you. However, since tomorrow is Friday, I guess you and Kenna will just have to wait out the weekend in the Caymans until the bank opens on Monday."

Kenna and Elana glanced at each other but failed to suppress their smiles.

Zwarnick continued. "Sierra, I had Annaliese leave early to compile and encrypt files for me, which she needed to do from Curaçao, where her secure state-of-the-art lab is located. Since I don't want anything loaded onto our systems until I get the okay from IT, I've asked Annaliese to put the information on portable encrypted hard drives. You've proven to be an expert in hard drive security. I need one of our agents there looking over her shoulder, and to bring them to Washington."

"I'm going to Curaçao?" Sierra asked.

"You'll drop off Kenna and Elana in Grand Cayman, and then you'll fly into Willemstad. Annaliese will have you covered once you're there."

"Does *she* know that?"

"She's the one who insisted I assign it to you."

"Nice."

"Mardi and Joe—that was great work. Once you pack up the Ops center, I promise I won't call you all weekend. Lieutenant Avedon, if you ever get the urge to play with more sophisticated toys, I'd be happy to put in a word at the FBI. They heard about you taking down Dixon Chase and have expressed interest in meeting you."

"Huh. FBI. Wow." Carly tried it on and nodded. "I'll think about it."

"Hunter, that was great work last night."

"Thanks. Turns out that Leopard—the big cat, was a big puss."

"Don't say it," Zwarnick laughed. "I have to go. I want all of your reports tonight."

The screen went dark.

"Remind me to put the American taxpayers on my Christmas card list this year," said Sierra.

"So, Sierra," said Elana. "How do you feel about seeing Annaliese now?"

Sierra beamed. "Is there ever a wrong time for your dreams to come true, Alice?"

Elana glanced at Kenna. "No, Vouvray, there isn't. And with that, I'm going next door to write my report."

Hunt looked at Kenna and sighed. "So, shall we go and get this over with?"

"Sure," she answered. "Call Maman and Uncle and let them know we're on our way."

"Where are the aspirin?" asked Joe.

"Yeah," Mardi chimed in. "Where are the goddamn aspirin?"

* * *

Hunt and Kenna drove through the open gate of the Van Bourgeade estate, only to find Uncle and Phyllis awaiting them outside the front door. Phyllis grabbed Kenna with the same intensity as the night that Kenna had boarded Uncle's yacht in Jamaica. They kissed on both cheeks, and Kenna waited patiently for Phyllis to stop squeezing her tightly—to stop uttering every idiom of gratitude in French. Then, she did the same to her son.

"Well done, *mes enfants*!" Uncle said before he kissed Kenna's forehead. "Shall we go inside, children?"

Hunt's shared knowing glance with Kenna spoke volumes to her. Neither one of them had to voice their amusement at how Uncle still saw them as children—his children.

"*Mon Dieu!*" Phyllis said when Kenna sat at the kitchen table in her sandals. "Look at your feet! And those bruises on your face—and your hands."

"Phyllis, are you crying?" Kenna asked.

Phyllis wiped away her tears and then placed a freshly baked French plum cake on the table. "Of course I'm crying. Look at you!"

Kenna stood and wrapped her surrogate mother in her embrace. "It was a small price to pay for averting Chinese infiltration and a global financial crisis, Maman."

"And for killing your parents' assassin," Uncle said softly. "Perhaps now you will find the peace that for so long has eluded you, *mon chou*."

Kenna smiled, but her eyes spoke remorse, sadness. "Perhaps," she admitted. "Uncle, I'll be living at my Jersey Shore beach house full time, so I'll be vacating your villa in Jamaica."

"Move in here with me," said Phyllis. "The Jersey Shore doesn't have your family nearby."

"I've spent a lot of time there this past year. I like the serenity and the lack of pretense. Also, it places me smack in the middle between you and Uncle. I promise to visit often, Maman—it's only a five-hour ride."

"A five-hour *airplane* ride," Phyllis retorted.

"What's the difference if I had to drive for five hours? It's the same five hours. I'll charter a jet if I have to. Promise."

"Mom," Hunt began, "this is Kenna you're talking to. Have you ever known her to not follow her heart?"

"Yes," Phyllis replied.

"When?" Hunt asked.

"All those years ago when she gave up on Alex Winthrop."

Kenna spoke up. "I disagree. My breakup with Alex forced me to follow my heart to my music."

"Well, just look at how that turned out," Phyllis said with disdain.

"I'd say it turned out pretty well for Steel Eyes, and for millions of her fans," said Kenna.

"Maybe for Steel Eyes, but not for Kenna Waverly," Phyllis retorted. "While Steel Eyes was adored, Kenna has remained alone for all these years."

Kenna fell silent. Her mother was right.

Phyllis shook her head. "And you're not even dating Annaliese!"

Kenna grinned. "No, but now that my parents can rest in peace, my heart is free to pursue someone else—someone I'd like to know better."

"Oh? Who?"

"Elana West," Hunt chimed in. "The dancer FBI consultant."

Phyllis smiled. "When do I get to meet her?"

"Right after we take care of an errand in the Caymans for Vince Zwarnick. How about if we come for dinner?"

Uncle laughed. "Looks like I'm sticking around a while longer, eh?"

"Hey, Mom," said Hunt, "how about if I bring Devon? You can meet her too—we'll make it a family affair."

"Sold!" Phyllis sighed, picked up the pie knife, and served Kenna the first and largest slice of her favorite dessert.

CHAPTER FORTY-SIX

Kenna waited for Elana at the hotel's beach bar, sipping a Cabernet whose balance and complexity rivaled her own. Island calypso and reggae music filled the spaces between her thoughts, and the sunset had put to bed all that had come before it.

The eye-catching brunette sauntered off the narrow cement path that wound along the sand, and Kenna caught her breath at the sight of her. They locked eyes as their smiles connected. Elana's windswept hair—dark once again like the Alice that Pascale had known—created a stunning contrast to her soft blue eyes. Tastefully accented in blue liner and a wisp of mascara, they simply sparkled. Graceful in her feline motion, the royal blue halter dress shimmered and flowed with her gentle curves. Kenna drank in the sight of her, and watched her eyes until Elana sat on the stool next to her.

"That's the woman I know," Elana said. "Blondish, jaw-dropping, and mine for the night."

"I'm flattered, Alice," Kenna teased.

Elana closed her eyes and inhaled the salt air. "Is there anything more perfect than this, Pascale? Here. Now. With you?"

Kenna placed her hand over Elana's. "I'm going to pretend that wasn't a rhetorical question and answer it." She cleared her throat. "No, there isn't anything more perfect than this, here, right now with you, Alice."

"Are you hungry?" Elana asked.

"Ravenous."

"Hungry enough to save room for lots of dessert?"

"Depends on what's on the menu," Kenna said.

"I'm on the menu."

Kenna grinned—felt her face suddenly become warm. "I hope we don't run out. Of dessert."

"I doubt we will."

"That's good to know because there's a little something new I'd like to try."

"Oh?" Elana smiled.

"It occurs to me that in my vast Wonder Woman experience, I never got the opportunity to give anyone a lap dance."

Elana laughed. "You're right."

Kenna continued. "It doesn't seem quite fair really. All those lap dances you had given to me, and I've never once returned the favor. Well, I mean if you can take it."

Elana deadpanned her. "I can take it."

"How do you feel about room service, Alice?"

"For breakfast, Pascale?"

"No, for dinner."

"Like *now?*"

"Like right now."

Elana stood. "Make the arrangements. I'll see you when you get there. For dessert, I'll have the *femme brûlée.*"

"What if that's not on the menu?"

"It's on the menu."

Elana sauntered onto the beach and back toward their villa.

Kenna placed their order and finished her wine. When she opened the villa door, candlelight flickered, augmenting the moonbeams bouncing off the water.

Elana lay back on the chaise under a ceiling fan. "When will dinner be here?"

Kenna smiled. "Soon come."

"It better be *sooner* come or the waitstaff is going to get an eyeful."

Kenna went to her and sat on the side of the chaise. She stroked Elana's hand then looking into her eyes, she said, "Do you think we're getting any closer to that kiss we've wanted for so long?"

"If you kiss me now, a knock on the door will interrupt it."

"Hmm. I don't think dinner will be here *that* soon."

"Who said I thought it would be here anytime soon?"

"You're an impossible tease. But then, you've made a gorgeous living at it. Which brings up a good question—how do I know who I'll be kissing?"

"Who would you rather kiss? Alice or Elana?"

"Can't I kiss them both?"

"Nice—very diplomatic."

"Who would you rather kiss? Kenna or Pascale?"

"I see what you mean. Tough choice. It's starting to sound like a foursome."

There was a knock at the door.

"Remember, counting Wonder Woman, it's a fivesome."

"No, that would just be an orgy."

"Hmm. Good thing we have until dessert to figure it out," Kenna said as she rose and answered the door.

"Good evening," said the waiter as he entered.

"How did you get this here so quickly?" asked Kenna.

"Miss West ordered it earlier," the waiter replied.

Kenna unsuccessfully tried to hold back her grin. "Very sneaky, Elana. Well played."

"We'll be dining on the veranda," Kenna said.

"Very good." The waiter set the table, but as he reached to remove the silver domes from the china, Kenna stopped him.

"We'll take it from here," she said, and waited for him to leave.

Elana stood and joined her on the terrace. Kenna took her hand and breathed in the salt air, listened to the gentle waves gracefully slide onto shore. She turned to Elana and tenderly stroked back her hair. She leaned in far enough to feel the woman's breath on her lips, an inch away from her longtime fantasy come to life. Elana slipped her arms around Kenna's waist and coaxed her closer. Kenna first placed her lips against Elana's with the lightness of a feather; then, embracing the woman, she melted into her and took her breath away.

Kenna held her tight, kissed her deep and mercilessly— Elana gasping as she yielded to the steel-eyed spy. Kenna's lips slid onto Elana's neck, her hands moving up her back and then down onto her streamlined rear. Her firm touch caused Elana to toss her head back so that Kenna could continue kissing every part of her neck and cleavage.

Kenna leaned her back against the wall and pressed against her as their tongues played against each other. Certain she had made her point, the spy pulled away. She stepped toward the villa and turned to look over her shoulder at Elana. Her playful smile beckoned the stripper to follow her.

Kenna waited for Elana to join her in the bedroom before she pressed Play on the stereo. The slow and sultry bass line throbbed like her heartbeat.

In the lights,
When the bass pounds soft and low
And the girl's someone you know
She wraps her legs around it
You wrap your mind around her

"This song is the gift that keeps on giving," said Elana.

"We can't get away from Steel Eyes," said Kenna, shaking her head.

"Why would you want to? She was the sexiest rocker ever."

"I don't stand a chance against an icon like that."

Elana put her arms around Kenna. "I don't know, Pascale. I really don't think she has *anything* on you."

Kenna grabbed Elana and kissed her hard and deep. Finally, Kenna thought, for the first time since I created her, Steel Eyes is a distant second to Kenna Waverly.

In that instant, she could feel the shift inside of her. At last, she had gotten a glimpse of balance—even if for only that moment. For so long, Kenna had lived the life where when Steel Eyes won, Kenna Waverly lost. The years of anonymity had taken their toll on her, never able to be her complete self. Always living in compartments. Either she was Steel Eyes, or Kenna, or the Mossad spy. But here, with Elana the FBI agent, with Alice the stripper—who had captivated her long ago—she could let go and finally be the woman that she had become.

Elana had seen her at her most vulnerable, and at her strongest. She'd even seen her upon waking, and yet she was still interested. She pulled back, gazed deep into Elana's eyes and released the passion she had restrained for far too long.

Lingering in their long overdue kiss, Elana gently bit the spy's lip, and then sensuously devoured Pascale's neck. Chills raced up and down Kenna's body in a stream of delight. And now, she knew why. At last, Kenna deciphered the mystery of why their connection had been—had remained so strong. Like her, Elana had also had to live two disparate lives. Like her, Elana craved the ally who could make being with each of her, feel like being with all of her.

Pascale led Alice to the upholstered chair, and to the tune of "She's Outta Control," she gave Alice a teasing, sizzling lap dance. She sensuously stripped down to her bra and panties, straddled Alice on the chair, and threw her long blond hair forward and then back. Looking down into the woman's eyes, Wonder Woman pressed her cleavage to Alice's mouth, ran her fingers through the woman's hair. Alice gripped Pascale's ass and pulled her closer, removing the lap dancer's bra before placing her warm mouth on Kenna's breast. Kenna flinched from the sensation, then pushed her other breast against Elana's luscious lips.

You tease me with your eyes
You move against my thighs
Then you climb into my soul
We're both

So outta control.

Afterward, their bodies lay entwined in bed—Kenna on top of the woman she had fantasized about for so long; the woman who had touched her to depths she couldn't have imagined. This woman—whom she had waited for years to simply kiss.

Elana rolled on top, pressing Kenna into the bed with her body, kissing her way along her breasts and abdomen—and then farther down until Kenna moaned.

"Elana," she whispered, "I've never stopped fantasizing about what it would be like with you. You're incredible." And then Kenna gave the stripper complete control over her. Moved with her, against her, under her. Vulnerable and open, she touched Elana from her most private places, both emotionally and physically—swallowing Elana's every whim as the taste of music, and then artfully giving it back to her in fuchsia, turquoise and all the golds of a Caribbean sunrise. Kenna pulled the woman closer, so that she could feel every part of their naked bodies against each other, teasing her, wanting her—craving her.

The walls they had hidden behind for so long came crashing down in an overload of relentless hunger. For hours, their bodies succumbed to what they already knew they had *always* known about each other, but had never tasted—every curve, every grasp for the intangible.

The intangible nuance, Kenna thought. Again, fate smiled on her—allowed her to bargain for shelter where the intangible nuance could be touched—tasted. Then she gave herself to Elana, one more time.

CHAPTER FORTY-SEVEN

Late the following morning, Kenna joined Elana on the beach, and lay back next to her on their oversized lounger.

Elana took a sip from her umbrella drink and reached for Kenna's hand. "I can't stop replaying last night," she said softly. "You were intoxicating. Might have even blown my mind—twice." She continued to stare out to sea.

Kenna sighed. "Only twice?"

"Two out of five ain't bad for mind blowing, Pascale."

"You taught me a few things too, Alice."

"Like what?"

"I'm much more fond of dessert than I ever knew."

"Hmm, which one was your favorite?"

"I'm extremely partial to the *femme brûlée*." Kenna sighed. "We have one more day and night here after today. What would you like to do with it? We don't have to collect the documents from Cayman Continental Bank until Monday."

"I still can't believe I finally scored the Caymans!"

Kenna glanced over at her. "*We* scored the Caymans. Personally, I scored so much more."

"Scored *in* the Caymans is more like it," Elana said under her breath. She rolled to her side and kissed Kenna's shoulder. As she slowly pulled away, she slid her sunglasses down her nose and met Kenna's eye. "I'd like to spend the night on a boat—just the two of us."

"Ah, early fishing?" Kenna said, straight-faced.

"Sure—if 'early fishing' is a euphemism for rocking the boat—"

Kenna interrupted, "Which would be yet another euphemism for ravaging your body."

"Mmm, my kind of fishing trip," Elana said.

"My kind of euphemism," added Kenna.

"Yep, Pascale—light on baggage, heavy on romance." Elana paused and let it all sink in. "You know, if I had to have *my* skin in the game, I'm glad yours was in it with me."

"You're going to make me blush."

"Pascale?"

"Hmm?"

"Do you think you'll ever get back to LA?"

"Yes, but not for a while. I've decided to make some big changes for the first time in a long time."

"Sounds mysterious. Exciting."

"I'm ready to make home base stateside instead of Jamaica."

"That's a big change after seven years. Where will you go?"

"To my beach house at the New Jersey Shore."

Elana got quiet.

"You okay, baby?"

"Yes. For a second, I forgot that all we have is the present moment. But that doesn't mean I want it to end."

Kenna squeezed her hand. "The present is all anyone ever has. This op was a constant reminder."

"Yeah."

"Alice?"

"Hmm?"

"Vanilla or chocolate?"

"Um, chocolate. Why?"

"I want to make sure it's on board," said Kenna.

"A boat?"

"The boat where we're going to spend the night, you know—euphemising."

"And here I thought you were more...the champagne and caviar kind of spy."

Kenna grinned. "Wait till you see what I can do with ice cream."

"Are you really going to get us a boat?"

"It's an island. Of course I'm getting us a boat. Did you really think after we both finally admitted how long we've waited to kiss, that I had plans to stop once we started? If you liked me on land, wait till you have me on the water."

Elana laughed. "Challenge accepted."

Kenna stroked Elana's cheek and looked into her eyes. "It's odd. Being with you makes me feel safe."

"You are safe, Kenna."

The beach attendant approached from their right and smiled down at them. "It's time for your couple's beach massage."

"Thank you," Elana said.

They gathered their gear, and had no sooner taken three steps before Elana's phone rang. She glanced at the number but didn't answer the call.

"Who is it?" asked Kenna.

"The home office." Elana grinned at her. Then, with the summertime windup of a seasoned pitching ace, she hurled the phone as far into the sparkling sea as she could. She took Kenna's hand, and as they meandered along the shoreline toward the beachfront cabana, Kenna's phone rang next.

She stopped, turned it off and put the device back into her pocket.

Elana kissed her lips and laughed. "You really are quite the *practical* spy, aren't you?"

"Just wait until later, when you fall victim to my evening tactics."

Elana sighed. "Later can't come soon enough."

* * *

Toward the end of the day, Kenna gathered their belongings and was placing them by the front door of their villa when the concierge knocked.

"Miss Waverly, all the arrangements have been made," he said. "The driver has been waiting patiently, ready to bring you and Miss West to the marina where your boat is docked."

"Sorry, I know we're an hour late." Kenna smiled. "Would you please bring these suitcases to the car? We'll be down shortly."

Elana entered the living room from the bedroom while tying a scarf around her ponytail and putting on her straw hat. "I'm ready," she said, grinning.

In the backseat of the taxi, Kenna's phone rang for the fourth time since they had left the beach. "Maybe I'd better take this, Elana. They keep calling from home."

"Can't we just give it one more day before we have to get back to reality?"

The taxi pulled into the marina about ten minutes later. "We're here," said the driver.

"Thank you." Kenna tipped him handsomely and took their bags.

They picked up their instructions from the broker they were to meet, and walked toward their boat slip. As they prepared to board, Kenna's phone rang again.

"We have to take this call, Elana."

"Why?"

"Because it could be really important. Hello?" Kenna said. "Hello? What? We have a bad connection. I'll call you back."

"Who is it?" Elana asked when Kenna hung up.

"Hunt," she replied. "I'd better walk back onto land, see if I can get a better signal. You can board if you like—I'll make this as quick as I can."

Elana put one foot on the cabin cruiser's deck and rethought it. "No, that's okay, I'll go with you."

They walked back up the pier, farther and farther until they reached the marina's entrance, where Kenna finally got a signal on her phone. She placed the call and waited for it to connect.

BOOM!

A deafening explosion behind them rocked the pier. The clatter sent people racing off their boats as the Harbormaster sounded the alarm. Kenna's phone flew from her hand when Elana tackled her.

When Kenna and Elana stood up, they turned to see cinders flying, and bits of hull scattered as the all-consuming fire engulfed the torched boat. They stepped in the direction of the blast.

Elana looked at Kenna. "That was our boat!"

"Yeah. With any luck, it will be a while before they figure out we weren't on it." Kenna quietly picked up her phone off the ground, took Elana by the hand and got into the nearest taxi. "It's time for us to get the hell out of here."

Bella Books, Inc.

Women. Books. Even Better Together.

P.O. Box 10543
Tallahassee, FL 32302

Phone: 800-729-4992
www.bellabooks.com